DIVINE POSSIBILITIES

Book One: The Divine Series

Divine Possibilities

Patti Barone

Cover design: Leonard Brown

www.divinepossibilities.net
2010

ISBN 1-453-79785-8
EAN-13 9781453797853

I want to extend special thanks to my friend, Kristy. With one simple question, she set in motion something much bigger than I could have imagined. Thanks!

Thank you to all my friends and family who read every page almost the minute I typed them. I am not sure I would have continued on this journey without promptings to give you more, especially when I left you hanging at the end of a chapter.

I am grateful for Vickie and Kim. I looked forward to Mondays when I could share the latest chapter and get your feedback. You helped make a possibility a reality.

I would also like to thank Brenda Colijn, Ph.D., Professor of Biblical Interpretation and Theology at Ashland Theological Seminary, for our theological discussions and for editing portions of the final manuscript. Finally, thanks to Leonard Brown for designing the cover and for creating the official Divine Possibilities website (www.divinepossibilities.net).

Thank you Triune God – Father, Son, and Holy Spirit.

To all the angels in my life (Hebrews 1:14).

Chapter Zero

Catherine struggles to wake. Her head is pounding. Her mouth feels like sandpaper, and her breathing is labored. The room is dark except for a small beam of sunlight streaming in from the rip in the window blinds. The bedroom floor is covered with dirty clothes. Drawers are open with their contents spilling out, and the stench of discarded food and alcohol permeates everything.

Unknown to Catherine, two pair of eyes are watching her: the demon, Pexov, crouches by her feet while the angel, Sarephah, hovers near her head. Anxious for victory, Pexov rises to his full height and glares at the mortal he's been assigned to conquer. Catherine stirs slightly. With one hand grasping her sword, Sarephah moves forward to protect the human assigned to her care.

These bitter rivals are in a battle for Catherine's heart, mind, and soul. They follow her every move and perceive her every thought. They have no real power in and of themselves. No. In many ways, Catherine controls her own destiny. Their only source of power comes directly from her when she yields to their influence.

Catherine has no idea that the battle for her soul is nearing completion. The fight between these two opposing spiritual beings is intensifying because Sarephah is running out of options and Pexov is running out of patience. Neither wants to lose this battle; neither wants to go before the throne of their Master to explain what happened to Catherine. Whatever it takes, one will win and the other will lose. And the prize is Catherine. But one will win only when Catherine chooses.

Surrendering to God or following a destructive path is not an easy choice, but fortunately for Catherine, choice is still a possibility. What Catherine doesn't yet realize is that with every choice she makes Pexov or Sarephah will gain the upper hand, and eventually, she'll either be enslaved by the evil that seeks to destroy her or freed by the good that wants to save her.

What will Catherine choose?

Chapter One

Half asleep and still half drunk, Catherine squints to see her alarm clock. 6:02. Pondering the time, she tries to concentrate but her mind is fuzzy. She hesitates and wonders, *is it morning or evening? What day is it?*

After a few moments, she musters some energy. "Ok, Catherine, get a grip."

She runs her fingers through her stringy, matted dark hair. Nausea sweeps over her so violently that she leans forward and lays her head in her hands. After a minute, the feeling passes and she sits up again. She waits for the next wave, but is spared another attack.

Something catches her eye.

A bottle of whiskey sits upright on the table with enough left for only a few gulps. She knew it had been full the night before. She hadn't planned on drinking the entire bottle yesterday, only enough to "feel good."

She picks up the bottle and studies its contents. "Almost empty. What happened?"

Pexov smiles. He knows what happened. Catherine succumbed to his influence once again.

The image of the almost empty bottle stuns her. She stares at it in disbelief and mutters to herself. "I could have sworn I only had a few sips. This can't be." Her head is spinning and she desperately wants something to make her feel better. She slowly climbs out of bed.

The light on her message machine is blinking. Two messages. She groans, "Great, now what?" She turns away from the blinking light and all the responsibility that will come if she checks those messages.

Ambling down the hallway toward the kitchen, Pip, her six month old cat, meows for breakfast. "Hold on, Pip. Mommy's not feeling so well." She stops near the entrance of the kitchen and stands there not knowing exactly what she wants. She stares aimlessly. No coherent thoughts come to her. She simply doesn't know what to do next.

Pexov speaks into the air and sends an onslaught of negative thoughts to Catherine. *Here you go again messing everything up. You are a waste of a human being. Nobody drinks like you. Might as well have another drink because life isn't getting any better.*

Catherine covers her ears with her hands trying to physically stop the thoughts that assault her.

Sarephah watches intently. Her influence has been weakened since Catherine's decision to drink last night. Sarephah knows it will take time for Catherine to be able to hear the soothing words of the Divine Three, whom mortals call God. The only option now is to focus on Pexov.

"Pexov, get away from her!"

Pexov slowly turns his head to acknowledge his archenemy. "Hello, Sarephah. Can't you see that I'm just trying to help? You know as well as I that she's trapped in her own perverted, alcoholic delusion and can't possibly make a good decision."

Sarephah glides past Pexov to move closer to Catherine. "You know nothing about helping anyone, let alone helping Catherine. You are not welcome here."

Pexov eyes blazed red. "YOU have no say on whether I am welcome here or not. Only Catherine can send me away, and she has no idea that I *or* you exist. Her ignorance is my greatest gain and your greatest loss."

"Pexov, you are a liar to the very core. I do have some say in the matter. And I wouldn't count on Catherine's ignorance for much longer. The Divine Three are never willing to lose one of their own."

Pexov, who was crouching in the corner, springs up and growls, "Catherine is NOT one of His. Never has been and never will be. The Ruler of the Kingdom of the Air won't allow that. Not now. Not ever."

Towering over Pexov, Sarephah declares, "Satan has no hold on this precious child."

Pexov laughs, "HA! How can you say that? Look at her and her miserable life. The Divine Three have obviously deserted this one." Satisfied for the moment, Pexov crouches back into the corner to wait for the next opportunity to torment Catherine.

• • •

Catherine suddenly feels extremely weak and tired, but Pip needs to be fed. She searches the drawers for some cat food. Pip meows like he hasn't eaten in days when, in fact, he is fairly well kept in spite of Catherine's inability to take care of herself.

"Okay Pip. Give me a minute. I can't find your food."

Pip meows with more intensity.

"Didn't I just feed you? Oh, my head hurts."

Shaking now, and with Pip weaving in and out of her legs in affection, Catherine opens one more cabinet and finds the only thing that will keep Pip quiet and happy: whitefish and tuna supreme.

"Finally. Okay, here you go, Pip."

A delighted Pip meows before hungrily attacking his food.

"You're welcome."

The thoughts that bombarded Catherine earlier linger and linger like festering sores. *I* am *no good,* Catherine thinks. *I should just have another drink and forget everything. Who cares, anyway?* Watching Pip eat, Catherine decides to finish off last night's bottle, find some more, and go back to bed.

Catherine shuffles down the hallway toward her bedroom.

Sarephah smiles. "Good. I have a little more time."

Pexov smiles. "Good. She's running out of options *and* time."

• • •

Sarephah stands over eight feet tall, with kind eyes, a large sword, and a demeanor that demands attention. Catherine never sees her and never will. The Divine Three don't work that way, at least not with everyone. They like their ministering angels to work silently and creatively, especially with humans.

Sarephah knows she needs just a little more time to work with Catherine. After last night, the options left for Catherine are dwindling. Her job is in jeopardy. The bills aren't being paid. Her friends are disgusted with her. Her family is distant. Catherine is utterly alone and with little hope of anything better.

Sarephah thinks maybe, just maybe, in light of this dire set of circumstances, the Divine Three will take control of this situation and force Catherine to make the right choice, which is to accept their help and follow them.

Thinking out loud, Sarephah says, "I must go before the Divine Three and plead for Catherine's life. Pexov will pursue her relentlessly, and Catherine is in no shape to resist him and the hatred that he spews." Sighing, Sarephah mutters, "I fear this battle may be costly."

• • •

Pexov shivers with excitement and anticipation. As he watches Catherine sleep fitfully, he snarls to himself, "Catherine is so pitifully weak. No one cares about her, which makes my job much easier. Hmm, yes, I must make sure she knows this."

Moving closer to her bed, Pexov senses that the end is near. "Yes, she is close to fully succumbing to the power of her own choices. I have been successful. Her will and her thoughts are almost mine." This thought gives him some comfort and slightly eases his persistently agitated mind.

Catherine stirs, but never fully wakes. The alcohol, still raging through her body, seems to have taken on a life of its own. Catherine will not wake for many more hours.

Pexov returns to the corner, crouches low, and with his cold blue eyes still fixed on the unconscious Catherine, rests quietly, for he knows it is only a matter of time before Catherine's thoughts and ultimately her actions are under his complete control. "My master will be thrilled with my superior abilities, absolute brilliance, and magnificent creativity in destroying this forgotten and worthless mortal. And, my reward will be sweetened since I will have also defeated Sarephah, the powerful and beloved servant of the Divine Three."

• • •

Later that day, Catherine stirs again. Her breathing is labored, her skin clammy, and her whole body trembles uncontrollably. Alcohol poisoning is a silent killer with little regard for its victim. The choice to drink last night and again this morning has many consequences for Catherine. As the alcohol rages through her body, it begins to send messages to her vital organs that render her weak, confused, and literally fighting for her life. In fact, she will struggle to wake or even take the smallest breath.

Opening her eyes slightly, Catherine tries to draw in a deep breath, but feels a vise grip around her chest. Alarmed, she sits up a little straighter and again tries to fill her lungs, but she can barely breathe. Concerned by her inability to catch her breath, she rises fully upright in bed and begins to panic. Completely awake now, she frantically takes small, short breaths. She feels light headed. Realizing she's on the verge of passing out again because she can't quite catch her breath, Catherine concentrates on breathing. "Breathe" she whispers to herself again and again as if in this meditative state and with the rhythmic cadence of her voice she can control the amount of air that enters her lungs. Several agonizing minutes later, the panic subsides slightly, but her breathing is still difficult and worrisome.

Suddenly, Pip jumps on the bed, startling Catherine. "Pip!" Catherine, seething in anger, yells, "What are you doing? Get off the bed. NOW!"

She pushes Pip away. Turning and hissing at his obviously deranged owner, Pip jumps off the bed and scurries out of the room. Catherine is stunned by Pip's response.

"Hey, Pip" she yells, slightly out of breath. "I'm sorry honey." No response. "Well, who cares anyway. I feel like crap."

Swinging her legs over the side of the bed, Catherine musters all the strength she has and stands up cautiously. She sways side to side and immediately sits back down. "What is wrong with me? I never feel this bad after some drinks. What did I do last night?"

Looking at the now empty bottle, she's jolted back to reality. "I guess I just drank on an empty stomach or something. Yeah, that's it…I should have eaten before I drank." Convinced of this lie, she slowly stands back up. This time she keeps her balance and moves hesitantly toward the blinking light on the message machine she avoided earlier.

Standing next to the night stand, she wrestles with her thoughts. *I guess I better check these. How did I get home last night? Where are my clothes? And what are these hideous clothes I have on now? What did I do? Did I go to work?*

Pondering this last thought, Catherine has a few vague memories of yesterday morning. *Yes, I did go to work. Oh, that can't be good. Why don't I remember anything?*

Catherine has experienced blackouts before. These are times when actions are taken but never experienced, when emotions are displayed but never felt, and when thoughts are conceived but never born. In the past, she viewed them as amusing incidents in which events happily disappeared from consciousness without the entanglement of responsibility. She never cared what she did or who she hurt. After all, Catherine reasoned, if she couldn't remember anything, then maybe it never really happened. Oh, yes, she knows about these long stretches of time lost to her memory for all eternity. But her blackouts are increasing, especially lately. They feel different to her now.

She realizes, with some angst, that her actions in a blackout exist as actual events in the reality of others, even though she cannot recall them. What she so easily laughed off before because she simply didn't care has begun to haunt her. In fact, she will soon be forced to confront the reality of her actions, even though her own memory of them has been erased. For the first time ever, she will have to account for what she has done and said during these blank spots of existence. She will have to reckon with those whom she's hurt.

Unknown to Catherine, the worst part is that each blackout removes all resistance to the influences that seek to destroy her. Pexov gains strength by these unnatural occurrences, while Sarephah losses strength. Yes, blackouts are the playground for evil: an evil that she can't fight because she doesn't know it exists.

Catherine pushes the listen button on the message machine. Beep. "Hi Cath. This is mom. Where are you? I just got a call from Mrs. Taylor. She said you missed Tommy's music lesson tonight, and your dad says you missed another dinner with him. Are you okay? You seemed down the last time I saw you. Do you think you need to see a counselor or something?"

Catherine rolls her eyes. *Why does she always think I need to see a counselor?* With sarcasm dripping from every word, she says to herself, "Yeah I need a counselor all right. Maybe I can get some good meds to get rid of this headache while I'm at it."

Her mom continues, "Okay, well, honey, call me. Your dad and I are worried. Bye." Click. Beep.

Putting her hands to her head, Catherine rocks back and forth. "Yeah, I bet dad is worried. He's worried about what board meeting he needs to attend. Note to self, call mom…tomorrow."

She hits the listen button again. Beep. "Hello Catherine, this is Vickie. We need you to come in and talk about what happened yesterday at work. I have scheduled a meeting for Thursday at 10:00 am. Since today is Tuesday, we thought that would give you time to…umm…to…well…to get yourself together. Until then you are officially suspended and not permitted to come onto the property without expressed permission from myself or Mr. Nielin. All right, well…umm… yeah…umm… we hope you're you doing okay? I'll see you Thursday, bye." Click. Beep.

Catherine's stomach drops. *I knew that wouldn't be good. I am definitely not drinking again. I can't image what I did. Suspended!?* Looking down at her baggy pants and oversized shirt, she realizes she's wearing the uniform of the kitchen staff from the hotel. *How did I get these?*

Pexov, roused by the news Catherine has just received, flies into action. With targeted precision, he speaks into the air. Immediately Catherine shivers and wraps her arms around herself. She sits down on the side of the bed.

Slowly several thoughts occur to her. *I couldn't have done anything that bad. Come on…they must be overreacting. I just had a few drinks, after all. I don't have a problem. My mom has the problem. Yeah, she's the alcoholic. Not me. She's the one who almost died from cirrhosis of the liver. I am nothing like her.*

She pauses for a moment. More thoughts come, but this time they are coming from Catherine alone. Pexov has done his job.

I'm going to lay low for a couple days and deal with work Thursday. In the meantime, I deserve to relax. In fact, I deserve a little drink to celebrate my two days off. I'll feel better with a couple drinks. Yeah, I'll deal with work later.

Catherine pushes herself up off the bed, steadies herself, and begins to walk toward the kitchen, and oblivion.

Chapter Two

Standing in the bedroom with Catherine, all Sarephah can do is watch her go. The powerful angel has been there all morning silently interceding for her, but Pexov has the upper hand right now. Sarephah can wait no longer. She moves swiftly through the barriers of earth's atmosphere and glides into the spiritual realm of the heavenlies. In an instant, she's in the world she loves best – the Kingdom of the Divine Three.

All beings, angels and demons, acknowledge and refer to the God of all creation as the Divine Three, because they are experienced as three in the unity of one essence. Although they are perceived in various ways, Sarephah understands them best as three - Author, Word, and Text - writing one story.

The Author is the creator and sustainer of all that was, is, and will be. The Word, who always is, was made flesh and dwelt among mortals and died for their cause, and the Text moves within and above guiding each mortal's existence. Together they each make one everlasting story of creation and humanity. They are never separated and never combined; always and forever one as three.

The Divine Three rule together as One from the area of the heavenlies known as Nede. Sarephah goes straight to Nede and the great throne room. Nede is unlike any other place in the heavenlies. Demons are permitted to roam freely in all areas of the heavenlies except Nede. To Sarephah's knowledge, no demon, including the chief demon Satan, has ever crossed the highly guarded borders that lead to this special place since the great rebellion. All day, every day, guardian angels line the entire perimeter with the intent to keep out those beings that choose to completely reject the Divine Three. By everlasting decree, only those who choose to belong to the Divine Three are permitted to enter.

As Sarephah is on an urgent mission, she moves without haste into the presence of the Divine Three. There is no waiting because time ceases to exist here. The Divine Three sit ready to accept any and all who come for courage, guidance, and strength without the restrictions of earth's time constraints.

"Greetings, Sarephah! We are pleased to see you. Sit with us and tell us why you have come."

Sarephah, feeling the overwhelming love and power of the Divine Three, relaxes visibly at their words. She happily moves closer to receive their embrace before she sits down across from the throne.

Speaking quickly and barely taking a breath, Sarephah begins, "I have come on behalf of Catherine. She desperately needs your help. Well, more than just your help; she needs you to take control of this situation. She is in real trouble, both physically and spiritually. Oh, and let me tell you about Pexov. He is…" The aura of the Three moves over Sarephah and she stops in mid-sentence.

The Divine Three, radiating warmth and love, calmly say to Sarephah, "Sarephah, you do not have to plead for Catherine's life. We have neither deserted nor forgotten her. We are pursuing her with a powerful and relentless love. And, yes, we know that Pexov, Satan's agent of death and destruction, is currently wielding much power over our dear precious child." Sarephah smiles and relaxes at this declaration.

Bolstered by these words of encouragement regarding Catherine, she confidently asks, "Oh, good. Then you will take charge now that you see how bad things are and force her to accept your love? Because you know that she will turn to Satan and be destroyed if you don't step in and make her accept you."

The Divine Three are silent for what seems like an eternity, and then finally speak. "We cannot force Catherine to accept our love, Sarephah. In fact, at this point we do not know what she will decide to do. Her future is made up of divine possibilities but not forced actualities. We must allow her the freedom to determine her own destiny. We will pursue her and encourage her to come, accept our love, and follow us. But what we can never do is command her to come, accept our love, and follow us."

Sarephah is stunned. "You mean you don't have control over her? Does that mean you are not all-powerful?"

Patiently, the Divine Three ask, "Why do you speak of power in terms of control?" They continue, "Our power is made perfect in the weakness of humans. For Catherine, our power will be displayed in her choice to accept her own weakness and then our love. Our power is our love. Our power in the life of Catherine is our love for her. Our power is patient, not wanting any to perish. Therefore, we must wait for Catherine to choose us."

Confused by this response, Sarephah begins to feel frustrated at the Divine Three's answers. She asks with exasperation, "Don't you want to save her? Don't you want to spare her the miserable existence she is living?"

The Three respond with equal passion, "Salvation has already been accomplished through the Word. Our choice has always been to save all of our creation. Our love is powerful. Our love saves. Our love does not, will not, and cannot force or control. Love requires freedom, and freedom requires risk. Catherine must decide to accept our gift of salvation by her own freewill."

There is another long silence. Sarephah contemplates the Three's words. Finally, with tears in her eyes, Sarephah cries, "But she doesn't seem to have the capacity to do anything beneficial for her life, let alone make the one crucial decision that will determine her destiny. It doesn't seem right."

Immediately Sarephah is surrounded by the incomprehensible love of the Three as their aura of them washes over her. She feels strengthened, encouraged, and oh, yes the love is exhilarating.

The Three finally speak, "Sarephah, we know your heart and we know Catherine's heart. We are NOT giving up on her. Even as we speak, prayers are coming up for her. Remember that love must be given freely, both our love for Catherine and her love for us. This freedom we allow humans is risky, for we know that they may and do chose to reject our love."

"Satan and his demons have used this freedom against us from the beginning. In fact, many things entice humans away from us when their freedom to choose us is constrained by their own sin, their love for the things of the world, the social context in which they exist, and evil."

"We are in a battle against every evil that stands against the good, just, holy, and pure plan for humanity. Evil, that which actively seeks destruction of the good and that which continually rejects our love, is real because freedom to choose is real. Yes, this battle for the souls of our creation is very real for us precisely because the freedom we allow our creation makes it real."

"It is important for you to realize that we actively pursue each and every one of our precious children. At the same time, we must wait on each and every decision because the freedom we give them to choose their own way makes the *personal outcome* of each battle unknown to us in actuality. We know only the divine possibilities. We have accounted for each choice that was, is, and will be made, but we can only respond to the actual choice, not the possible one. We know the plan we have for Catherine, but we know this plan only in its potentiality."

Revived by this increasing knowledge of the Three's purpose and plan, Sarephah inquires, "So you can't just fix Catherine because of your everlasting decree of freewill for all beings, natural and spiritual?"

The Divine Three respond, "Correct, we can only show her, with your help, the reality of her choices, our perfect love, and our divine plan for her. But, again, the plan will remain a set of possibilities until she chooses and makes them actualities."

The Divine Three's aura begins to pulsate with brilliant colors and Sarephah is comforted.

"Enough for now, Sarephah, Catherine needs us and you are one of our agents of love. Remember that our love is powerful but cannot be controlling. Stay vigilant and ready to act as we pursue her so you can help her see the truth in every situation she encounters."

"We fear that Catherine is near her end. Her choices are becoming limited in light of the person she has become. Ironically, she has become this person because of her choices. However, there are those who are praying for her and her mind is still open to the possibilities of love and goodness."

"Be quick in your return. Catherine is going to be confronted with more choices – choices that will determine her ultimate destiny."

Chapter Three

Vickie Reed is exhausted. It's the end of a long day at The Holden Suites hotel. As the Assistant General Manager she feels the weight of responsibility for everything at the hotel from the guests to the employees. Her management style is relaxed yet firm. She is passionate about what she does and believes that leadership done the right way involves lots of prayer and the application of God's word. In the business for twenty years, she thought she had seen it all. However, she's deeply troubled by one particular employee and the situation that occurred Monday.

Vickie slowly eases back, rests her head on the headrest of her chair, closes her eyes in contemplation, and with a sigh groans, "What am I going to do about Catherine Ash?"

Frustrated, she adds, "Her behavior yesterday was incomprehensible. I just don't get it and frankly, I am repulsed by what she did. And the fact that she involved so many employees in this…no…they are *not* at all happy about this. And I don't blame them."

Vickie pauses. She takes in a deep breath and slowly releases all the air out of her lungs. "Yet, I sense that I am supposed wait before I make a final judgment about her and her continued employment. I need to pray about this."

Suddenly her phone buzzes.

Kim, Vickie's genuinely and persistently cheerful administrative assistant, announces pleasantly, "Excuse me, Vickie. Don just called and wanted me to let you know that he will be a few minutes late for your 5:30 meeting." Kim has faithfully served as the confidant and assistant to Vickie Reed for over ten years.

Vickie smiles at Kim. *Nothing seems to upset her* muses Vickie. "Okay, thanks for letting me know. By the way, thanks for the extra work on the McGerty wedding reception. You really saved the day."

Kim responds, "Oh, thanks. Just another day at the office!" After a short pause, Kim asks, "Mind if I head home now? I'll take care of the reservation blocking first thing tomorrow morning."

"Sure, say hi to Dave for me."

Vickie eases back in her chair again and whispers under her breath, "Thanks God. I needed a few extra minutes to pray about Catherine." Vickie closes her eyes in prayer. She knows she needs some wisdom about the situation she's confronting.

After a moment of silence, Vickie prays, "Father God, maker of all that is good and righteous, I come to you seeking wisdom on a situation with one of your precious children. Catherine doesn't know you, but I know that you know everything about her. Please show me what to do to help Catherine. I'll be honest with you, God, I really don't understand all the aspects of the sinful entanglements that are weighing her down. But I do know that her drinking is out of control. I just don't understand why she continues to drink in light of her situation..."

Vickie pauses and a thought comes to her. *Don't focus on what you see, focus on what you can't see. Remember, what comes from the heart reaches the heart. Show her My love.*

Vickie smiles and continues praying, "Yes, okay, just love her. I get it. But how do I do THAT? All right, then help me to remember that you pursued me with your love while I was still a sinner…and even after I became a saint who still sins! Yes, I shall try to be as loving to her as you are to me. To you I lift all my praise. I love you with an everlasting love. Amen."

Sarephah stands near Vickie observing the work of the Divine Three. After smiling and nodding to acknowledge Vickie's faithful angel, she fades away silently and returns to Catherine.

Vickie sits quietly for a few more minutes, and then, after feeling a strong sense of peace wash over her, she finally opens her eyes. Glancing at the clock on the wall next to the window, she realizes that Don Nielin, the General Manager, should be arriving any minute. Their meeting this evening is about none other than Catherine Ash.

Vickie, encouraged by her prayer time, now feels compelled to keep Catherine employed and to direct her to get the help she needs, if it's not too late.

Don rushes into Vickie's office with his usual bluster. Although Don "gets things done," he sometimes forgets that being a good leader involves caring about and having compassion for his employees.

Without taking a seat, Don quickly states his position. "Hello, Vickie. I'm ready to discuss Catherine. Basically, I am totally disgusted by her actions. I cannot possibly allow an employee who displayed such total disrespect for herself, the staff, and the guests to continue working at this establishment. I believe the best course of action is to fire her immediately. We have to make it legal, of course. We will cite the latest example as the main reason. That should make HR and our lawyers happy. "

Barely taking a breath, he continues. "You know, she never really has lived up to the expectations we set for her. She's been here what…umm…let me think." Frustrated because he can't quite remember the length of Catherine's employment at Holden Suites, blurts out, "Oh, well. What does it matter how long she's been here? It's what she did yesterday that really matters. Don't you agree?"

Vickie is not bothered by Don's demeanor. She knows he's really an old softy. He just needs a nudge now and then to do what is best in some situations, especially when it comes to dealing with employee issues.

With years of practice, she waits patiently for Don to finish speaking before calmly saying, "Hello, Don. How are you?"

Don winces because he knows he can be abrupt sometimes. "Oh, yeah, right. Sorry. I'm fine, and you?"

Vickie smiles and laughs quietly. "I'm good, considering." Then, still smiling, but now with a slightly sarcastic tone in her voice continues, "Thanks for coming to discuss Catherine." Don looks at her with an apologetic smile. Pausing, she adds, "Come on, have a seat, and let's *really* talk about Catherine."

Don, embarrassed at his behavior and Vickie's redirection of the conversation, nods his head slightly, and then sits down with a heavy sigh.

"You know I am just so…so…I don't even know what words I can use to describe my feelings about this whole situation," Don admits.

Vickie nods in agreement. "I know what you mean. I'm wrestling with how I feel as well. I agree with you that she showed little respect for some of our best employees and for herself. The whole situation was really ugly and scary. It is important to note, however, that no guests were involved."

Pausing slightly to gather her thoughts, "I see something in Catherine. I can't fully explain it…but I really think there is still hope for her."

Don interjects loudly "Her drinking needs to stop!"

Vickie agrees and adds, "It's obvious to us that she has a problem with alcohol. However, Catherine is in a serious state of denial of this glaring fact. Listen Don, we might be the only ones who can help her. She's young: twenty-six, I believe. I know she lives alone and doesn't have a good relationship with her family. I think her only friends are the ones she's met here. But after what she did Monday night, I'm sure they're reluctant to have anything to do with her. She's a good employee, notwithstanding the events of Monday. And by the way, she's been with us six months."

Don wrinkles his brow, shakes his head, and throws up his hands in exasperation, "How do you know all this?"

Vickie smiles. "I've talked with her! I've also watched her interact with the guests and other employees. She's a good kid. Yeah, I admit she's in real trouble and I can't condone her behavior. But, I firmly believe she's worth keeping. I'll work with her and direct her to get some help as a condition of her continued employment."

"All right...*all right*....you've convinced me," Don declares reluctantly.

Vickie sighs inwardly and silently thanks God for this opportunity to help Catherine. "Thanks, Don! I'll handle everything."

Don stands up, turns, and walks toward the door. He stops abruptly, whirls around, and gestures angrily with his index finger pointing at Vickie, "This is IT. One more mistake and she's out. No questions asked. Understood?" he says firmly, but with a hint of compassion.

"I understand. Thanks again, Don. Good night." Vickie hears a muffled "Good night" as Don marches quickly down the hallway.

"Okay, God. Thank you for granting Catherine a second chance here. Please help her to accept this offer of grace. Oh, and *please...please* help me to know what to do next," Vickie prays earnestly.

The minute this prayer is spoken, the Divine Three send the very essence of their presence to help Sarephah, who is tending at Catherine's side, and an overwhelming sense of peace envelopes Vickie. After a brief moment of reflection, Vickie picks up pen and paper and begins outlining a plan for Catherine.

Chapter Four

Pip thoroughly enjoys stalking imaginary prey scattered throughout the house. He is especially excited to hunt down menacing dust-bunnies or rolled up pieces of paper that pose any threat to him at all. Yes, Pip, the ruler of his vast domain, takes great pride in ridding the house of all dangling, discarded, or untended objects.

After destroying several ominous wrappers in the kitchen and taking down one lamp shade, Pip saunters triumphantly toward Catherine's bedroom. At the entrance of the bedroom Pip stops suddenly. Crouching low, he senses something foreign and potentially dangerous in the corner.

Pexov's eyes flash red. Pip rises up on his paws, curls his back, and hisses in the direction of the far corner. Pexov snarls back, but retreats into the realm of the heavenlies to avoid this unwanted nuisance.

Catherine, startled by the commotion, rolls over onto to her side. Resting on one elbow she says groggily, "What's going on?" while wiping the sleep out of her eyes.

Pip, still in the cat-fight position with bushy tail, raised back, and large saucer eyes, nervously surveys the room.

After Catherine's eyes adjust to the brightness of the room, she sees Pip and relaxes a bit. "Hey, Pip. What's up, honey?"

Pip hesitates when he hears Catherine's voice. He is weary of his inconsistent owner and scared of the unknown threat lurking in the corner.

Catherine pats the bed and calls out, "Come on up here, Pip." But fear gets the better of him. Pip takes one last look at the corner, turns swiftly, and races out of the room. Catherine's too tired to care."Whatever. Crazy cat." She moans while falling back onto the bed.

• • •

It's late Wednesday morning when Catherine wakes from her alcohol-induced sleep. She's feeling better physically, but is a wreck emotionally, and very much still in denial about all the trouble she is in. Sarephah waits by Catherine's side ready to exert some influence over her after being strengthened by the meeting with the Divine Three. The benefit of Pexov's temporary retreat into the heavenlies is that there is no hindrance whatever to the loving presence of the Divine Three. Their power begins to fill the room. Sarephah is relieved and declares, "It's time."

After taking a much needed shower and putting on some relatively clean clothes she gathered off the bedroom floor, Catherine feels revived. She mutters to herself as she catches her reflection in the bathroom mirror, "You know, I feel pretty good today considering how crappy I felt yesterday."

She grabs her cup of coffee, walks into the family room, plops down on the couch, and clicks the power button on the remote. Flipping through several stations, she finally lands on one of those 24-hour news channels. Uninterested, restless, and discontented, Catherine sighs. She has no one to call. No boyfriend. No special confidant. No friend of any sort, really. She's irritated that no one from work has called, especially Kurt.

Taking advantage of the quiet moment, Sarephah springs into action by sending her aura and thoughts into the air.

Several seconds later a surprisingly pleasant feeling invades Catherine's consciousness. She ponders this feeling for a moment. She's incapable of naming this feeling, let alone analyzing its worth and value for her tattered soul. It feels good, peaceful even, but it's so foreign to her that it's almost uncomfortable.

She puts her coffee cup down, points the remote at the television, and pushes the off button. Silence fills the room. Pulling her legs up to her chest, she wraps her arms around her bended knees, and spends a moment just sitting there.

A thought comes to her. *Maybe I should call mom.* Before she can begin to act on her thought, the phone rings. Slightly startled, Catherine says jokingly, "Ooo, that's weird. I think about calling mom and the phone rings."

Thinking the phone call must be her mom she quickly reaches for the receiver, notices the caller-ID, hesitates, and frowns. "Uh, oh. This won't be good."

For a split second Catherine contemplates letting the answering machine pick up the call, but at the last minute something inside her convinces her to answer it. Sarephah smiles triumphantly.

Once her decision is made to face what's on the other side of the line, she snatches the phone from the table, hits the talk button, and says with as much confidence as she can muster, "Hello?"

"May I speak with Catherine Ash?" barks the lady on the other end of the line. Recognizing the voice of Blanche, the receptionist at Sanitiz's Music Emporium, Catherine winces and says haltingly, "This is Catherine."

With obvious anger in her voice, Blanche states bluntly and definitively, "Catherine, we have decided to terminate your teaching contract with us due primarily, but not exclusively, to your failure to keep commitments with your students. This includes the latest incident in which you missed your scheduled teaching time with Tommy Taylor on Monday. You will receive your last paycheck covering the previous week's roster of students, less the ones you missed, of course, on Friday. Oh, by the way, Tommy really liked you and was quite upset about losing his 'favorite teacher' as he put it. But we feel we are making the right decision under the circumstances. If you have any questions, you can call Sam. Okay, well, that's all. Good Bye." Click.

Catherine pushes the off button on her phone and slowly places it on the table. A tear comes to her eye. Regret…remorse…inadequacy, all feelings she is so familiar with, fill her entire being. The weight of them is heavy, so very, very heavy.

Sarephah is sad, but knows that Catherine must continue her descent to the bottom in order to have enough willingness to accept help from the Divine Three. This is just another small step along the road to surrender. Sarephah speaks into the heaviness.

A mist of reflective aura surrounds the contrite Catherine, permitting her to gaze into the sins of selfishness and irresponsibility. This angelic aura is like a roomful of mirrors in which there is no hiding from the images they display.

For one brief moment, and for the first time in a long time, she sees a small piece of truth about herself without the fog of denial. *I was wrong to let Tommy down like that. He is such a good kid. I've missed so many appointments over the past few months. I never thought of how this would affect Tommy or any of my students. I know I'm irresponsible. I don't keep commitments.*

Almost as quickly as she recognizes these truths about herself, Catherine can't bear it any longer. She wipes away the wetness in her eyes with the back of her hand, takes in a deep breath, and with steely determination wrestles the truth back into submission.

Trying to hide from her exposed conscience, she defiantly declares, "Well, it's their loss. I'm a good teacher. I'm sure

Tommy will get over it. It was a stinking part-time job anyway." Sarephah withdraws the reflective aura.

By early-afternoon, Catherine is fully recovered from her battle with the truth. Winning this decisive battle gives her confidence to call her mom. Pip, also fully recovered from his encounter with Pexov, sits next to Catherine as she dials her mom's phone number. Being in a reflective mood, she thinks about the dynamics of her family while waiting for her mom to answer her phone.

Catherine is the third of four children by Nancy and Scott Ash. There are the twins, Andrew and Nicole. Both are twenty-nine and married: Andrew to Bridgette and Nicole to Devon. Andrew and Bridgette have one son, Bryan. Catherine used to party with Andrew and still feels a false sense of closeness to him because of this.

Nicole and Devon are expecting their first. Nicole never drank much, but quit completely once she started attending that mega church on the west side. Nicole now believes drinking alcohol is ranked amongst the greatest of all evils. Needless to say, Catherine and Nicole don't get along.

Megan is the youngest at twenty-two and closest to Catherine. Megan genuinely misses the old Catherine: the person she used to be before she started drinking.

Catherine's mom, an admitted and recovering alcoholic, just celebrated four years of sobriety. Although she doesn't attend church every Sunday, she lives out the spirituality of the AA program. She has a big heart, but is a little headstrong and controlling. Her constant prayer is that Catherine will see the light and come to AA with her one day.

Nancy recognizes all the classic symptoms of alcoholism in her second daughter because, as she likes to put it, "I've been there and done that." Against the wise advice of her sponsor, Nancy Ash believes it is her mission in life to save Catherine by getting her to see that she's powerless over alcohol and that her life is unmanageable. Unfortunately, if Nancy stays on course with this mission, she may not only lose the battle about alcoholism, but the entire war for the life of the daughter she deeply loves.

Catherine's dad, Scott, is the Chief Technology and Communications Officer at MedTech Communications, Inc. Scott is a decent, honest, hard-working man, and loyal husband. Reaching his dream job has been both thrilling and costly for Scott. He loves what he's doing and the respect he receives at work. However, his work takes him away both physically and emotionally from his family.

There was a time when Catherine and her dad were very close. Not anymore. Catherine loves her dad, but detests the executive. There are many wounds that must be healed to save this relationship.

"Catherine Olivia Ash! It's about time you called. I have been worried sick. How are you?"

Jolted back to the present by the overly excited voice of her mother, Catherine rolls her eyes and seriously questions the sanity of her decision to call. "Hi mom… I'm fine. I don't know why you worry so much. Please, would you just chill out."

Disregarding Catherine's disrespectful comment and tone, Nancy continues. "Why did you miss your lesson with Tommy Taylor? Samantha and I are good friends, and she's really disappointed that you didn't show up again for her son's lesson. What's going on? Were you drinking again?"

"Of course not!" Catherine lies. Gripping the phone a little tighter, she quickly comes up with a plausible story. "I had car trouble going to work, someone had to drive me home… and…. umm… in the midst of all the commotion, I just forgot to call to cancel."

There is a long silence. "Hmmm…well, anyway, you should call and apologize for missing the appointment," her mom urges.

"Yeah, I plan on doing that later today," Catherine says with a sincere tone and lying lips. Pexov, her master teacher in the areas of lying, manipulating, and deceiving, would be proud of his protégé.

Changing the subject, Nancy asks tentatively, "Listen, do you want to come over for dinner tonight? Everyone will be there. We're having a celebration of sorts. Nicole and Devon just got their ultrasound pictures and are going to tell us whether they're having a boy or girl."

Catherine is immediately angry. *Why am I just now hearing about this? Did they plan this without me? If I hadn't called, I probably wouldn't have been invited. It's pretty obvious they don't want me around.*

"Ummm…I don't know…I'm so busy with everything here" Catherine explains unconvincingly.

"What things? Come on, Cath. It will be good for you to get out of that apartment for once. Just come," Nancy urges.

Sarephah whispers into the air. There is a long pause. A thought comes to Catherine. *Family time isn't all bad. It's lonely here anyway.*

"Ohhh, alright. What time should I be there?"

"6:30," her mom says and adds, "Do you want Andrew or Dad to come pick you up since you're having car trouble?"

Catherine almost forgot her most recent lie. She recovers quickly, "NO! I mean…no thanks. I got it fixed today. They did such a good job it's like nothing was ever wrong with it," Catherine says with a grin.

"Okay, see you at 6:30, and don't be late. And Catherine, I hate to say anything but…ummm….we'd like it if everyone remains sober for the evening. You know how Nicole can get. Okay?"

Rolling her eyes again, Catherine remembers why she really hates spending time with her family. "Sure. Whatever. See ya later. Bye." Click.

After Catherine finishes the conversation with her mother, she decides to lie down. She figures she needs all the energy she can get to make it through a family dinner. Also, a short nap may help with the killer headache she still has from the last two days of drinking.

As soon as she lies on the couch, Pip takes the opportunity to snooze on a soft surface and jumps onto Catherine's stomach. "OOPH!" Catherine moans.

"Well, hello Pip. You wanna join me for a nap?" She inquires.

Pip meows loudly.

"Okay, get settled then." After enduring the predictable ritual in which Pip circles and circles before finally lying down, Catherine enters into a restless sleep.

• • •

Sarephah and Pexov have been listening in on the phone conversation.

Pexov sneers, "I'm glad Catherine's going to the 'celebration dinner,' since time with the precious family stirs up lots of emotions, and lots of excuses to drink."

With a little sadness, but with love in her eyes, Sarephah responds, "I'm glad she's going to the dinner as well, since Catherine needs to learn the truth about her effect on this family."

"I'm curious, Sarephah, why such interest in this...this...worthless piece of decaying flesh?" Spittle falls from Pexov's grotesquely swollen lips as he speaks.

Pexov is about five feet tall, emaciated, and gray. His eyes are red when angry, which is most of the time, and cool blue during less agitated times. He moves freely between earth and the heavenlies. Yet, he lives in constant fear because he is required to account for his movements and actions anytime his master, The Ruler of the Kingdom of the Air, summons him. His only respite from the terrors of his master is when he successfully destroys a soul and offers it as an unholy sacrifice on the altar of the eternal death.

"I mean, really," Pexov continues, "she is nothing. Now, I can *see* spending time on someone important. Why not focus on someone, say, who will influence thousands of people. Someone like…mmm...like…a pastor of one of those mega churches would be worth your effort. Why all the trouble for a small time drunken loser like her? *Please*. Don't you have anything better to do?"

Sarephah, though completely repulsed by Pexov, calmly replies, "Every mortal is precious in the sight of the Divine Three. They will never forsake nor leave their children no matter how far away they run from their presence. They pursue them with a holy and perfect love."

"WHATEVER! I've heard it all before," Pexov screams.

As his eyes begin to change to a fiery red, he roars, "I WILL have this one, and there is NOTHING you can do to stop me. I am too powerful and too smart for you. I will DESTROY HER."

Sarephah responds with righteous anger, "NO! You will not destroy Catherine."

"YES…I…WILL," Pexov yells while reaching for his weapon: a long rod that tapers at the end to make a long, sharp knife.

Pexov stands with both legs spread wide and thrusts his weapon toward Sarephah. Sarephah swiftly moves out of the way of the strike and pulls out her sword. They begin to circle each other as opponents often do before the fight begins.

While maintaining a safe distance, Sarephah takes the opportunity to question Pexov. "I'm curious as well, Pexov. What happened to you? Why did you follow Satan at the great rebellion?"

Pexov responds, "COME ON! Why do you *always* bring THAT up?"

Still circling and thrusting his weapon at Sarephah, Pexov adds with a sneer, “I wanted more.”

Deflecting a blow, Sarephah shouts, “More what? We had everything in the presence of the Divine Three.”

Pexov lands another blow on Sarephah’s sword, but Pexov’s flimsy weapon bends, and he loses control of it for a moment.

After struggling to catch it, he gains control again, raises his weapon, and just before swinging hard, he shouts, “I wanted more of EVERYTHING” C*RACK.* The sound of the weapons colliding reverberates in the heavenlies.

“I wanted more POWER…more CONTROL…more FREEDOM.” To emphasize each phrase, Pexov swings his weapon at Sarephah, but she deflects each blow.

Sarephah goes on the offensive by pushing Pexov back with a wave of resistance streaming out from her sword. Pexov staggers back a few steps, gains control of himself, raises his weapon again, and resumes circling Sarephah, but from a safer distance.

Watching Pexov intently, Sarephah says in frustration and with some sadness, “We were friends before you followed that traitor. Was it worth it?”

“Yes, it was worth it. I am FREE, which is more than I can say for you. YOU have to follow rules and be *loving.*” Pexov spits out those last words as if they burn his tongue.

“You are so deluded, Pexov. My freedom has not been hindered at all by following the Divine Three. I just use my free-will for good, NOT for evil.”

Then, stopping momentarily, Sarephah lets down her guard, and says softly, “The Divine Three loved you…and so did I.”

Trembling with rage, Pexov yells, “I never wanted your love *or theirs.*” Charging wildly toward Sarephah, he swings his weapon…CRACK!

“STOP! DON’T HIT ME!” Catherine screams as she raises her arms to cover her face. Sitting up, panting, and sweating, she frantically searches her memory for the cause of the horrendous terror she feels.

Pip scrambles off her lap and scurries out of the room.

Catherine's eyes dart around the room, horrified she will discover something or somebody ready to attack her.

She sees nothing.

She slows her breathing to listen for a noise or voice. Pausing again, she hears nothing.

Dread of impending doom overwhelms her.

She is terrified.

Sarephah moves out of Pexov's range after she expertly deflects the last blow. "The Divine Three love all of their creation. I will forever praise the eternal One who was, is, and will forever be. They are worthy to be praised. Holy, holy, holy is their name."

Pexov is repulsed and defenseless when the praises of the Divine Three are lifted up in his presence. He glares at Sarephah, then slowly retreats into the dark depths of the heavenlies to prepare for the next battle.

Sarephah smiles victoriously. She turns toward Catherine, takes in a deep breath, and breathes out a protective aura around Catherine.

The intensity of the nightmare begins to fade for Catherine. A safe feeling slowly overtakes the fear and panic. "It's okay...breathe. You're okay…breathe. Nothing is here. It was just a nightmare. I'm alright." But the anxiety will linger long after reassuring herself that it was just a nightmare.

She finally stands and looks at the clock. 6:00. "Crap!" she yells. With a hint of sarcasm, she thinks *I better get going. Don't want to be late for dinner.*

As she heads for the door, she murmurs to herself, "I need a drink."

Chapter Five

"Guess who's coming to dinner?!" Andrew whispers in Nicole's ear.

Nicole, his twin sister, turns around slowly, looks at him wide-eyed, stomps her foot, and exclaims, "NO!"

"Yes!" Andrew replies and turns quickly, trying to avoid the inevitable tirade this news will bring.

Nicole grabs his arm and spins him around. "Who invited *her*? And…how did she know we were all having dinner here tonight? For once, can't we have just *one* peaceful family get together?" Nicole spurts out with a combination of frustration and anger.

Andrew laughs. "Ah, come on. It's always much more fun when Catherine shows up."

"FUN?" Nicole interrupts angrily. Waving her arms to accentuate every word, she exclaims, "What is so fun about watching our drunken sister make rude comments to everyone, start arguments with whomever happens to get in her way, cast blame on everyone and anyone she's ever met for *her* problems, and then leave the house in an uproar? Oh, yeah that's really fun stuff, Andrew."

"That's a very good description, sis!" He chuckles, and then continues a little more seriously. "Hey, I have no problem with

Catherine coming over. She's part of the family, whether you like it or not. Deal with it."

After patting her on the shoulder in a mock show of sympathy, he hurries off to join his wife, son Bryan, dad and brother-in-law in the other room.

An obviously distressed Nicole, whirls around, stomps her foot again, and heads toward the kitchen.

"Mom! Did you invite Catherine to dinner tonight?"

Megan, the youngest daughter, looks up from the magazine she's browsing, and says, "Really, Catherine's coming? I haven't seen her in ages." Then adds under her breath, "I wonder how she's doing?"

Nancy shuts the oven door, turns toward Nicole and sighs, "Yes, I invited your sister."

"WHY? You know how she gets, and this is supposed to be mine and Devon's night." Stomping her foot again, she whimpers, "She's going to ruin everything."

Nancy puts her arm around Nicole and gently guides her over to a chair and sits her down. Joining her across the table, she tries to console her daughter. "Calm down, Nicole. It's going to be okay. I know as well as you do how Catherine can get, but I specifically told her that there would be no drinking tonight."

"Oh, like *that* will do any good. YOU of all people should know how drunks are…" She stops mid-sentence. Nancy lowers her eyes. Nicole reaches over and grabs her hand. "I'm sorry, mom. I shouldn't have said that. Catherine just makes me crazy." She sits back and sighs heavily.

With every muscle starting to tense, Nancy tries to remain calm. Secretly, she is just as worried as Nicole about Catherine causing a scene tonight, but does her best to keep her fears to herself, while at the same time, reassuring her daughter.

Megan jumps into the conversation, "Nicole, don't be so dramatic. You're the one causing the scene now, not Catherine. I think it's good that Catherine's coming tonight." Then looking at her mom with a worried expression, she wonders, "Although, I do hope she hasn't been drinking. How was she when you last talked with her?"

Nancy gets up to check the casserole. She sighs. "Well, I think she was sober when I talked with her but…she missed…umm…some appointments recently, and I'm almost certain it was because of drinking." Nancy returns to the table and sits back down. "I don't know. She needs help but…she has to *want* help."

No one says anything for a minute. Defeat, frustration, anger, and worry loom heavy in their hearts. Finally, Nancy says softly to Nicole, "If Catherine causes a scene tonight, your father and I will ask her to leave. We won't let her spoil your night, Nicole."

Poking his head around the corner, Scott hesitantly asks, "Hey, I just heard Catherine's coming for dinner. Is that right?"

"YES!" they all three shout simultaneously. Nancy expresses worry, Nicole anger, and Megan concern.

Scott holds up his hands, "Whoa, sorry I said anything."

Nancy jumps up from the table, "All right, enough about Catherine for now. Why don't you two girls join the others while I finish up in here."

After Nicole and Megan are out of sight, Scott puts his arms around Nancy and gently questions her. "Aren't you concerned about how Catherine might be when she gets here? Remember the last family dinner."

"Yes, I remember," Nancy says softly.

After some moments, she sighs wearily. "Oh, Scott, I just want to help her. She's really going downhill fast. She missed dinner with you Monday. I found out she missed another music lesson with a student. Plus, I think she's in trouble at work."

Scott looks concerned. "How do you know she's in trouble at work?" he asks.

"Trust me, I'm an alcoholic. She can't be doing well at work with the amount of drinking she's doing," Nancy states knowingly.

Scott moves away from Nancy, sits down heavily at the kitchen table and hangs his head for a moment. Finally, he looks up and asks, "What do you think we should do?" Nancy sits down next to him. They are both weary from the battle. After a long wait, she sighs, "I really don't know."

• • •

The heaviness in the house is exhilarating to the demonic presence that surrounds this family. Pexov is uniquely concerned about Catherine, but he is joined by demons that have similar influence on the others in the family. Catherine's family believes the only problem is her drinking. However, the problem is infinitely greater and more profound; it is a spiritual fight for her soul.

• • •

Catherine waits in her car one block from her parent's house, trying to muster enough courage to spend an evening with her entire family. She's still shaken from her afternoon nightmare, worried about losing her job at the hotel, and tired of never measuring up to the expectations of everyone.

She takes another swig of liquid courage from the whiskey she purchased on the way over. "I am so tired of everything in my life. And I *really* don't want to spend an entire evening talking about how good everything is for everyone, but me," she mumbles to herself.

She sits for a few more minutes staring at the clock on her dash and taking several more large gulps of whiskey. With increasing intensity, the alcohol begins to relieve her anxiety, bolster her courage, and dim the depression.

Her thoughts are becoming distorted. *What is the point of my life? No one cares, and frankly, I don't care either. Why do*

I have to go in there and be with a family that doesn't want me around? They treat me like dirt. I need to be around people who care about me. Hmmm...I wonder what Kurt is doing?

Catherine takes one more satisfying gulp, puts her car in drive, and forgets all about dinner with her family.

As she drives off, Sarephah gazes onto the scene, shakes her head, looks over at a triumphant Pexov, and then enters the presence of the Divine Three.

Chapter Six

Sarephah joins the multitude of angels gathered at the foot of the throne praising the Divine Three. Encircling the throne is a luminescent cloud pulsating with brilliant colors. Lightning flashes illuminate the faces of the faithful mortals who are enjoying the eternal rewards of their earthly choices. Peels of thunder rumble and rattle praises to the maker of all creation. The voices of the angels and mortals blend to create a majestic and powerful choir. "Holy, holy, holy, is the Almighty Three in One, who was, and is, and is to come" is being chanted joyfully as hands are raised and bodies sway in exuberant gratitude.

Suddenly, the Divine Three rise from their throne. The pulsating cloud rolls up into the realm above, and their aura, which looks something like rushing water, moves rapidly throughout the heavenlies washing over every living thing. In an instant there is silence.

No sound is heard anywhere in the heavenlies, including the depths of eternal death. The stark contrast from the previous moment is shocking. Everyone kneels in anticipation of what is to come.

In the far distance there is a muffled sound. It is faint. It is weak, but it is beautiful. All ears strain to hear the call of the one who caused the Divine Three to bring silence to the heavenlies.

Finally, the clear voice of a mortal reaches the ears of the silent gathering. The multitude hear this voice express faith in the Author of all life, confess a heartfelt belief in the sacrifice of the Word, and ask for the presence of the Text to write a new story for their life. One soul has made the momentous choice to renounce their sin, turn away from evil, and seek a new way. Immediately, the saving aura of the Divine Three goes out from them and enters the newly saved soul. "Let us rejoice! One of our precious children has been forgiven and has accepted our love. They are blessed to join the assembly of the redeemed for all eternity," shouts the Three. Jumping to their feet in celebration, laughter, shouts of joy, and praises ring out, and all who are gathered dance to the sound of a soul reborn.

A little while later, Sarephah positions herself at the feet of the Divine Three simply to be in their presence. She finds these times comforting, peaceful, and enriching. The Divine Three are pleased to have her so near. Although perfect love weaves in and through the Three to create one essence which needs no other, love for and by their creation is supremely cherished. The Three bask in the glow of the love given them by Sarephah, for they know it is her free choice to give. While they drink in the sweetness of love freely given, Sarephah rises on the wind of love gratefully received.

"Sarephah! How is our faithful servant?" inquires the Three.

"In your presence, I am utterly joyful," she responds with arms stretched wide in adoration. "Please, may I sit with you a bit longer?" she requests.

A rush of the Three's aura washes over her as they respond, "We are honored you ask to sit with us. Not many seek only our presence. Be still and know that We are One." Sarephah sits fully enclosed in the soothing wind of their aura and rests.

In a place where time is unbound, it is difficult to speak of time in measured, orderly increments. Yet, it is appropriate to say that Sarephah is fully blessed after spending considerable time resting in the presence of complete and perfect love.

Finally, Sarephah shifts reluctantly out of the soothing aura, stands up, stretches, and looks toward the edge of the heavenlies where a porthole makes earth visible. She remembers Catherine. Shaking her head, she approaches the Three with one question, "Why do some reject your love?"

There is a place deep within the essence of the Three that groans for all those who reject them. Upon hearing this question posed by their beloved Sarephah, they are collectively flooded with memories of the original plan of the Author, the sacrifice of the Word, and the work of the Text. Finally, representing the one essence, each replies in a distinct voice, together making a single harmonious melody.

The Author declares, "Our eternal power and divine nature have been clearly displayed from the creation of the world."

The Word continues, "I, representing the Divine Three, took on mortal flesh to reach that which was Our own, but Our own did not receive Us."

The Text finishes, "Although humanity knew Us, they neither glorified Us nor gave thanks. They suppressed the truth and therefore, their thinking became futile, and their foolish hearts were darkened."

All three speak with one voice, "Since they did not think it worthwhile to know Us, We permitted them to follow their own depraved minds, weakened by sin and every kind of evil and choose wickedness and evil over our love."

Pondering these truths spoken by the Divine Three and curious about the risks of freewill for mortals, a wide-eyed and still somewhat confused Sarephah inquires, "Is it true to say that those who reject you do so when the truth of who you are is suppressed by their freewill, thus making them into the type of people who will continue to suppress the truth? Then, over a period of time, the people they become can only make sinful choices because those are the only choices they are able to choose?"

She pauses to catch her breath, and then continues with another question. "Does that mean their freewill is no longer free since suppressing the truth begins to limit their choices?"

The Three remain silent for a moment. "Sarephah, it will be best to start from the beginning, and then proceed to answer your questions."

Sarephah sits down again, opens her heart and mind to experience the knowledge given by the Three, and waits expectantly for what they will teach her.

The Three speak as one, saying, "In the beginning, we created mortals in our image. They were whole and complete in every way we desired. In addition, we bestowed upon them freedom of the will, uninhibited, but not all powerful. We furnished them with a human nature to experience their human existence with each other, and a soul to experience their spiritual existence with Us. In fact, we uniquely designed their nature, will, and soul to work together for complete relational connectivity with all living things. Placing them in comfort and safety, we protected them from all that was beyond their capacity to understand or experience without harmful consequences. We were pleased with our creation and enjoyed our time with them."

"We must include some details about Satan, the Morning Star – son of the dawn, who could not accept our love or our limits. Envy whispered to him that he deserved to rule over all creation; pride shouted to him that he could indeed become that ruler. In the end, his being was consumed with every wickedness and evil. He and his followers were cast out of our presence by our righteous decree. It was Satan who tempted the first mortals born of our creation and interrupted our relationship with all mortals thereafter."

"Once our two first born were tempted and made the decision to seek after that which was forbidden by our love and for their protection, human nature was forever imprinted with the memory of good and evil, and the guilt of this rebellion. Because of the actions of our first born children, innocence was lost and all mortals thereafter inherited a tarnished nature and will. As a consequence, at some point within the soul of mortals, they must wrestle with a nature and will that either pulls them away from us or draws them toward us."

The Three pause for a moment. They sense Sarephah's understanding and continue.

"Sarephah, We want you to understand that the desire within a mortal's soul to seek evil or good does not happen right at the moment life begins. At the beginning of each mortal's earthly existence, their stained nature is inactive because it has no outside influences upon it to direct it one way or another. Their will is completely uninhibited because their nature is newly born. Over time, however, influences such as events, environment, heritage, and most importantly, spiritual forces begin to awaken the memories of good and evil sleeping deep within their soul. A soul awakened by these influences begins to form their nature and stir the will to move in the direction it most desires."

"A nature molded into our image becomes increasingly holy, and therefore, the will, consisting of desires and choices, becomes holy and good. However, a nature molded into the image of evil becomes increasingly sinful and corrupt, and the will becomes wicked and evil. Thus, a wholly corrupt nature chooses evil and rejects Us."

Pausing for a brief moment, they state, "We have answered your question about why someone rejects us. We will now answer your question about the freedom of the will."

"A mortal's will works freely within the boundaries set by their nature. Let us explain further. A mortal's nature and will are intertwined to govern their thoughts and actions. Their will is bound to and controlled by their nature. Yet, their will often determines the character of their nature. And, it is the soul that animates their spiritual life. All three work together in pursuit of either good or evil."

"Therefore, when a mortal's nature is molded fully into our image, their will is shaped as well to seek only the good. In contrast, when a mortal's nature is molded into that of an idol or something just as sinister, then their will is shaped likewise. An evil nature desires evil; a holy nature desires that which is holy. Mortals have freewill, but their will, programmed by their nature, is compelled to choose what their nature demands."

Sarephah sits up straighter when the Three finish speaking. Thinking of Catherine now, she asks, "If Catherine persists in following her will, which has been formed and now controlled by her sinful nature, how can she ever change and follow you?"

With love for Catherine permeating every word, the Divine Three quickly respond, "Catherine must use her will to go against her sinful nature and begin to choose a different way. However, she cannot do this alone. She needs supernatural help to do this. This is why we continually pursue her and work to awaken her soul so she can recognize the spiritual forces working for and against her."

"In addition, she must be enabled to recognize her sinful nature in order to respond just enough to see the truth about herself, her inability to change her life, and the love We offer. This is a spiritual struggle unlike any she will ever encounter, because when her will is called upon to reshape her nature, the battle is fierce. She needs a reversal in her thoughts and desires, but her nature will fight against this, and so will the spiritual forces out to destroy her."

"However, if she cries out for help, we will come to her, restore her soul, renew her nature, and reshape her will. Her rebirth, the cleansing of her soul from the stain of sin, will happen instantaneously, but the memories of sin and its effects will linger. Then over time, her nature will be molded into our image by the working of the Text residing in her soul. Ultimately, her freewill shall yearn to follow only that which is of Us."

Sarephah is extremely pleased when she hears this news, but just as she begins to ask another question she hears an agonizing, terror-filled scream rise up from the depths of the heavenlies - a place known as the eternal death.

Alarmed, she asks wide-eyed, “What is that?”

The Three’s aura dims ever so slightly, and they moan quietly. With extreme sorrow, they begin, “Sarephah, we have opened your ears so you could hear the cry of a soul being sacrificed at the altar of Satan in the eternal death. Satan has taken another soul. We know the one he has taken, and the grief we feel is inexpressible. Their sinful nature chose to follow its wicked and evil will and to continually reject Us.”

They pause reflecting on what is ahead for Catherine. “Remember what you have just heard, and why it happened. Go back to Catherine. Sin is crouching at her door and desires to have her. And Pexov holds a knife to her soul.”

The Three’s aura brightens again as Sarephah rises to leave.

Another scream shatters the silence.

Chapter Seven

As Sarephah departs, the Three send out their aura of knowledge, transmitting a divine message for several prayer warriors. The Divine Three are gearing up to battle Satan, the once mighty but fallen angel, for the soul of another precious child. For they know Satan and his horde are ruthless and relentless in their pursuit of mortals.

The Three declare, "To survive, Catherine needs divine help, an enlightened heart, and spiritual eyes. For her struggle is not against flesh and blood, but against the rulers, against the authorities, against the powers of this dark world and against the spiritual forces of evil in the heavenly realms." Immediately several messenger angels are dispatched.

• • •

Vickie glances at her watch, frowns, and hurries her pace. "Oh, boy, I'm running later than I thought this morning," she whispers to herself. She waves to the front desk staff as she walks in the front door of the Holden Suites, but doesn't stop to talk.

What is wrong with me? I'm never late. I just can't seem to get focused this morning. There's something unsettled with me, but I can't figure out what it is. She sighs and shakes her head, then enters the elevator.

While pushing the button for the corporate offices on the fifth floor, a verse suddenly pops into her head. *For our struggle is not against flesh and blood, but against the rulers, against the authorities, against the powers of this dark world and against the spiritual forces of evil in the heavenly realms.* "Huh...what's that supposed to mean?" she wonders.

The elevator stops, the doors open, and Vickie exits still pondering the verse that seemingly came out of nowhere. She's greeted by her administrative assistant Kim.

"Morning Vickie!"

Distracted, Vickie barely hears her. "Huh...ah...sorry. What did you say Kim?"

Kim repeats her greeting. "I just said good morning." Concerned Kim asks, "Everything okay?"

Not wanting to discuss her uneasiness, Vickie responds, "Yeah, sure. How are you this morning?"

"Great!" Kim practically shouts. Vickie smiles at her exuberant secretary, shakes her head, and turns toward her office.

While Vickie is unlocking her office door, Kim inquires, "Did you hear about the Longwell reception last night?"

Turning around slowly, Vickie looks at her secretary with a worried expression and says cautiously, "No. Why?"

"I guess it got pretty wild. You may want to check with Greg. He was the Manager on Duty last night."

Sighing and pushing the door open, Vickie says over her shoulder, "Thanks, I will. Listen, I need to work on something. No interruptions for the next half hour. Thanks Kim." Before Kim can respond, Vickie shuts her door.

While hanging up her coat, she sees her Bible on the bookshelf and grabs it. Holding the Bible against her chest, she whispers a silent prayer, asking for help finding the verse. She sits down at her desk, puts her phone on hold, and opens her Bible. She pauses before she begins intently searching her memory for the exact reference of the verse that came to her in the elevator.

Suddenly, she remembers. "It's from Ephesians" she says victoriously. Hastily flipping through the New Testament, she finds the letter to the Ephesians. "Let's see...I think it is somewhere in chapter six. Yes, Ephesians 6:12."

She reads the verse silently, and then sits back in her chair. "Okay, so what am I supposed to make of this particular verse popping into my head? Does it have anything to do with my meeting with Catherine this morning? God, are you trying to tell me something?" Vickie bows her head in prayer. The angel assigned to this mission begins speaking into the air.

• • •

On the other side of town, Nancy Ash is beginning her morning meditation, something she learned to do after joining the program of Alcoholics Anonymous. Normally these times of quiet and reflective mediation are peaceful and soothing for her. This morning, however, she has only one thing on her mind: Catherine.

Catherine's absence last night was almost as disruptive as her presence would have been. Relief was felt in the air, but worry settled in everyone's heart. No one spoke about it openly. No, to do so would have been too uncomfortable, and they think, pointless. After all, what else can be said or done about Catherine? They've encouraged her to seek help in every possible way: counseling, anti-depressants, self-help books, doctors, horoscopes, seminars, church, and yoga. You name it; they've tried it.

Nancy can't give up on her daughter though. She remembers how bad things got when she was drinking, and how Scott and some close friends never gave up on her. But what really drives her, if she is honest with herself, is that she feels somehow responsible for her daughter's struggles. This guilt pushes her to go to any lengths to rescue Catherine from the disease of alcoholism: a disease that runs deep in Nancy's biological family. Even her AA sponsor, Sherry, hasn't been able to redirect this thinking, yet.

By all accounts, Nancy is a Christian. To Nancy, God is not simply a "higher power" but the Almighty Creator God. Yet, she prefers the spiritual simplicity in her AA program over the dogmatic complexity she finds in Church. She's comfortable using both her Bible and her program-approved meditation books to improve her conscious contact with God. Her constant prayer is for knowledge of God's will and the power to carry it out.

Working hard at listening during her time with God, Nancy waits patiently for some divine word. The problem today is that she keeps thinking about Catherine and not listening for God's voice.

Then, suddenly she senses something. She quiets herself. She listens. A thought comes. *For your struggle is not against flesh and blood, but against the rulers, against the authorities, against the powers of this dark world and against the spiritual forces of evil in the heavenly realms.*

She pauses. She listens for more. Nothing. "Hmmm....I know that verse is from Ephesians. I think chapter six." She ponders this for a minute longer.

Another thought comes. *Alcohol is but a symptom. It is an illness which only a spiritual experience will conquer.* "Yes, that's from the A.A. Big Book. Okay, God what are you trying to say to me? I'm listening. Is this about Catherine?" The other angel dispatched for this very purpose speaks into the air. Nancy reaches for her pen and paper and begins journaling.

• • •

About the same time Nancy and Vickie are deep in prayer, Catherine is waking with a splitting headache, a guilty conscious, and a surly disposition. She spent the evening drinking alone after Kurt brushes her off. All other calls to various drinking and non-drinking buddies go unanswered, providing her with plenty of reasons to be angry and resentful. But what Catherine can't quite face is the awful truth that no one really wants to be around her. When she's dry, she's barely tolerable; when she's drunk, she's downright unbearable. Yet for an alcoholic like Catherine, the opposite is true. When she's dry, life is unbearable; when she's drunk, life is barely tolerable.

What many don't realize is that Catherine needs to drink just to feel normal. She's caught in the vicious cycle of alcoholism in which the drink manipulates her nature, and her will desires the next drink.

It's a beautiful sunny morning, but Catherine's too busy feeling sorry for herself to notice. Her high tolerance for alcohol helps her shake off the effects of last night's drunk, and she falsely believes she is ready to face whatever will happen during her meeting at work.

She dresses conservatively, wearing a fairly clean, but slightly wrinkled, black pant suit. After putting on knee-highs, ripped at the toes, and her tattered black shoes, she stands before her full-length mirror.

She sees a worthless human being.

Pexov sees a pathetic mortal.

Sarephah sees a beloved child.

The Divine Three see a lost soul.

Pip comes up behind Catherine, rubs his head against her leg in affection, and interrupts the moment. Barely acknowledging Pip, she takes one last painful look, and then turns away from the mirror. She grabs her coat, rubs Pip on the head, and heads out the door. Both Sarephah and Pexov follow.

Catherine arrives ten minutes early for her meeting with Vickie, which is a major miracle since she's normally late for everything. Scared, but unwilling to admit it, she enters the hotel through the service entrance in the back. Hoping she doesn't see anyone, she rushes through the hallway to the elevators. Out of nowhere, she hears someone yelling her name.

"Catherine!"

She keeps going, pretending she doesn't hear anything. The last thing she wants now is to face any employees, especially this particular one. Picking up her pace, she mutters "this sucks" under her breath.

"Catherine! Hey, it's Ben. Wait up!"

Catherine walks even faster down the hallway, and finally stops right in front of the elevators. She pushes the up button, silently hoping the elevator doors will fly open so she can escape the always inquisitive Ben, the maintenance manager at the Holden Suites.

It's too late.

Catching up to her, he slows down and comes up behind to her. "Hey, Catherine," Ben says slightly out of breath. "How've you been? I haven't seen you since…hmm….since Monday."

Catherine rolls her eyes, turns around to face him, and responds, "Good. I've been real good. I just took a couple days off," she lies. She doesn't make eye contact with Ben when speaking to him, and turns back around as soon as the last word is spoken.

"I was a little worried about you. We were all worried about you," Ben says calmly.

"Yeah, well there's nothing to worry about," she mumbles without turning around to face him. Ben isn't bothered by Catherine's response. He's seen it plenty of times before.

Talking to her back, since she won't turn around, Ben asks, "Are you feeling better?"

Without turning away from the elevator doors, she lets out an exasperated sigh, "Yes."

Ben continues boldly. "You know. I used to drink. I used to drink a whole lot. I drank so much that I would have times where I couldn't remember what I had done or said." He waits a moment to let this information sink in, and then asks solemnly, "That ever happen to you?"

Catherine whirls around, looks at him angrily, and responds. "Ben, I would appreciate it if you would just leave me alone." She turns back around, hits the up button a couple times for emphasis, crosses her arms, and wonders why this stupid elevator is taking so long.

Unfazed, Ben forges ahead with his story. "Yeah, drinking really messed up my life."

Catherine cringes.

"All I can say is that I thank God I finally surrendered and got sober. I could only do it through the help of...well...God and working the program of Alcoholics Anonymous," Ben testifies.

She cringes again, shuffles her feet, hits the up button a few more times, but says nothing.

There's an awkward moment of silence. Finally, Ben breaks the silence. "Listen, if you ever want help let me know." Just as he turns to leave, he smiles and adds, "By the way, an angel sent me to talk with you...oh, and this elevator is out of order."

Trying to act cool and unaffected by this news, she walks slowly toward the steps, pushes the door open, and enters the stairwell. When the door shuts behind her, she collapses against it. *What was that all about,* she wonders? *I didn't need that just before this meeting. Ben is so weird, and now I know why.* She starts the climb to the fifth floor, contemplating Ben's announcement about the angel. *An angel sent me to talk with you. Okay, Ben, whatever.* Sarephah smiles.

Catherine reaches the fifth floor out of breath, out of patience, and almost out of time. She bursts through the door with a loud bang. Embarrassed by her less than graceful entrance, she hastily shuts the door, and adjusts her suit jacket under her coat.

She's greeted by a somewhat subdued Kim. "Hello, Catherine. Please have a seat, and I'll let Vickie know you're here,"

Kim states with little of her usual enthusiasm. Catherine takes off her coat, sits down, and tries to smooth out the wrinkles in her pants. Her hands are sweating, and she feels nauseous.

Kim knocks on Vickie's door.

"Enter!" Hearing Vickie's response, Kim opens the door, pokes her head in, and says quietly, "Catherine's here."

"Thanks Kim. I'll come out and get her when I'm ready," she replies. When the door shuts, Vickie closes her Bible, lays it to the side, and picks up the detailed plan for Catherine she just finished. She whispers one more silent pray for strength and wisdom, stands up, and heads for the door.

Catherine fidgets in her seat under the watchful eye of Kim. A couple employees walk by, stop talking, and look away when they see who's waiting for Vickie, but Catherine barely raises her head to notice. She's still not sure what happened on Monday, but she's very sure it wasn't good.

The wait is excruciating. Pexov smiles.

Catherine looks up when Vickie's door opens, and her stomach does a full triple somersault with a half-twist.

"Hello, Catherine." Vickie says with a business-like tone. While holding the door open, she motions toward her office, and says solemnly, "Come in."

Catherine can barely catch her breath.

There are few moments in one's life that are truly life altering; Catherine is about to experience one of them.

She stands and walks into the office.

Vickie shuts the door.

Chapter Eight

Catherine plops down heavily, and slumps in the chair opposite the desk, while Vickie walks around to her chair and sits down. Vickie looks at her notes, sets them aside, and looks up at Catherine. Catherine fidgets under Vickie's gaze and wonders; w*hat did I do to get here? Oh, why can't I remember? I wish I could run out of here.*

Vickie intentionally pauses before she begins. *God, she looks so miserable. Help her to accept what she is about to learn, and the plan you have for her.*

"How are you feeling?" Vickie finally inquires.

Why does everyone keep asking me that? "I feel good." Catherine responds in a weak and unconvincing tone.

Vickie raises her head slightly and casts a curious look toward Catherine. "I'm glad to hear that." Leaning forward in her chair, she continues, "'cause you weren't doing very well on Monday." Leaning back in her chair again, she calmly asks, "Can you tell me what happened on Monday Catherine?"

This is it. What do I say? No, I don't know what happened on Monday. "Umm…well…I wasn't feeling well, so I took some cold medicine…and…" Vickie raises her hand to stop Catherine.

With a stern tone, Vickie declares, "Catherine you were drunk when you showed up to work on Monday. Cold medicine had nothing to do with your condition." She leans forward, places her elbows on the table, and clasps her hands together, and rests them under her chin, and asks, "Do you want to try again?"

Catherine sits up straighter, adjusts her suit jacket, looks down, thinks for a moment, and then starts again. "What I meant to say is that…umm…yes, I did have a few drinks." Leaning forward for emphasis, and talking more rapidly, she continues, "but I really think that the combination of the alcohol and cold medicine…ummm…you know…really made me feel worse, since I only had a drink or two."

Vickie sits unaffected, but silently prays for patience and compassion.

Sitting back and looking down, Catherine says quietly, "I know that I shouldn't have been drinking before coming into work that day." Adding for good measure and with all the sincerity she can muster, "It won't happen again. I promise."

Vickie sits back in her chair after waiting what seems like an eternity to Catherine. Finally, Vickie locks eyes with Catherine and states emphatically, "You're right on both counts. Yes, you should *not* have been drinking before coming into work, and yes, this will not happen again on hotel property."

"Yes, absolutely. This will not happen again," Catherine adds, nodding her head in agreement. *This is going better than I thought.*

Continuing to look directly into Catherine eyes, Vickie inquires, "Catherine, I am going to ask you again. Can you tell me anything about what happened on Monday?" Vickie is confident, based on her research that Catherine was most likely in a blackout, and has no recollection of what happened.

What! I thought this was almost over. Why is she asking about Monday? I DON'T KNOW! Squirming in her seat, her hands are sweating, and her heart is racing. *How do I get out of this?* Weakly she says, "I...believe...that I...came to work...umm..." She adjusts her suit jacket and thinks of something to say.

Sarephah sends her thoughts into the air. *Tell her the truth.* Catherine is startled by this thought that comes out of now where.

Pexov counters with his messages of deceit. *Tell her nothing. You don't need this crappy job.*

Tell her the truth.

Tell her nothing. Quit this stinking job.

Catherine is paralyzed by the thoughts streaming into her brain.

Vickie waits patiently, for she sees the struggle that Catherine is waging in her mind. Vickie remembers the verse from Ephesians 6:12, and prays that Catherine can win this battle.

Vickie senses that Catherine needs some encouragement. She says with a compassionate tone. "Catherine, your job is on the line here. I need you to be as honest as you can with me right now."

For Catherine being honest is a foreign concept, yet she isn't stupid, and knows that telling the truth might just get her out of this jam. And, maybe, get Vickie off her back.

Tell her the truth. Sarephah's voice is slightly louder than Pexov's.

Catherine takes a deep breath and practically whispers, "I don't know what happened on Monday." Adding with her eyes cast down, and embarrassment in her voice, "I can't remember."

Bolstered by this small victory, Vickie relaxes visibly. *One battle won.* "I appreciate your honesty," she says with sincerity. Picking up her notes, she glances at item #2: Monday night.

"I believe it's important for you to know exactly what happened Monday when you showed up for our staff meeting drunk," Vickie says somberly. Adding for emphasis, "I don't think you can fully appreciate the seriousness of this situation until you know the truth."

Catherine nods her head slowly. *Let's just get this over with.* "Okay," she says weakly. Sarephah stands ready. Pexov eyes glow red.

Vickie gathers up her personal notes, interviews from the other staff, and the outline she created this morning after her prayer time. She begins factually, "On Monday, at exactly 2:00 p.m., the weekly staff meeting commenced. All managers and supervisors were present, except one."

Looking up from her notes, she nods toward Catherine. "You were the only staff member absent at the start of the meeting." Vickie declares.

Continuing, she states, "At approximately 2:15 p.m., the last staff member made her appearance." Putting down her notes, she fixes her eyes on Catherine. "It was apparent from the moment you walked into the meeting that something was very wrong. After taking a seat, you quickly became disruptive by throwing mints across the room to other employees, and then whispering loudly to the person next to you, which was, by the way, Ben Towland." Remembering her agitation about this, Vickie pauses slightly. Catherine looks down, concentrating on her hands in her lap.

Resuming, Vickie says, "After approximately ten minutes, you abruptly got up and left the meeting. When you didn't return in a reasonable time, *I,*" emphasizing the "I" makes Catherine look up, "sent Betsy to see where you had gone, and if you were all right. The meeting was finally adjourned without Betsy or you returning. I didn't learn the next part of the story until about a half hour later that day."

Leaning forward in her chair for emphasis, Vickie says firmly, "This part was conveyed to me by your co-workers when I interviewed them yesterday." Catherine cringes and slumps in her chair. *How bad does this get?*

Looking back at her notes, Vickie states, "Betsy found you passed out in the main bathroom. She was concerned that you were injured, but once you came to, it was apparent bruises were the worst of your physical injuries at that point." Pausing, Vickie looks up at Catherine to see how she's handling this information, knowing it gets much worse.

Confident that Catherine is listening, though very uncomfortable, she forges ahead. "You became quite agitated when Betsy suggested that you were drunk and needed to be driven home." Glancing up from her notes, she adds, "Apparently, you used a few choice words that I won't repeat." Catherine slumps a little further in her chair. Pexov smiles.

"Marie, the restaurant supervisor, entered the bathroom and saw what was happening. She immediately contacted housekeeping to get a key to a room, so they could get you out of the bathroom in case any hotel guests walked in, and to have time to figure out what to do with you, since you were being quite, how shall I say it…boisterous. Finally, Betsy and Marie met Kris from housekeeping, opened one of the rooms, and hid you from other guests."

Leaving the story for a moment, Vickie asks, "Have you noticed how many employees are involved in this story so far?"

Catherine sits up slightly, nods solemnly, but says nothing.

"Good. I didn't want that fact to go unnoticed."

"Again, I want to emphasize that I had to interview three employees, Betsy, Marie, and Kris, for this part." Catherine nods again.

"Shortly after you arrived in the room, you started throwing up." Vickie pauses. Catherine lowers her head.

"You threw up all over yourself…all over Betsy…all over Marie…and all over Kris. They eventually got you into the shower to minimize the mess you were making. After attempting to clean themselves, they sat you in the shower, and sent Kris to get something for you to put on, since your clothes were ruined. I believe they ended up getting one of the uniforms of the kitchen staff."

Vickie sighs, "Word gets back to me, and I head up to the room they put you in. By this time, Ben and Kurt show up thinking they're just going to take you home. The plan was that one would drive you, and the other would drive your car. However, as you can imagine, they walked into much more than they bargained for." Vickie relays firmly.

Catherine tries to withdraw into herself to avoid hearing more of this awful story. She frankly doesn't know if she can take it anymore. She sits silently, head lowered, and begins to shut out every thought, every emotion, and every word coming from Vickie's lips.

She's jolted back to reality. "Catherine! Are you still with me?" Catherine looks up quickly, and nods her head affirmatively. "Good, 'cause you need you to hear the *whole* story," Vickie says sternly.

"When I arrive in the room, you are undressed, under the covers, and unconscious. I can see the concern on everyone's face as I enter the room, so I move closer to where you are lying. Betsy is the most upset, and frantically tells me that you stopped breathing!" Vickie pauses to catch her breath as she recalls this moment.

"As the senior staff member, they looked at me to assess the situation," Vickie remembers. Shuddering, she states quietly, "I was very scared for you, because you did stop breathing for a moment. We just couldn't revive you." Looking directly at Catherine, almost into her very soul, she adds, "We thought you died."

Vickie waits to see Catherine's response. Catherine, head down, foot bouncing, and arms folded, does nothing but wait for Vickie to continue.

Pexov smiles because he loves the pain Catherine's feeling; Sarephah frowns because she knows how painful this is for Catherine.

Noticing Catherine's lack of response, she continues the story more calmly. "Finally, after shaking you and waiting several agonizing moments, you took several small breaths. You continued to breathe, but each breath was extremely slow and labored."

Vickie picks up a pamphlet called "Alcoholism" and hands it to Catherine. Pointing to the pamphlet, Vickie declares, "I have since learned that your labored breathing was a symptom of alcohol poisoning."

"Anyway, we were relieved that you were breathing, but we were all still quite concerned. We watched you for about ten minutes. In our ignorance, and since you continued breathing well enough, we felt you were out of imminent danger. We discussed calling an ambulance anyway or maybe your father" pausing as Catherine looks up, "but we finally decided to let you sleep it off for a few hours, and then later assess the situation further. It was a very difficult choice to make under the circumstances, and frankly, I am not sure we chose the right one, since learning more about the dangers of alcohol poisoning."

"The night was very chaotic. Your breathing was very slow. I decided to maintain a vigil, fearing you would lapse into a coma or something. In addition, I needed to attend to Betsy, Kris, and Marie. I hope you can appreciate how extremely upset they were." Vickie says. Adding, "I finally got them a change of clothes, and sent them home."

"Once we could tell that you were breathing more normally, and not falling back unconscious, it was agreed that Ben would drive you home in his car, and Kurt would drive your car. Apparently, Ben got an earful driving you home, and they both had some trouble getting you in your apartment. I didn't relax until they reported back to me that your car was in your carport, and that you had been unceremoniously deposited on your couch."

Vickie sighs, gathers her thoughts, and reigns in her emotions. After composing herself, she asks, "Do you want to know what was the most shocking about this entire event?"

Catherine winces. *No! I don't want to know.*

"When you finally woke up, you remembered the retirement party we were having for Jim and wanted to get more to drink!" Vickie tries not to look as appalled as she feels when Catherine looks up at her with little emotion.

Somewhat taken aback by Catherine's lack of emotion or remorse, Vickie falters for a moment. *Doesn't she see the severity of this? Is it too late for her?* A thought comes. *A man judges the outside, God judges the inside. Your ways are not my ways. Love her as I have loved you.* Vickie smiles inwardly, and instinctively understands what she is to do next.

At the same time, Catherine is lost in her own thoughts. *I can't let her see how this is affecting me. Stay strong. I'll just make sure I NEVER come into work after drinking. That's what this is all about. I shouldn't have come into work that day.*

"Do you have anything to say or any questions after hearing what I just told you?" Vickie inquires gently. Catherine shakes her head slowly, indicating she has nothing to say, and no questions to ask.

"Okay, well." Resting her hands on the table, she says, "I'll let you spend some time on your own mulling over the story I just relayed." Catherine relaxes a little, but gets a worried expression on her face. Vickie notices her change in expression, and asks curiously, "Is everything okay? Do you have a question after all?"

Barely lifting her head, Catherine nervously asks, "I...was...umm...wondering if I still have a job?"

Vickie is silently relieved that Catherine is concerned about her job. She was worried Catherine was too far gone to even care.

"Well, frankly, that depends on a few things," Vickie states firmly. Picking up the plan she outlined for Catherine, she holds it up in front of her. "See this document?" Vickie asks.

Catherine glances up. "Yes."

"This piece of paper outlines the conditions for your continued employment at Holden Suites. There are only two conditions." She puts her right index finger on her left index finger as if counting, and proclaims, "First, you can never drink anywhere on the grounds of Holden Suites, or come onto the property after drinking."

Catherine relaxes. *Oh, that's easy.*

Vickie puts her right index finger on the first two fingers of her left hand, and proclaims, "Second, you must attend counseling for your drinking."

Catherine grimaces. *WHAT!*

Vickie continues, ignoring Catherine's obvious disapproval of the second condition. Shuffling through the papers on her desk, she pulls out a single piece of paper, and studies it. "Here," handing the paper to Catherine, "I have researched these two counseling agencies, and they both have counselors specializing in addictions."

Catherine stiffens. *You have got to be kidding me. I am not that bad.*

"Vickie, I'm feeling much better. I really think Monday was just a onetime thing. I'm confident that it won't happen again. Counseling seems a bit extreme," Catherine sputters out.

Vickie is unmoved; she expected this response based on her prayer session this morning. "I am not sure you heard me correctly, Catherine. These two conditions are not optional, IF you want to stay employed at Holden Suites. Either you go to counseling, or you're fired," she states emphatically. Sitting back, she waits for Catherine's response, while saying a silent prayer. This is another battle that must be won.

Catherine is genuinely torn in spite of the fact that refusing counseling means losing her job. In her head, she hears Pexov shouting, "Quit. This job isn't worth it. They can't force you to go to counseling." At the same time, she hears Sarephah proclaiming, "They are trying to help you. You are worth it. Accept this offer before it's too late." This last thought, *before it's too late,* echoes in her head,.

Looking intently at the names of the two counseling agencies and the pamphlet on alcoholism, the scene in the hotel room flashes before her mind's eye, and Catherine reluctantly makes her decision. "Okay. I'll go to counseling," she announces in a reserved and quiet tone.

Vickie sits back in her chair. *Thank you, God.* Vickie smiles. "You made a very wise decision Catherine." Reaching for her notes, she adds, "I have a couple final items. You are on indefinite probation. I will require weekly status reports from your direct supervisor. You are being reassigned. Your new title is Banquet and Special Events Coordinator under the supervision of Sarah Mitchell." Putting down her notes, she picks up the master schedule for banquets and special events. "Looks like Sarah scheduled you to start work Saturday at 3:00 p.m. Do you have any questions?"

"No," Catherine responds.

Leaning forward and putting her hands on her desk, Vickie sighs. She hesitates, but remembers what God said earlier, and takes a chance. Speaking with an equal measure of intensity and compassion, Vickie says, "I'm willing to give you a chance Catherine. I think you're worth it." Pausing to wait for Catherine to make eye contact, she adds, "I hope you think you're worth it too."

A tear forms in Catherine's eye. She strains every muscle, reigning in her tears and the emotions bubbling to the surface. She wants to feel the compassion extended to her by Vickie, but can't without also feeling the shame of what she did on Monday. The only way to get through this, she believes, is to remain numb to any and all feelings.

Vickie stands up, indicating the end of the meeting. Catherine stands up and turns to leave. "One more thing before you go. I would like you to set up your first counseling session within the next few days. Here," handing Catherine a piece of paper, "I almost forgot the counseling tracking sheet I created. You must get this signed by the counselor after each appointment. I expect you to go weekly for three months. I will not monitor what goes on in the counseling sessions obviously, but I will be tracking your adherence to this condition of your employment. I will want to see this sheet once a week. Any questions?"

Catherine almost rolls her eyes in utter disgust of this intrusion, but stops herself in time. "Okay, whatever you say. I don't want to lose my job. I'll make an appointment soon."

"Good! Take care, Catherine. I'm available if you have any questions or concerns." With that, Vickie sits back down as Catherine walks out of her office. *Okay, God. I did everything you told me to do. Now, she's in your hands.*

Pride allows Catherine to walk out of Vickie's office with her held head up; shame does not allow her to make eye contact with anyone.

Chapter Nine

Once Catherine reaches her car, she loses the battle to restrain her emotions, and begins to shake with gut-wrenching sobs. She weeps at the shame of losing her dignity and self-respect. The innocence once believed in ignorance is replaced by the guilt now provided by knowledge.

The removal of the cloak of darkness concealing the events of Monday's blackout rouses her buried conscience and stirs her dark and weary soul. The intense anguish she feels is her soul struggling to find its way in the blackness that engulfs her.

While enjoying Catherine's sobs of agony, Pexov stiffens in fear. He instantly realizes he is being summoned by his master who sits on the great throne of eternal death. *What does He want! I can't leave NOW! I am sooo close to eliminating this mortal. Why do I have to answer to him anyway?*

Pexov contemplates ignoring this intrusion, but the sudden increase in the intensity of the fear he feels startles him. Obediently, yet reluctantly, he fades into the realm of the deep depths of the heavenlies, and steps into the presence of pure evil.

"Don't...you...EVER...ignore...my...summons," Satan hisses slowly and deliberately. Suddenly, Pexov feels an intense burning all over his body as Satan's fiery aura engulfs him in a ball of flames. Pexov screams in agony, drops to his knees, and curls up in a fetal position to protect himself. Just before Pexov succumbs to the fire and heat, Satan withdraws his aura.

Pexov rolls over slowly, gets on his knees, and lowers his head. With arms stretched out, he bows at the waist, acknowledging the presence and power of his master. "Mighty, mighty, mighty is the Ruler of the Kingdom of the Air, who rules all creation, now and forever more."

Satan sits on his throne surrounded by hideous creatures and vanquished mortals who succumbed to his influences. "Stand up! Come before me, and report on your mission."

Pexov rises unsteadily to his feet. After taking one tentative step, he shuffles toward the throne, pushing through the slithering creatures covering the floor. When he stops, the creatures wrap themselves around his legs, holding him in place.

The throne is on a raised platform, covered with writhing black creatures of all shapes and sizes. To Pexov, the throne looks alive with all the movement. The darkness is oppressive. One single light behind the throne shines on the back of Satan, casting a long shadow. Stepping into Satan's shadow, Pexov can barely see his master, but his master can see him perfectly.

"When will you give me Catherine?" Satan roars. His voice sounds like the blast of air coming from a furnace.

Pexov cowers at the sound of Satan's voice, but his own evil and hatred drives him to remain in control. "She's at her end. You will have her within days," he declares. Pexov has no idea if he can deliver on this promise, but lies come easily for him, even in the face of an evil powerful enough to destroy him in seconds.

"Hmmm…very well…go back and plunge your knife into her soul. Kill every good thing within her. Bring to life her desires for sin and every kind of wickedness so hatred will reign supreme in her heart. The evil she desires will consume her nature, drive her thoughts and actions, and determine her destiny.

Then another soul will be ripped out of the hands of the Divine Three," he yells triumphantly. Then fixing his gaze on Pexov, he hisses, "Do…not…fail…me!" Pexov bows slightly. Impatiently, Satan roars, "GO!"

• • •

Catherine arrives home weary from crying, and is greeted by a meowing Pip welcoming her home. Abruptly pushing Pip aside, she says angrily, "Get away from me, Pip! I'm not in the mood for you." Pip scoots down the hallway to the safety of another room. After dropping her keys on the counter, she heads directly toward the alcohol she keeps in the kitchen. *I deserve a drink after that crappy meeting.*

Nancy Ash sits in her car looking at Catherine's apartment. She was just about ready to leave when Catherine drove up. *What am I doing here? Are you sure about this God?* She wrestles within herself for a minute or two. Finally, resolving to follow God's will in this, or at the very least, act on her mother's intuition, she gets out of the car and walks up the steps. Taking a deep breath, she rings the doorbell.

• • •

Sarephah encounters Pexov in the realm of the heavenlies just outside the depths of the eternal death. Sarephah knows she must detain Pexov until Nancy speaks with Catherine.

"Hello, Pexov. I hear you lost another soul today to the Divine Three. How did your master take the news?" Then, noticing how awful Pexov looks she adds, "By the way, why do you look so…ummm…charred?"

Pexov wants to ignore this comment and finish his mission, but his pride and anger, as always, get the better of him. "I hear YOU lost *several* souls today to the Ruler of the Kingdom of the Air. How did YOUR master take the news?"

Sarephah smiles, knowing she just bought some time.

• • •

Catherine grabs an unopened bottle from the cupboard, hastily twists open the top, and raises the bottle to her lips. "Ding…Dong." The noise of the doorbell startles her. She spills some of the whiskey down her chin, curses, and angrily sets the bottle down on the counter, spilling more.

"Who in the crap is ringing my door bell? This is all I need, some lousy door-to-door salesman or something. Whatever, I'm ignoring it. Go away."

She wipes the spilled whiskey off her face with the back of her hand, and then grabs a paper towel to clean up the spill on the counter. Raising the bottle to her lips, she hears, "Ding…Dong." Again she spills whiskey down her chin when the door bell rings. "This just sucks. Leave me alone."

Catherine thinks she hears her mom's voice. She stops and listens intently. "Catherine" is heard faintly behind the door. Yep, it's her mom. "What is my mom doing here? Oh, great. It's probably because I didn't show up for dinner last night. I do NOT want to see her."

She hears, "Catherine, are you okay? Can I come in for a minute? I know you're home," coming from the direction of the front door. Realizing she can't get rid of her mom, she quickly wipes her mouth again, screws the lid onto the bottle, puts it back in the cupboard, and heads for the door.

Catherine angrily swings the door open and glares at her mom. "What are you doing here mom?"

Unfazed, Nancy responds, "Hello to you, too. Can I come in for a minute?"

"Ummm…I'm kinda busy right now." She says looking back toward the kitchen.

"Busy doing what? I just saw you drive up."

"What do you mean, you just saw me drive up? Are you watching my every move?" she says angrily.

"No…I…well…okay…listen, Catherine, this may not make sense to you, but I was...told," Nancy pauses. *God, what do I say? I can't tell her YOU sent me.* After a moment she continues, "I just felt led to come over to talk with you. Come on, can't I spend some quality time with my daughter?"

Catherine is suspicious, but finally lets her in. "Fine. Come on in." Heading down the hallway, she calls over her shoulder, "And don't say anything about the apartment. I haven't had time to clean today."

Nancy glances around at the mess, but refrains from making a comment. Moving to the couch, she smells the whiskey that Catherine spilled a few minutes ago. *Has she been drinking already this morning?* Sighing and shaking her head, she moves discarded papers and one empty plate from the couch and sits down.

"So, what up?" Then remembering how she missed the family dinner last night, she looks away and adds reluctantly, "Sorry I missed dinner last night. Umm…I wasn't feeling well."

Nancy's heard all her daughter's excuses before, even used some herself. "You could have called."

"Right…yeah…okay…next time I will be sure to call," she says a little too flippant. "Is that why you're here?"

Knowing this is not the time to point out all the inconsistencies of her daughter's behavior, Nancy stays focused on why she's here. "No, I just came to spend time with you, see how you're doing, catch you up on family news, and…who knows what other topics might come up." Nancy looks away, trying not to show how nervous she is. *God, I need some help here.*

Catherine rolls her eyes. "You came over here at 11:30 in the morning just to have some quality time with me? You aren't going to yell at me for missing dinner, and get on my case about drinking like you always do. Really?" she says cynically.

Nancy reacts to Catherine's comment. "I do *not* always get on you about drinking and your behavior."

"Please mom. Reality check. Yes, you do."

Just before Nancy begins to follow this argument to no purposeful end, she stops. A thought comes. *What comes from the heart, reaches the heart. Tell her about my love.*

Holding up her hands, Nancy urges, "Please, Catherine. I really did not come here to get on your case about anything. I…came to talk with you about…something with me."

"Are you all right?" Catherine asks genuinely. Nancy is still suffering some physical consequences of her alcoholism, and in spite of her general apathy toward everyone, Catherine does in fact worry about her.

"Oh, yes. I'm fine; nothing to worry about." Changing the subject, she quickly adds, "By the way, since you missed dinner, and I'm not saying anything about that," she reassures, "I thought you might want to know that Nicole and Devon are having a little girl, Katelyn! Isn't that a pretty name?"

A girl. Wow! Katelyn. That is a pretty name. Internally, Catherine is excited for her sister and brother-in-law, but can't bring herself to openly express her feelings about it; it's just too uncomfortable. "That's great. I'm happy for them," she says flatly.

Nancy is puzzled by this less than enthusiastic response, but ignores it for now. "The doctor says everything looks great. You should see the ultrasound pictures. It was so detailed. You could see all the tiny toes and fingers…"

Catherine cuts her off. "Mom, that's all nice to hear, but like I said, I am busy and..."

Nancy interrupts, "Okay, sorry. I just got a little excited. Oh, Megan says hi. She misses you." Catherine rolls her eyes and crosses her arms. Nancy gets the hint.

"Well…anyway. I guess I do have something about me to talk about," adding quickly "but it's all good." Catherine waits impatiently.

"This morning, I was doing my morning meditations, and I read a story. It applies to me, but I also thought of you, and wanted to come and share it." Nancy is cautious and tries to read the expression on her daughter's face. She senses no overt hostility and tries to continue.

Catherine asks impatiently, "Is this a story from your A.A. books or the Bible, 'cause either way, I really don't have the time."

"It's from the Bible. Please, Catherine, it's a good story. Just indulge me. I feel like this story is my story, but...maybe you can see yourself in it, too."

Catherine just wants to get back to that bottle. She agrees to hear the story so her mom will leave. "Okay, go ahead," she says, glancing back at the kitchen.

Encouraged that Catherine agrees to hear the story, Nancy utters a silent prayer and begins. "This morning, I was reflecting on how sick I got from drinking. Although that's not a pleasant thought, I always feel gratitude about finally accepting help and getting sober." Nancy shifts nervously as Catherine begins to look bored and indifferent. *Please God, let her hear this story of your love.*

Nancy continues tentatively. "Over the past three years, I've rejoiced with my A.A. friends and with you guys for each day of sobriety. You don't know this, but in A.A., when someone reaches a month or year milestone in their sobriety, the whole group celebrates. Someone usually bakes a cake; congratulations cards are given; we whoop, holler, and clap as they announce the days, months, and years of continuous sobriety. We generally make fools of ourselves celebrating this miracle. We celebrate the fact that a lost soul found their way to A.A."

"The celebration is even more special because we realize how many people prayed us into the rooms. But the story I read this morning gave me a much deeper appreciation of the search for lost souls, and of the celebration that happens when someone turns from their destructive ways to follow a new way."

Catherine sighs heavily. *I'm glad you're sober, but what does this have to do with me? Hurry up!*

Nancy sees Catherine's discomfort, but knows she must continue. "This morning, I stumbled upon a parable about a shepherd with a hundred sheep who left ninety-nine of them just too search for the *one* that wandered away. The shepherd of course is God, and I believe the parable says that God cares so much that he will do whatever he needs to find those who are lost due to drinking, drugs, or whatever; anyone can fill in the blank to name any sin."

Nancy points to herself for emphasis as a tear of gratitude forms in her eye. "God searched for me…me…little ole me. God loves me that much. I now believe I didn't just show up in A.A., even with all your help. I was found by God and brought back to him, and I guess, in a way, he brought me to the other sheep in A.A."

As she wipes the tear away, she continues excitedly. "Then, I read how God celebrates with all the angels in heaven when one lost soul is found and returned to the flock. Wow, I thought we had celebrations in A.A. I can't imagine what a celebration in heaven would be like. I like the fact that God is so intimately involved with all of us and how he even celebrates for us."

Nancy continues more calmly. "I believe that God pursues us even when we walk away from him. He loves us too much to let us just wander in the wilderness of our pain and destructive habits; whatever they are. Catherine, I believe God is pursuing you right now. And I really felt like I needed to tell you this story today." *Okay, I told her your story, God. I hope she heard it.*

Catherine is at the end of her rope emotionally. Physically, she is starting to experience withdrawal symptoms, since she hasn't had a drink since last evening. She's sweating, shaking, and very, very irritable.

"Interesting story, mom." Standing up to end this torture, she states abruptly, "I really hate to end this…umm…time of storytelling, but I really do have to get some things done. Thanks for coming over."

Nancy is crushed. "Did you hear my story? Don't you have any comment?" Nancy asks.

"No, not really. I get it. God, the shepherd pursued you and brought you into the A.A. sheepfold. That's great mom. It's good you're sober." She crosses her arms defiantly and adds, "You said you weren't going to discuss my drinking or any other sin you want to mention, remember? I don't see anything else to discuss. Besides, I'm tired and I don't feel well." Catherine walks toward the door while Nancy reluctantly gets up and follows her.

Okay, God. I don't know if that went well, but she's in your hands now. Nancy gives Catherine a hug, which feels more like hugging a stone than a human, and says softly, "Honey, if you need anything, or want to talk, please call me. Okay?"

"I'm fine. I'll talk to you later." Catherine closes the door, almost hitting her mom in the process.

Nancy wipes away a tear as she gets into her car. *God, what happened? I thought I was supposed to talk with Catherine, and tell her the story from Luke fifteen. I thought she would say something or react somehow.*

Nancy starts the car, and as she begins to drive away, a thought comes. *You planted a seed; someone else will water it; I will make it grow.* The tears come more quickly now, but this time, they are tears of hope. Nancy looks at her watch, notices the time, and heads straight for the A.A. meeting just down the road.

Back inside the apartment, Catherine drops heavily on the couch and puts her head in her hands. A million voices in her head are competing to be heard. *We thought you died. An angel sent me to talk with you. You threw up all over Betsy, Marie, and Kris. God is pursuing you. Ben and Kurt had to drive you home. You stopped breathing. I think you're worth it. We thought you died.*

"Stop! I can't take it anymore," Catherine screams.

Chapter Ten

Sarephah hears Catherine scream. She turns her head to listen. She notices that Pexov doesn't react. *Hmmm...Pexov doesn't hear her. His power has been weakened by his recent experience with Satan. It will take awhile for him to recover.* Without saying a word, Sarephah fades out of the heavenlies and settles by Catherine's side.

Catherine is angry, tired, confused, scared, and sick. She wants the voices in her head to stop. Mostly, she wants a drink, but the meeting with her boss, seeing Ben, and the conversation with her mom cause her to reconsider drinking, at least for now. She's caught in a horrible place of indecision; she doesn't want to drink, but she doesn't want to stay sober.

Catherine tightens her jaw, clenches her fists, and closes her eyes desperately trying to get rid of the pain by her own power. Sarephah wraps her aura tightly around Catherine and sees her relax, but only slightly. The pain is so great for Catherine that she barely senses any relief.

A thought, louder than the other voices, comes to Catherine. *You must make an appointment with a counselor in the next few days.* But Catherine pushes the thought aside, and lies down.

A couple hours later, Catherine wakes with a horrible headache, the shakes, and a queasy stomach. Despite feeling lousy, her first conscious thought is not about drinking; it's about calling a counselor. "Okay, already. I'll call the stupid counselor," she says to no one in particular; although, Pip looks at her, cocks his head, and meows with interest.

Catherine smiles slightly at Pip's reaction. "Do you think that's a good idea, Pip?" Pip meows and rolls over. "Eh…what do you know?" she says while slowly lying back down.

After a minute or so, the thoughts about the counselor nag at Catherine to the point that she can't ignore them any longer. She sits up very slowly trying not to disturb her already disturbed head and stomach. "Ohhhh….I…feel like…. like…I don't know what I feel like. I've never felt this bad. I need a drink, but…maybe I'll wait." Sarephah smiles and wraps her aura around Catherine even tighter. Since Catherine isn't fighting her, Sarephah is gaining strength, and her aura is keeping Catherine in a protective cocoon.

Catherine reaches for the slip of paper with the names of the two counseling agencies she left on the kitchen counter. "New Horizons Counseling…hmm. Great Shepherd Counseling…huh…interesting name." Remembering the shepherd and the lost sheep story, Catherine manages a slight smile and says, "Okay, I'll call this one."

Holding her aching head, she heads back to the couch and sits down slowly. "Maybe I should wait to call." She moans, "I feel awful." *You must make an appointment with a counselor.* "Are you kidding me? That voice. I can't get it out of my head! Okay, okay, I'll call."

Grabbing the phone off the table, she squints to read the information for the counseling agency, dials the number, and rolls her eyes at the absurdity of this whole thing. "I hope no one answers. What am I supposed to say anyway? Uh, hello I got drunk and threw up over my coworkers and my boss thinks

I need help," Catherine says mockingly. Before she can continue this train of thought a voice interrupts her.

"Hello. Thank you for calling Great Shepherd Counseling. How may I help you?" chirps the perky receptionist. Catherine cringes. *Oh, please, a little less enthusiasm.*

"Ummm…yes, I need to make an appointment with a counselor," Catherine manages to stammer out.

"Okay, are you new to Great Shepherd Counseling?" the receptionist asks in a sing-song voice.

"Yes."Catherine rolls her eyes again at the obnoxiously happy receptionist. *Take a chill pill lady.*

"Can I get your name and reason for your visit please?"

"My name is Catherine Ash. And the reason for my visit is umm…well…umm…my work said I need to see a counselor. You were one of the agencies they suggested. So I'm calling to make an appointment."

"I see. In order for me to put you with the appropriate counselor I need to know the nature of the problem," miss perky says.

Sighing in frustrated embarrassment, Catherine is unsure how to respond. "Well…if you must know…ummm…I guess the *nature* of the problem is….drinking." She says drinking so quietly and quickly that the receptionist asks, "I'm sorry. I didn't catch the last word. What is the nature of the problem?"

"Drinking," Catherine blurts out. *Drinking - like in I want to be drinking right now.*

"Okay. Great! Hold on for one moment."

Catherine closes her eyes and seriously considers hanging up. She nervously bounces her foot and wonders what is taking so freaking long. Pip swishes by her leg, but Catherine roughly pushes him away.

"Thanks for holding, Catherine. Elizabeth Sampson will be your counselor. She specializes in addictions. She happens to have availability tomorrow at 11:00 a.m. Should I book that time for you?" asks a slightly more serious receptionist.

"Tomorrow!" utters a shocked Catherine.

"Yes! Tomorrow at 11:00 a.m."

"Well…all right…I guess I can make it at 11:00 tomorrow," says a now worried Catherine.

"Great! We're located at the corner of Vine and Webster. Do you know where that is?"

"Yes" Catherine says unenthusiastically.

"Great! We'll see you tomorrow. Oh, and make sure to bring your insurance information. Thanks for calling Great Shepherd Counseling. Bye." Click.

Click. Catherine hangs up the phone and looks toward the kitchen. *One little drink. What would that hurt? Just one little drink.*

• • •

Pexov finally makes his appearance, but Sarephah knows he's too late. The aura surrounding Catherine is strong due to the willingness she showed by listening to her mom and calling the counselor. Sarephah is pleased with this shift, though slight, away from Pexov's influence.

Pexov sees Sarephah's aura completely engulfing Catherine, curls his lips, pulls in a deep breath, and with a roar sends flaming arrows to penetrate the aura. The aura holds strong. Pexov is stunned. He spins around and glares at Sarephah.

"That stupid protective aura won't stay strong for long. Her weak and pitiful nature hasn't changed one single bit, which means she *will* drink again. And when she does, I will once again regain control!" Pexov shouts with delight.

"At this moment, I am not concerned about her nature, Pexov. It is her will that concerns me and the Divine Three. As we speak, her will is being encouraged to explore positive influences. And that means she is able to resist *you*!"

"That's not possible" spits Pexov. "Her will belongs to her nature and her nature belongs to ME!"

"As always, you have no idea what you are talking about. Her will is just that, *her* will, not yours. What you fail to remember is that the Divine Three decreed that humans have freewill. With the Divine Three's help, Catherine is loosening the grip her nature holds on her will. Yes, she will drink again because right now, her nature demands it, but the big difference is that her will is starting to fight against her nature and YOU!" Sarephah yells triumphantly.

Pexov growls in disgust. "Then I must make sure that this new *freedom* she displays is ended and chained with binds that she can't ever break."

Chapter Eleven

Catherine actually feels a little better Friday morning after drinking Thursday night, because, without putting alcohol in her system, she suffers horribly from the sickness and shock of withdrawal. Pexov sees Catherine's drinking as a victory, but Sarephah sees no defeat in what happened Thursday night. Sarephah is pleased that Catherine's mind is beginning to fight against the mental obsession to drink, even though she's not yet physically able to deny what her body badly craves. As long as Catherine stays willing, even just a little, than Sarephah gains strength to assist her.

Catherine's decision to go to counseling is having two effects on her psyche: producing white-knuckle fear and red-hot anger. On one hand, she's afraid to learn about herself and what drives her to drink to the point she blacks out. She dreads the idea of facing the consequences of her actions and the intrusive questions of a stranger, even if that stranger is a trained counselor. On the other hand, she's furious that people just won't mind their own business. She doesn't see why she needs to talk to *anyone* about *anything*. She can take care of herself and her problems all alone, thank you very much.

Catherine is a poster child for those living in the lies they tell themselves. She tries to control every situation and circumstance, yet life seems so unfair and so unsolvable to Catherine. She walks through life and relationships with a sense of entitlement and detachment, yet she craves intimate relationships and commitment. Although she acts like she's got life all figured out, at the end of the day when she climbs into bed, she secretly wonders if she's living out some crazy curse of alcoholism, and therefore, doomed to live a miserable existence.

• • •

The sound of the bell startles Catherine when she pushes open the front door of the Great Shepherd counseling center. She jumps slightly, looks up, and then notices the crowd in the lobby. The noise of the bell is bad enough, but it's the stares of everyone in the waiting room that bother her more. Embarrassment radiates from her now flushed face. She lowers her head, stares at her feet, and then walks quickly toward the receptionist's desk with what feels like every eye fixed on her. She wishes no one was in the waiting room. If invisibility were an option, she would fade away in a flash. Catherine feels more shame and embarrassment walking into this office right now than she does for the blackout on Monday at work.

"Hello! Welcome to the Great Shepherd Counseling Center! How can I help you?" says the very energetic receptionist.

Catherine wishes the receptionist wasn't so obnoxiously loud. "Umm…yes, I have an appointment with Elizabeth Sampson," Catherine whispers, hoping no one but the receptionist hears her.

"Did you say Elizabeth Sampson?"

"Yes" Catherine mutters.

"Great."After glancing at the appointment book, she looks up and announces more loudly than Catherine thinks is necessary, "Catherine, since this is your first visit you need to fill out some paper work. Here you go." The perky receptionist hands Catherine a clipboard filled with various forms and questionnaires. "When you're done, just bring them back up to me."

"Okay." Catherine takes the clipboard, turns, knocks into a stand of self-help books on display. The display tilts and sways; she grabs it, but in the process of saving the book display, she loses her grip on the clipboard of papers. The clipboard is launched out of her hands; the papers rise into the air like confetti and then slowly begin floating to the ground. "Crap!"

Heads turn as Catherine frantically twirls around, trying to grab each paper before they hit the ground. Several papers hit the floor and glide in different directions. Catherine drops to her knees and scoops up the scattered pieces of paper. "This isn't happening," she mutters to herself.

"Are you all right?" the receptionist calls out, while leaning over the counter to see what happened. More eyes turn toward the paper drama being played out, and a couple giggles are heard.

Catherine picks up the last form, adds it to the others stuffed into her arms, and nods to the receptionist in response to her question. Hurrying to an empty seat, she sits downs and makes sure to avoid eye contact with everyone. *Could this possibly get any worse?*

It takes a few minutes for Catherine to recover, but she valiantly rallies and begins sifting through what appears to her as a mound of junk. She reads them off one by one: *General Information, Patient Confidentiality Form, Insurance Form, Health History, New Counselor Intake Form*. "This could take forever," she sighs.

Fifteen minutes later, Catherine finishes her mound of new patient paperwork, and thankfully, without further mishap, hands the clipboard back to the receptionist.

"Thank you. Take a seat, and Elizabeth will be out to get you in a few moments."

Catherine returns to her seat and, after several minutes, musters enough courage to scan the room and take in her surroundings while waiting for the counselor. The place is remarkably cozy, considering what she's encountered in previous visits to crises centers and psychiatric clinics.

This center is a quaint old house. The receptionist's area and waiting room look like a family room. There are several couches positioned next to a fireplace, a short hallway leads to a small kitchen, and a table and chairs are set up in what was probably the former dining room. She assumes that the counseling offices are behind the doors off the family room and upstairs. Several burning candles are producing a wonderful vanilla scent. Adding the final touches to the atmosphere, there is soothing music playing softly in the background. It's a far cry from the other counseling agencies Catherine's visited over the years.

Growing up in an alcoholic home and starting to drink in the seventh grade really messed with Catherine's head. Early on, she decided that life was painful and confusing because of the circumstances of her family and from several disturbing events in her young life. She began to seek protection from these hurts and disappointments, and for Catherine, that meant keeping every feeling deeply hidden in the safety of her own mind and, of course, drinking.

At nineteen, Catherine was officially diagnosed with a severe panic disorder after suffering horrible panic attacks when she returned home for the summer after her sophomore year in college. Twice, she ended up in a crises center after the torment of two nights of sheer terror. She was eventually referred to a psychiatrist who diagnosed her, prescribed some powerful drugs, and assigned her to one of his counselors. However, Catherine was more interested in the drugs she was getting than in the counseling being offered.

She hated counseling. The idea of opening up to someone was both frightening and violating. For Catherine, counseling was a battle of power, and she felt the only power she had was the ability to keep her secrets and feelings to herself. Protecting herself was not only important, it was absolutely necessary for survival. Needless to say, with this attitude, counseling didn't help.

During the entire time she spent with her first counselor, the topic of drinking never came up in the sessions, because Catherine wasn't drinking heavily at the time and didn't see the connection between the panic attacks and depression with her use of alcohol. She only attended the weekly sessions to get the drugs she needed to make it through the day. The drugs were especially helpful making it through those horrible nights: nights in which she lived on the edge of sanity, waiting for the dawn to break and relieve the awful anxiety that engulfed her like a black shadow.

The intense fear was evil in many ways, although she would never have looked at it that way. Catherine had no relationship with God, no spiritual longings, and no consciousness of good or evil. At the age of nineteen, she was living in a void between life and death, good and evil, black and white – it was all gray and completely lifeless.

Catherine eventually dropped out of college, and spent the next year sedated to ward off the panic attacks, confined to the house for security, and depressed about it all. All this time she remained dry of alcohol, mostly because the drugs did the trick, but also because she found two new obsessions: dieting and men. She decided that losing weight would solve all her problems, and finding a man would make her supremely happy; to her dismay, neither worked.

After a couple disastrous relationships and coming close to a complete emotional breakdown, she realized that her life was going nowhere. With the urging of her counselor and the security of her prescription drugs, she was able to return to school. And returning to school for Catherine meant returning to her life of drinking. This time, however, she had three new obsessions: drugs, diets, and dating – and not necessarily in that order.

"Catherine Ash?" The sound of her name brings Catherine back to the present and back to the reality waiting for her – another round of counseling. "Catherine Ash?"

Catherine looks up, wide-eyed and slightly irritated. Elizabeth Sampson immediately recognizes that deer-in-the- headlights look, smiles inwardly, and walks confidently over to where Catherine is sitting. Thrusting out her hand, she says, "Hello, Catherine. My name is Elizabeth Sampson. It's nice to meet you."

Catherine, somewhat taken aback by this introduction, extends her hand weakly, and without making eye contact, says "Hello."

"Come on back to my office."

Elizabeth Sampson has been a counselor specializing in addictions for ten years. She's been sober for fifteen years, active in Alcoholics Anonymous, and extremely good at counseling people in denial of their own alcoholism. Remembering what it was like when she got sober, she loves helping people get through this tough time just like others helped her. She's medium height with short dark hair and very fit. Working out is her passion and stress reliever, although her sponsor worries that her exercising might be a tad obsessive. But most importantly, Elizabeth loves God and brings her spirituality to her counseling sessions when it's appropriate – she lets God decide that.

Elizabeth stops in front of one of the rooms off the kitchen and gestures toward the room. "Here we go. This is my office. Come on in."

The office looks like it was previously the parlor of the old home. Against the wall and under a window is a couch, of course; every counseling office has a couch Catherine thinks. Several comfortable chairs are positioned across from the couch and on opposite ends of the coffee table. There are lamps sitting on two end tables, and Kleenex boxes are strategically place for those emotional breakdowns; Catherine rolls her eyes when she spots the Kleenex boxes. The room is intentionally setup to facilitate both individual and family counseling sessions. There's a nice, sweet smelling aroma filling the air and the lighting is low and soothing. In the corner is a desk and chair that's used as office space when Elizabeth is not in session. The room is safe and comfortable, but Catherine feels neither.

Quickly surveying the room, Catherine knows she must make the crucial decision on where to sit. It's all part of the power game she plays and can't afford to lose. The couch is way too therapeutic, so she avoids it. After a few seconds, she heads for a comfy, high-back chair that allows her to face the door in case she needs a speedy exit. Satisfied with her choice, she sits, raises all her defenses, and readies for the battle. Pexov smiles at Catherine's unwillingness to participate in this counseling session. He's pleased, because when her defenses against help are up, her defenses against him are down.

Elizabeth has been observing and assessing Catherine the minute she saw her in the waiting room. Without even hearing her story or knowing anything about her, Elizabeth already identifies three things about Catherine: one, she's fearful of intimacy; two, she's controlling; three, she's depressed. Elizabeth's seen it all before, and based on her experiences with others, is quite sure Catherine has no idea what's really wrong with her. Elizabeth whispers a silent prayer.

Sarephah waits for Catherine's response to the help she's being offered. She knows her aura of protection is growing weak, but because Catherine is here, she's still able to keep the aura securely around her. But she's not sure how long this protection against Pexov will last; that's up to Catherine.

After waiting for Catherine to pick a seat, Elizabeth takes the seat across from her in the other high-back chair. For one brief moment, they make eye contact. Elizabeth notices how lifeless Catherine's eyes are; Catherine notices how penetrating Elizabeth's gaze is. Catherine looks down quickly, hoping she didn't reveal anything. Elizabeth looks away after catching a glimpse of the spiritual war waging within Catherine's soul. They both know this will be a battle. But only Elizabeth recognizes the true nature of this battle.

Chapter Twelve

Elizabeth glances down at the paper work Catherine just filled out, and notices that she's been referred to counseling by her work. The reason listed is drinking. Elizabeth now knows how to proceed.

"How are you doing today, Catherine?"

"Fine."

"Good! Oh, by the way, I always like to ask how I should pronounce someone's name. Do you go by Catherine or Cathy or Cath?"

Catherine is slightly impressed that this counselor even cares about how to pronounce her name. "I prefer Catherine."

"Then, Catherine it is. I usually ask, because even though my name is Elizabeth, some people feel the need to call me Liz or Beth, or heaven forbid, Eliza. Ugh. I can't believe people sometimes. I think to myself, hello, didn't I just say Elizabeth?" Pausing for a moment, she asks, "Do you ever have that happen to you?"

This question disarms Catherine because she was expecting the typical counselor type questions like, how do you *feel* about that, or can you tell me how that makes you *feel*? Catherine raises one corner of her lip in an attempt at a smile and responds, "Yeah, that happens to me too. My mom sometimes calls me Cath, and I hate it." *Oops, idiot, don't talk about your mom.*

Even though Catherine mentions both her mom and a feeling that indicates a little animosity toward her mother, Elizabeth ignores it for now. She knows that too much, too soon, will send Catherine running.

"What's your family situation like? Married? Kids?"

"I'm single, no kids."

"Boyfriend?"

Catherine contemplates this question. *Not anymore.* "No."

Elizabeth notices the hesitation, but files it away for now. "Do you live alone or with a roommate?"

"I live alone. Well, I do have a cat, Pip," she adds with a slight smile.

"Pip. What a great name. How about your family? Brothers or sisters?"

Catherine sighs and fidgets in her chair. *What does this have to do with anything?* "I have an older brother and sister, twins, and a younger sister."

"Mom and dad divorced or still married?"

"Still married."

Elizabeth makes a mental note that Catherine's detached from her family, which is typical for an active alcoholic. She doesn't mention any of their names, but mentions the cat's name, interesting. No current boyfriend, but there's a story there. After getting all the information and all the reactions she needs, she changes the subject.

"Your paperwork says that you work at Holden Suites. Isn't that the really nice hotel downtown? I've never stayed there, but I've been to some events held there and to the restaurant a couple times."

"Yeah, it's the one downtown."

"What do you do there?"

"Well, I was the Shift Supervisor for General Operations…but I'm now the…the…" She can't quite remember her new title. Finally, she remembers, "My new title is Banquet and Special Events Coordinator."

Elizabeth knows there's a story behind this change in position, especially since she's coming to counseling because of work. Again, she ignores it at this point. "Do you like working at the Hotel?"

"I don't know. I guess it's okay."

"What would you rather do if you could pick any job in the world?"

Catherine is confused by all this small talk. She's not sure how to play this game. These questions aren't threatening, so she relaxes a little. Thinking for a moment, she says, "I've always wanted to be a radio DJ or own a jewelry shop. You know the kind where people can come in and pick out their own beads and make something. Something like that I guess."

Elizabeth notices that Catherine wears no jewelry. "Wow. That sounds like fun. Do you like to be creative?"

"Yeah, sometimes." There's no expression in her voice or light in her eyes.

"How come you don't have one of your creations on today?"

"I don't know. I didn't feel like it." *I really don't feel like doing anything.*

"I know how you feel. Sometimes, I just don't feel like doing anything either. Well, until you open the jewelry store or start your DJ business, I guess you'll just have to continue working at the hotel."

"Yeah." Catherine sits up a little and nods.

Elizabeth decides to move the conversation in the direction of the presenting problem. "You indicate in your new patient information that work referred you to this agency, and that the reason for the visit is drinking. Is that correct?"

"Yes."

Looking Catherine in the eyes, she asks with a soft and sympathetic tone, "Can you tell me what happened?"

Catherine looks down, twirls her thumbs in her lap, and asks, "How much do you want to know?"

"As much as you want to tell me."

Good answer, Catherine thinks. Still looking down, Catherine begins, "Well, I had a couple drinks, went into work, and got into some trouble."

"When you say, a couple drinks, what does that mean to you?"

"One or two."

"So in this instance, you had one or two drinks before going into work. Is that right?"

Catherine squirms in her seat and looks away. "More or less."

"How often do you drink?"

Catherine rolls her eyes and shrugs, "I don't know."

"Give me a ball park figure: once a month, once a week, once a day. Something like that." Elizabeth pushes this line of questioning to see how honest Catherine is willing to be in this first session.

"Ummm…I would say…maybe…once a week – usually only on the weekends."

"When you drink, umm, once a week and only on the weekends, do you get drunk or just have a couple?"

"I don't know. It depends."

"Depends on what?"

"On how much I want to drink," Catherine shrugs her shoulders as if this is the dumbest question she's ever heard.

"I see. The trouble you had at work, what day of the week was it?"

Catherine is sweating now. "Monday."

"I see. So what trouble did you get into at work?"

Catherine sighs, "Trouble with my boss."

Elizabeth stays patient. "Okay. So your boss sends you to counseling because you had a couple drinks, went into work, and got into some trouble. Is that about right?"

"Yeah. But, I think the main problem is that I went into work that day. I should have just stayed home. That's what this is all about," Catherine says angrily and crosses her arms.

"So you think the main problem is going into work not the fact that you were drinking. Is that right?"

"Yeah! I just should have stayed home and none of this would be happening."

"So drinking wasn't the problem?"

"I guess it contributed to *some* of what's happening to me. But, I still say that I should have just stayed home." Catherine is adamant about this fact.

"Okay. What time did your shift start that day…Monday wasn't it?

"1:00 p.m."

"Why were you drinking at 1:00 pm on a Monday?"

Uh,oh;, didn't see that coming. "I don't know?"

"Okay. Have you ever done anything like this before?"

"No! This is the first time I have *ever* had anything like this happen. Frankly, I think work is over reacting." Catherine tries defending herself.

"I see. I have to admit that based on what you've told me so far it does appear that they're over reacting. What do you think they should have done with an employee that came into work after drinking and got into 'trouble,' as you put it?"

Exasperated, Catherine states angrily, "I don't know. I sure wouldn't have sent them to counseling!"

Elizabeth smiles. "Fair enough. You don't seem very comfortable about the idea of counseling, especially for this minor trouble. Have you ever been to counseling before?"

Catherine rolls her eyes and begins to shut down. "Yes."

Elizabeth knows she's treading on thin ice, but wants to see Catherine's response. "I see. You must not have had a good experience with counseling. Can you tell me about it?"

Catherine notices that time is almost up, breathes a sigh of relief, and tries to redirect the conversation. "Are we almost done here? I really don't see the point in all this."

Elizabeth recognizes Catherine's attempt to highjack the conversation, but again, lets it go. She knows Catherine's not ready to open up, so she decides to back off on this first session. Glancing at the clock, she says, "Yeah, I guess we are almost out of time."

It's over? She's not going to pry or force things out of me anymore? Catherine is relieved. *Good, 'cause I'm done with this nonsense.*

"Do you want to continue with counseling?" Elizabeth asks, even though she assumes Catherine has no choice.

"Unfortunately, I don't have a choice."

Bingo. Catherine feels trapped. "Okay." Smiling, she adds, "Even though you don't have a choice to come here, maybe I can make this a better experience for you than your last time at counseling."

Catherine says nothing. She's done.

Leaning forward for emphasis, Elizabeth says calmly, "Catherine, I know you don't think drinking is a problem for you, so I'm wondering if you think you could stay sober until our next appointment."

Elizabeth knows that if Catherine is as far along as she thinks, this will be virtually impossible. It's the only way for Catherine to begin to see the powerlessness over her ability to stop drinking on her own.

Catherine's eyes grow wide and she shifts in her seat. "Sure. Whatever." Suddenly, she feels sick to her stomach, thinking about the possibility of not drinking for a whole week, let alone for the rest of the day. She's immediately angry and scared.

"Okay, then I'd like you to stay sober until I see you next week. You can make the appointment with Sylvia on your way out. It was nice to meet you, Catherine. I hope this wasn't too bad for you."

"Umm…it was all right."

Standing up, Elizabeth walks toward the door and opens it to let Catherine out. "See you next week."

Catherine practically races out of the room and calls over her shoulder, "Yeah, okay, see ya."

After Catherine leaves, Elizabeth shuts the door, grabs her notebook, sits back down, and assesses the session. Elizabeth chuckles to herself, "Typical active alcoholic, if her lips are moving, she's lying."

She begins writing up a list of symptoms of alcoholism Catherine displayed in this session: vague about the amount of drinking, definitely minimizes amount of drinking, drinking at inappropriate times, drinking alone, causing problems with work, depressed, drinking getting in the way of goals, distant from family, trouble with relationships, denial about the problem with work, angry, lying. She puts down her pen and pad. "Yep, she qualifies. Now I just need to get her to see the truth about herself, and the fact that all her secrets are keeping her a very sick young lady."

Catherine sits in her car and assesses the counseling session. "That sucked! Are you kidding me? Can you go one week without drinking?" she says mockingly. "I can if I want to…but…maybe I just don't want to."

However, secretly she is scared at the prospect of not drinking. She tries to remember how long it's been since she's been able to go more than a day or two without getting drunk. The only time she can remember is when she was hooked on those prescription pills.

It feels like the world is crashing in on her. The truth is she just wants the pain to go away and for everyone to leave her alone.

"Somehow I've got to get through this counseling crap. But I don't want to tell her about what happened at work. I don't want anybody to ever find out about it. How am I going to keep it all together?"

After thinking for a moment about her dilemma, she concludes that the best course of action is to say nothing. "I'm not saying anything to that counselor. It's none of her business. I'll drink if I want, and I won't tell her about it either. What's the big deal anyway? I know what to do; I'll just lay low for a couple weeks, and this whole thing will blow over."

With a renewed sense of determination and a heavy dose of false courage, she drives home with a firm resolution to take control of this situation.

• • •

Pexov watches the protective aura around Catherine dissolve. "Ha! Good. I knew that aura wouldn't last long. All I need to do now is make sure that loser keeps her flap hole shut like I taught her. The sin and evil inside her grows best in dark and lonely places of the soul." He rubs his hands together in anticipation of his victory. "Hmm…yessss…I can keep her drunk and stupid by making sure she stays SILENT! This little lamb will be slaughtered, because the shepherd will never hear her cry for help. But, she'll make lots of noise when I plunge my knife into her soul when the end comes. Oh, what a pretty sound that will be…hee…hee...hee."

Sarephah's worst fear comes true when the aura around Catherine crumbles. Sarephah is amazed at the capacity of mortals to tolerate sin and evil in their lives. In fact, she wonders why evil exists at all in this world since mortals appear incapable of releasing its grip on their souls once it takes root. "How can Catherine conquer the sin and evil inside her? The Divine Three are trying to help her but she continues to fight against their help. It doesn't make sense to me."

Come to us Sarephah. We have the answers you seek.

Hearing the voice of the Divine Three, Sarephah smiles, takes one last look at Catherine and Pexov, and steps into the presence of pure love.

Chapter Thirteen

Later in the afternoon on Friday, Catherine's depression deepens, even though only a couple hours ago she concocted a brilliant plan to take control of her situation. To her consternation, she quickly realizes the situation is greater than her energy level can manage. She prefers sitting alone and feeling sorry for herself over the more challenging prospect of actually doing something about her life. Besides, what is there to do anyway, she thinks?

In her mind, nothing will ever change about her or her life. And she's darn sure all the blame for her misery resides squarely on her family, her job, her ex-boyfriend, her friends, her drinking buddies, her boss, and anyone or anything else she can think of. It is inconceivable to her that she has any part in the mess of a life she's created. And even more tragically, she has no spiritual ability to discern that there are spiritual forces working for and against her; a fact that may cost her dearly.

Pip jumps on Catherine's lap and joins in on her little pity party, although somewhat reluctantly. He's not at all thrilled when his owner starts squeezing the life out of him while she moans morbidly about her loneliness and the fact that nobody cares.

"Nobody," she moans.

"Life sucks, Pip. Nobody cares about me. You love me though right?"

Pip can hardly breathe.

"You're lucky you're a cat. Cats have no problems. You just get to lie around and eat and lie around and…what else *do* you do, Pip?"

Pip cocks his head and lets out a squeaky meow, almost like a chirping sound.

"I thought so…nothing but a life of leisure with nooo problems. And look at my life…nothing but misery," she moans while a sappy love song plays a little too loudly on the stereo. Mercifully, Pip is rescued from the clutches of his distraught owner when the phone rings.

"Oh, brother. Who's calling now?" she says while turning down the music. She picks up the phone, recognizes the caller, sighs heavily, and hits the answer button. "Hey, Kelly. What's up?" she says with little enthusiasm.

"Hey, girl. What's ya doing?" Kelly, one of Catherine's drinking buddies from college, believes that life is one big party, and she doesn't plan on missing one single event.

"Just hanging out." Catherine falls back heavily on the couch.

"Where've you been all week? I called a couple times but you never answered or returned my calls," she says with a slightly irritated tone in her voice. "You missed some good parties."

Catherine is not in the mood for Kelly. "I was busy this week."

"Busy doing what?"

"Just busy, okay!" Catherine snaps.

"Okay, chill. Well, you're in luck because there's another party tonight at Joe's. You're going right?"

"I don't know. Who's gonna be there?"

"Well, I don't know *everyone* who's gonna be there, but I'm pretty sure *they* won't be there, if that's what you mean."

Catherine winces. "Shut up, Kelly!"

"What! I'm trying to be helpful. I know you won't go if he's there."

"Which he?"

"That's funny," Kelly laughs. "Glad to see you haven't lost your sense of humor."

"Whatever. I don't know. I'm not sure what I'm doing tonight."

"Ah, come on," Kelly urges. "It'll be fun, and if they show up, we'll leave. Okay? Come on," Kelly pleads.

Catherine's absolutely certain she's not going to any party where she may run into her past. No way. No how. Catherine feels sick to her stomach just thinking about facing either of them, but the only way to get Kelly off the phone is doing what she does best, lie. "Okay. I'll come."

"Woohoo! We're gonna have some fun tonight," Kelly hollers. "I'm planning on getting there around 8:00. It depends on Justin, of course."

"Of course," Catherine mumbles. "I'll get there about the same time," Catherine replies deceitfully.

"Okay, but you better be there. I know you, and you don't sound like you mean it."

"I'll be there! Quit bugging me about it."

"All right, all right. See ya later. Bye." Click

"Bye."Click

After hanging up the phone, Catherine stares at the half empty bottle on the coffee table in front of her. She reaches for it, holds it up for a closer look, and shakes her head. *This crazy liquid makes me feel so good, yet so bad. I hate it, but I love it. I don't want it, but I need it. Why? Why do I do this?*

She screws opens the lid, slowly brings the bottle to her nose, smells the alcohol, and then licks the edges of the opening just to get a taste. Suddenly, she throws her head back, raises the bottle to her mouth, and takes a large gulp. Closing her eyes, she feels the alcohol burning all the way down her throat to her stomach. She tries to block out the memories of what happened a couple months ago, but some memories have a way of making such a deep imprint that nothing takes them away, nothing.

• • •

Two things attracted Catherine to Mark: his amazing blue eyes and his equally amazing capacity for alcohol. It would be an exaggeration to say it was love at first sight, but it wouldn't be an exaggeration to say that it was love at first drunk. They met while drinking at the Crazy Eights, a bar well-known for catering to the college crowd, quarter pitchers, and live music every weekend.

Mark noticed Catherine mostly because she practically fell in his lap. While heading to the bar for another round, Catherine tripped and fell into him with all the grace of a drunken sailor. In a way that only drunks can, they both laughed hysterically when his drink spilled all over them. Later, they would agree that the moment was magical. Well, at least as magical as two drunks falling all over themselves can be. It wasn't long before they were inseparable.

Their romance consisted of drunken nights together, an occasional dinner out, usually something real fancy like the local dive, or hanging out at parties. They were obsessed with each other, which they equated with commitment. From all appearances they had a good thing going, but almost like clockwork, they fought about some petty issue, got drunk, forgot what they fought over, and made up with each other by getting drunk all over again. It was a perfect relationship for two people incapable of anything more. Catherine wasn't sure if what she had with Mark was necessarily love, but the companionship eased the ache of loneliness and boosted her fragile self-esteem.

Mark was an easy going guy who rarely got angry, but jealousy did sometimes put him in a foul mood. Catherine never tried to purposely make him jealous, but her ego needed an incredible amount of stroking, and since Mark wasn't always up for the task, she looked elsewhere. For Catherine, flirting was just a game, a way to make her feel pretty and desirable. For Mark, her flirting was a slap in the face. Catherine's flirting would eventually burn her and him as badly as a child playing with fire.

A couple months ago, when Catherine felt especially unappreciated and unattractive, Greg gave her what she longed for: attention that she wasn't getting from Mark. Greg was engaged to Carla, Mark's sister, but that never stopped them from what they believed was innocent flirting. However on this night in particular, the combination of physical attraction, unrestrained desire, and lots of alcohol was poisonous.

Greg and Catherine spent most of the evening getting sloppy drunk and falling all over each other, which irritated Carla and infuriated Mark. When Mark confronted Catherine, she reassured him that she and Greg were just having fun and that he should lighten up a little. But later, as drinking games were being played downstairs, Greg whispered to Catherine to meet him upstairs in one of the rooms. She did.

Mark went looking for Catherine when he realized she was gone way too long and that Greg was nowhere to be seen either. It didn't take him long to find them, and what happened next was fueled by both alcohol and rage.

Catherine still remembers the look in Mark's eyes when he flung open the door to expose them in their sin. Mark took three long strides across the room and, just before he hit Catherine, he paused long enough for Greg to jump up and deflect the blow. The fight that ensued was short, but horrifying. Mark hit his target, which was mercifully Greg not Catherine, enough times to eventually ease his rage and allow him to regain some semblance of composure. While backing up toward the door, Mark seethed with anger and told Catherine she was a whore and could go to hell for all he cared. His last words were directed at Greg to stay away from his sister or he would regret it.

Catherine hasn't seen Mark or Greg since that fateful night. Rumor has it that Greg and Carla made up and plan to be married later this spring. She hasn't heard anything about Mark and wonders how he's doing. Regret, guilt, and remorse about her behavior haunt her daily. Over the years, she conveniently adjusted her standards of right and wrong to fit her behavior, but she never thought she could sink so low or feel such shame.

Raising the bottle to her lips one more time, she swallows hard, and waits for the sting of her pain to lessen and the memories to fade away, even if only temporarily. Her last conscious thoughts that night reveal a soul tormented by the evil consuming her and the good fighting to set her free. *What kind of person have I become? What's happening to me? How bad can this get? There's got to be something better than this. I need to find a better way.*

• • •

Sarephah turns to the Divine Three after watching the scene of Catherine's life unfold before them. "Why?" Sarephah asks dejectedly. "Why does Catherine have to suffer so much? You talk about divine possibilities, but all I see is pain and misery."

The Divine Three listen with patient understanding.

Looking back at Catherine, who finally passed out, she asks impulsively, "Why is there so much sin and evil in Catherine's life? In fact, why is there so much evil and sin in the world?" Pausing to contemplate the next question, one she's wondered about for eons, she tentatively asks, "Why did you create the tree of the knowledge of good and evil?"

Chapter Fourteen

A strong wind blows up and swirls around Sarephah in a display of the Divine Three's wrath over a world that was, could have been, and is still yet to be. Sarephah is not scared by this demonstration; she's seen it before when the Divine Three are displeased with their creation. Finally, the wind subsides and the Author speaks. "You have asked difficult questions, Sarephah. I, speaking as the creator, will answer your questions. Please let us walk together. I have something to show you." The Divine Three are never separated, but when necessary, one of them will move in front of the others to become the most visible manifestation of the Three.

The Author takes Sarephah's hand and in the blink of an eye they're standing in a beautiful, lush forest. The birds are happily singing their songs and flying from tree to tree in a choreographed display of aerial gymnastics. Sensing the presence of their creator, they swoop down and hover over the Author, chirping excitedly as if welcoming Him home for the first time. As the birds fly away, more animals stick their heads out from behind trees, from under rocks, out of holes, and out of bushes. Each animal pays homage to the creator in their own special way. The Author laughs heartily at this reception, remembering how it was meant to be. Sarephah smiles at the scene unfolding before her.

As far as the eye can see, the land is painted green with an assortment of bushes, trees, and grass. Dotting the landscape are brilliant colors created by a million different varieties of flowers and plants. Butterflies float and flutter gracefully in the air. One cheerful butterfly lands softly on the end of the nose of the Author and tickles him. "What a silly little creature," He giggles while gently picking up the butterfly and sending it on its way. The land is beautiful and flawless except for one barren spot directly in the center.

A gaping hole, stretching over fifteen feet wide in diameter, is the only sign that a tree once grew there. It was a majestic tree: taller than any of the other trees except for one other. This tree's fruit was both precious and poisonous.

"Sarephah, do you see this spot?"

"Yes. Is this not where the tree of the knowledge of good and evil used to stand?"

"Yes. But it is no more as you can see."

"I remember the day it was burned with the fire of betrayal."

The Author moves closer to the hole and motions for Sarephah to join him. They both sit in silence for a moment.

The Author stands and gazes out onto the endless range of white-capped mountains. Finally, he turns and looks down at Sarephah. While motioning toward the hole he says, "I created one tree to hold all the knowledge of good and evil. I did not create one tree with the knowledge of good and another tree with the knowledge evil: good and evil grow on the same tree. In fact, knowing only one without the other is impossible, because neither can exist on its own."

"Without a true choice between good or evil, there is no real decision to make and thus, freedom to choose doesn't exist. In effect, true freewill requires that the knowledge of good and evil be forever linked. Therefore, there was only one tree."

The Author sits down across from Sarephah and looks directly into her eyes. "The tree of the knowledge of good and evil was intended for spiritual beings only, *not* for mortals," he states forcefully, with an emphasis on the word not. The ground trembles slightly with the volume of his voice.

A tree appears suddenly after the Author sweeps his arm in a motion as if painting a picture. Sarephah sits up wide-eyed and the Author says, "When I created this tree, I did not create *actual* good or evil; I created the *potential* for good and evil. Spiritual beings, like you Sarephah, were created above mortals in your capacity to understand everything about good and evil in its potential, without experiencing its actual form. In other words, you did not need to experience actual good and evil to know its full potential. Spiritual beings could eat all the fruit they desired without actualizing good or evil."

"Let me give you an example. You have perfect understanding of envy without actually becoming envious. The choice to actually experience envy is yours to make, but it does not happen automatically after eating the fruit."

"Only one being, the greatest of all the angels, chose to make potential evil an actuality. Wickedness was found in him by his choice to experience evil instead of only knowing of evil. Satan, the Father of all lies, is the creator of actual evil. Once evil was actualized, the nature of spiritual beings was completely altered. Angels who experienced actual evil became evil; they are now demons."

"I see now what happened to Pexov. Is it wrong to be sad for him?"

"No, Sarephah. It is not wrong. He was your friend."

"So, how did the tree affect mortals?"

The Author looks at the tree, snaps his fingers and the tree dissolves until nothing is left except a gaping hole. "Mortals had *all* the knowledge they needed when we created them. Our perfect plan for them did not include the burden associated with the good and evil contained on that tree. Even *potential* good and evil was too great for them, so for their protection we warned them. Mortals were never supposed to partake in the fruit of this tree, because once their human nature had knowledge of the potential of good and evil, actualizing good and evil could not be prevented."

"For example, when the fruit was eaten, they knew all about shame *and* would eventually experience shame. And because good and evil grow together on one tree, actualizing the good without evil was impossible."

"Once freewill, a risky but necessary gift from Us, was used against Us and the fruit was eaten, actual evil could no longer be restrained in the forest or in mortals. Mortals were banished from this paradise, and thus actualized evil entered the world through the sin of our created first two and brought with it unthinkable pain and suffering."

"In addition, since our first two mortals did not think it was necessary to honor Our will, all mortals struggle with a desire for potential good and evil within them *and* the joys and pain associated with actualizing either one. This struggle will continue until the final day."

"In the world, evil, actualized through Satan brings incredible pain and suffering. However, evil will not have the final say. Good, actualized through sacrifice of the Word, brings perfect love and grace. Although good and evil are in a constant battle, by the power of the Word, victory over evil becomes possible for those who choose to accept this Word: actualized good. In fact, it is only by the indwelling of actualized good within the soul of a mortal that evil can be defeated."

Sarephah smiles at this, and it gives her hope for Catherine, but she wonders when evil was actualized in Catherine. "Is there a point when potential evil is actualized in each mortal? I'm thinking specifically of Catherine. Could she have prevented her own suffering?"

The Author holds out his hand and Sarephah takes it. In a flash, they are standing in the past watching a young Catherine encounter the evils of alcohol for the first time.

It's a beautiful summer night just before dusk gives way to darkness. Catherine is twelve years old and unburdened by choices between good and evil. Catherine and her best friend, Lisa, who lives only several houses away, are walking through the streets of the neighborhood. While catching up on all the drama that only twelve years old can understand, Lisa's brother, Samuel, comes staggering down the street toward them.

"Heyyy…girthhs," yells Samuel.

"Oh, no. Not again," Lisa moans.

"What's wrong with your brother? He's acting funny. Ugh…gross… he's getting sick right in the middle of the street." Wide-eyed, Catherine looks at Lisa, "What's wrong with him?"

"He's drunk again."

"Drunk?" Catherine steps back fearful, watching Sam cautiously.

"Come on, let's get out of here. He gets mean when he drinks." Just before turning to run, she looks at Catherine with fear in her eyes. "He scares me when he's like this." Lisa whispers while grabbing Catherine's hand.

"Okay. Let's go."

After running several blocks, they find their usual hiding place and sit down to catch their breath. "Don't ever drink, Catherine. I see how it makes my brother, and I don't want that to happen to you," she says sternly.

"My mom drinks all the time, but she doesn't act like that. Why does your brother get so drunk?"

"I don't know. All I know is that when he's drunk, he's a different person. As far as I'm concerned, alcohol is bad news. It's no good whatever. So don't drink, ever. Okay?" Lisa pleads in a hushed tone.

"Okay," Catherine whispers.

The scene fades away and Sarephah looks back at the Author.

"Was that the only warning Catherine got? That didn't seem very convincing."

The Author looks onto the horizon and says, "No. There were many warnings along the way, but this one made a deep impression on the twelve year old Catherine." He sighs and adds, "She took the warning seriously at the time, but unfortunately the memory of this, and many other warnings, faded over time. The good in her was never nurtured, so evil began to stir. Finally, one day temptation comes along and is stronger than her willingness to resist. Come, Sarephah, and witness the fateful day."

Less than a year later, Catherine's new best friend, Sonya, arranges a sleep over at her house one weekend during the school year. Catherine met Sonya at the start of seventh grade, and they quickly became friends. Catherine likes how daring Sonya is and secretly envies her passion to live life to the fullest. What Catherine doesn't know is that Sonya lives in a house where evil has touched her literally and figuratively. To ease her pain, Sonya's discovered what alcohol can do for her and has already gotten drunk on several occasions. Catherine has no idea what awaits her when she enters that house for the first time.

"Hey, Catherine, I'm so glad you came. We're going to have so much fun," Sonya says excitedly while helping Catherine with her overnight bag. Heading into the basement, Sonya drops off the bag and proudly shows off the room they will stay in that night. The room is her brother's bedroom and comes complete with full size refrigerator.

"What's that?" Catherine asks while pointing at some sort of handle coming out from the side of the refrigerator.

Sonya smiles. "That's the tap for the keg." Opening the refrigerator she gestures dramatically at the contents and says, "Look at that. A keg of beer." She says it as if it's the most natural thing in the world to have a keg of beer in your refrigerator. Handing Catherine a mug, she says, "Come on. Let's get the party started." Sonya starts filling up her mug completely oblivious to Catherine's hesitation.

"What are you doing?" Catherine asks. She's starting to get nervous about all this, but in some ways she's also kind of interested.

"I'm filling up my mug, silly. Come on. Have some with me. It's fun," Sonya urges.

Catherine hesitates. "I don't know. Drinking is wrong. It makes you change and everything." Catherine isn't sure she believes that, but it's the only thing she can think of to say.

"You're darn right it makes you change, but change for the better. You feel happier, forget all your problems, and just laugh and have fun. There's nothing wrong with drinking. I've done it a few times already. You'll never know how good it is till you try it."

Catherine just stands there, so Sonya takes the mug out of her hand and fills it to the top with yellow, foamy liquid. Handing it back to Catherine, Sonya says, "Here, what have you got to lose? Live a little."

Catherine frantically tries to think of one reason why she shouldn't do this. Nothing comes to her. *My parents drink all the time. They've never said drinking is wrong. Sonya says it's fun. I'll never know till I try it myself.* Raising the mug, she says to her friend, "Here's to living life." And with that she takes her first drink of alcohol.

Several hours later, Catherine is so drunk she can barely stand, but just like Sonya said, she laughs and has fun. See, what's so bad about drinking, she thinks. However, little does she know that she just awakened a monster within her; potential evil is actualized.

The scene slowly fades away. The Author puts his hand on Sarephah's shoulder, and they are back once again in the lush forest next to the spot where the tree of the knowledge of good and evil once grew. "Did you notice how similar Catherine's fall was to the fall of the first born of creation?" asks the Author.

"Yeah. Just like your first mortals, Catherine was warned to stay away from sin, or should I say, the proverbial tree. She does for a time, but then temptation comes along, and she takes a bite of the forbidden fruit, believing that it won't harm her."

"Well put, Sarephah."

"So now that evil has taken root, what can be done? She doesn't seem to be responding to your love."

"As long as Catherine has breath and is willing, there is hope for her. Evil is conquered in three stages. First, expose it; this is the job of mortals with Our help. Second, extract it; this is Our job with the mortal's cooperation. Third, extinguish it; this is the work of both mortals and Us working together. Catherine is at the first stage. She must be willing to expose her sin and evil and ask for help. Only by confession will she find peace and know the truth about herself; this truth will set her free."

The Author slips back into the circle of the Divine Three, and they take Sarephah back to Nede. Sarephah is overwhelmed by all she's seen and wonders, "What should I do now?"

"You will know what to do when the time comes," they reassure. "Some chapters in Catherine's life are complete. But the end of Catherine's story has not yet been written. We, as the Author, Word and Text, stand ready to write a new chapter for her. She will be turning the page shortly, and the sheet will be empty. Evil wants to write the next chapter, but Good still holds the pen."

"May your will be done." Sarephah steps out of the heavenlies and back into Catherine's story.

Chapter Fifteen

It's five in the morning and Catherine's lying in bed wide awake. Pip is perched on her chest enjoying her strokes of affection. His purring, which sounds like a tiny motor, slightly calms Catherine's frayed nerves as she lays there contemplating her life. She's not doing well in her new position and has been called into Vickie's office several times. It's always about her attitude, but being pleasant to the customers is not easy when you feel so incredibly miserable. Mark hasn't called and, even though she didn't expect him to contact her, she misses him. In reality, what she misses is having someone in her life. She thinks that if Mark doesn't want her anymore then maybe she needs to find someone who does. Frankly, at this point, anyone will do, because the ache of loneliness is excruciating; not even drinking takes away that pain.

In the past month, she's only managed to string together two or three sober days. The most baffling part of her drinking pattern lately is that her capacity for alcohol changes every time she drinks. On some days, three or four drinks get her sloppy drunk, but on other days, a twelve pack doesn't even make her tipsy. It feels like alcohol is toying with her, intentionally trying to keep her off guard. Catherine still thinks she can control this monster, but lately she wonders if this monster just might be too big for her handle on her own. Her counselor's been suggesting A.A., but she's holding back. Fear, denial, and anger are worthy opponents in this struggle. Fear tells her she can't get sober, denial tells her she doesn't need to, and anger tells her she shouldn't have to.

Across town, Nancy Ash is also wide awake, but instead of lying in bed she's up making coffee for her morning devotional time. Sensing the need to intercede in prayer for Catherine, she flips through the Bible to find the verses that keep rolling around in her head: Colossians chapter one verses thirteen and fourteen. After taking a sip of coffee, she slips on her glasses and reads, "For he has rescued us from the dominion of darkness and brought us into the kingdom of the Son he loves, in whom we have redemption, the forgiveness of sins." *Darkness: I was certainly in darkness.*

Looking up, she whispers, "Thank you God for rescuing me. Please rescue Catherine. I am so worried about her." A tear forms in her eye, but she wipes it away with the sleeve of her bathrobe. *Catherine is in such darkness. I can see it in her eyes; they're so lifeless. They tell us in A.A. to look at newcomers eyes and Catherine has those eyes.*

Nancy reads the rest of chapter one silently and then goes back to the spot where Paul begins a prayer. She reads verse nine out loud, "For this reason, since the day we heard about you, we have not stopped praying for you and asking God to fill you with the knowledge of his will through all spiritual wisdom and understanding."

"Ummm…if that prayer is good enough for Paul, then it's good enough for me. I'm making that part of my new daily prayer for Catherine." *God, I sense you telling me that Catherine's about ready to make some decisions about the direction of her life, especially her drinking. I pray that you fill her with knowledge of you, your love for her, and your desire to rescue her from the dominion of the darkness of alcoholism. I also ask that somehow you could open her heart to…to...feel my love.*

The tears are flowing again, but this time she doesn't bother wiping them away; there are just some things worth crying over. *Please God, give me back my daughter.*

• • •

Pexov hears the prayers for Catherine. "Oh, how repulsive are the ramblings of mortals. They need to shut their yappers and stop the incessant whining. When will these pathetic mortals learn that prayer does nothing?" Pexov snarls.

Sarephah also hears the prayers for Catherine. The crackle and popping sounds emanating from the power surging through the atmosphere as the prayer ascends to the throne of the Divine Three is exhilarating. She twirls and laughs, knowing that the minute prayers are spoken for Catherine they are heard and she gains strength.

"You're just worried, Pexov, 'cause you know that The Divine Three hear every prayer and that prayer changes many things. As a matter of fact, here is one thing prayer changes: your ability to spread your evil and wickedness. Every prayer said for Catherine weakens you and strengthens me." Sarephah twirls around a couple more times to emphasize her point.

"Catherine's gonna need more than some words spewing out of the mouths of a few weeping mortals to help her. The loser doesn't even want help." Turning toward Catherine he says, "You must be slacking on your job, Sarephah, 'cause your little project doesn't look so good." He turns back to look at Sarephah. "Oh, and you conveniently keep forgetting that the ONLY thing that can weaken me is Catherine, and she's too ignorant to fight against me."

"I guess I see things differently than you, Pexov. I can see you growing weaker with every prayer that is uttered on her behalf. Whether you admit it or not, Catherine is moving in the direction of good, which means she is indeed fighting against you and the evil you represent."

"Are you kidding me? I think you actually believe she's getting better."

"I believe in the power of the Divine Three and their ability to rescue her from your clutches. As her will to change grows stronger, the ability to accept help grows stronger. Someday, if Catherine reaches out her hand for help, the Divine Three and I will be there."

"Hmmph…*if* Catherine reaches out her hand for help, I'll grab it first and drag her straight to hell – the altar of the eternal death."

Pexov glares at Sarephah, but his weakness forces him to retreat back into the depths of the heavenlies. He thrusts his head back, screams in anger, and disappears into the darkness from which he came.

Sarephah turns toward a now sleeping Catherine and breathes out an aura of protection upon her. Once the protection is in place, she sends out comfort and encouragement for the journey ahead. Catherine has no idea that while she sleeps Sarephah's whispers of love are reaching the depths of her soul. Catherine's heart is being opened to hear the voice of the Divine Three and the message They bring through the prayers and direct intervention of their chosen agents.

Sarephah knows that what comes from a heart filled with love reaches the heart prepared by that same love. This makes her mission even more critical, because Catherine can only hear what love has to say when her heart is softened. And for Catherine, what she hears will challenge everything she's ever believed.

• • •

Megan, Catherine's little sister, is both anxious and excited to see her big sister. They rarely get together anymore, so she's surprised when Catherine agrees to meet her for lunch. She's concerned about her and prays for her often, but admits she doesn't understand her sister at all. Megan drinks a little with her college buddies, but never gets drunk and wonders why her sister so often does.

Drinking is a touchy subject. She's knows better than to bring it up at lunch. It's been a rough road with her sister and she sighs heavily remembering some of the more unpleasant times. *God, I've seen this all before with mom. I don't know if I can do it all over again with Catherine.*

In the midst of her reflecting she's brought back to the present by the brake lights of the car in front of her. "Whoa," she yells while slamming on the breaks to avoid the car that stopped at the red light. "Slow down," she whispers to herself. Grabbing hold of the wheel, she shakes off the anxiety of the near miss. The light turns green, and she heads one more block to the parking lot of Slammin Sammy's Sandwich Shop.

She turns into the first parking spot she sees, shuts off the car, takes a deep breath, and mutters, "Okay. Here we go." At the same time she opens her door she notices Catherine pulling into the parking lot. Megan looks at her watch, looks back at Catherine's car, and smiles. "Hmm, on time. I'm impressed, sis," she says under her breath.

Megan's genuinely glad to see her sister, but also guarded 'cause she's never sure which Catherine is going to show up. Over the years, Megan's gotten good at making quick assessments of Catherine's prevailing mood and adjusts accordingly to avoid unnecessary confrontations. Living with an alcoholic for most of your life will do that to you.

"Hey, Sis!" Megan yells to get Catherine's attention. Catherine looks over, smiles slightly, and waves.

Catherine is also genuinely glad to see Megan, but she can't get past her own pain to express it appropriately. "Morning," Catherine says.

Megan is a hugger, so after sensing no overtly negative vibes, puts her arms around Catherine and gives her a big sisterly hug. "Good Morning!" she shouts while holding the hug and swaying back and forth. Catherine's heart stirs unexpectedly by this display of affection and holds onto Megan longer than normal. Megan notices this and when she lets go, she looks into Catherine's eyes and instantly knows why her sister agreed to have lunch: she's hurting.

"It's really good to see you. I'm so glad we could arrange our schedules to meet for lunch. It's been way too long since we've gotten together," Megan says. Taking Catherine by the arm, they walk toward the front door of the restaurant.

"Yeah, it has been a while."

"What made you pick Sam's?" Megan wonders, though she suspects it's because they used to meet here all the time.

"I have good memories here," she says quietly. "Plus, they have good food," she adds with a little more enthusiasm.

The restaurant is a favorite of the college crowd, so the atmosphere is very laid back. There's several students working on laptops in the booths lining the wall, and a group of students are gathered around a table discussing the concept of duty in Kantian ethics. The sign right inside the door reads, "The Hostess is off duty. Seat yourself."

Spying an open booth in the corner, they grab it and congratulate themselves on such a good find during the lunch hour. After quickly glancing over the menu, Megan puts her menu down and declares, "I'm gonna have the chipotle chicken wrap *with* the fries."

"Good choice. I think I'll have the same."

They both lay down their menus and sit in silence for what feels like an awkwardly long time. Thankfully, the waitress stops by to take their order and momentarily breaks the silence. After ordering, there's another long stretch of uncomfortable silence.

Finally, Megan asks with the exuberance of a college student, "Did I tell you how excited I am to be graduating in 150 days? Not that I'm counting or anything." Megan smiles broadly just thinking about graduating with a degree in Instructional Design and Educational Technology.

"That's great. How'd the interview go at Holsted Academy?" Catherine asks.

"Good, I think. It's hard to tell sometimes, but I answered all their questions, and they seemed to like my answers. I even got the chance to show them how I would tie learning objectives to assignments within their specific Intelligent Learning Platform." She pauses, "Am I boring you with this stuff, 'cause I could go on forever."

"No. I want to know what you're doing. It sounds interesting."

Catherine is saying all the right things, but her demeanor is saying something entirely different. It's not that Catherine is bored: she's simply preoccupied by her own stuff. Self-centeredness is one trait that blossoms with the alcoholic lifestyle. In every situation, she constantly asks herself, "What about me?" Her second question is equally narcissistic, "How does this affect me?" To make matters worse, she has no idea how self-absorbed she really is.

"You just seemed like you were off in your own little world."

"Sorry. I'm not feeling very well today."

This is one of Catherine's standard answers, right up there with, "I'm tired." Both are equally evasive and unchallengeable, with the added bonus of potentially eliciting some sort of sympathetic response, which in turns feeds her self-centeredness. It's a wonderfully viscous cycle that Pexov encourages.

"So, anyway, how are you doing?" Megan keeps the question intentionally vague.

"Okay, I guess."

"I was wondering 'cause I heard about Mark."

"What!" Catherine asks wide-eyed, "Why, what did you hear?"

Megan's surprised at Catherine's reaction. "I just heard that you guys broke up. Someone said you guys had a big argument or something at a party, but that's all I heard."

Catherine visibly relaxes. "Yeah…umm….yeah that's about right."

"So how are you doing? Do you miss him? I didn't know him very well, but you guys were together for about six months."

Catherine tears up unexpectedly. She's not sure if it's because she misses having Mark around or because Megan seems genuinely concerned. She blinks back the tears and says, "I miss him a little, but whatever. I've got too much going on to sit around and think about Mark."

"Really? So what else is going on with you?"

Catherine wasn't expecting that question and struggles to answer. "Umm…well…you know...things."

"Okay," Megan says slowly and looks doubtfully at Catherine. "Are you sure you're doing all right?" Megan treads lightly, but she really wants to know how her big sister is doing. "You seem out of sorts. Anything I can do to help?" Smiling, she adds, "I'm a good listener."

Tears again well up in Catherine's eyes. She hates to cry, and is irritated that she can't seem to control the tears right now. She blinks a couple times, but a tear falls anyway. Quickly wiping it away she says, "I'm fine, really."

The ache inside her paralyzes her. She's kept so much inside for so long she has no idea where to start or what will happen if she does say anything. Fear of letting anyone in is still greater than the pain of keeping everyone out.

"Well, I hope you know that I'm here if you want to talk." Megan says a silent prayer, but doesn't press Catherine any further.

"Thanks." They lock eyes in a compassionate gaze that seems to validate both Catherine's pain and Megan's concern. They both know this part of the conversation is over, but they also somehow know that this won't ever be over until Catherine takes down some of her walls.

Realizing it's time to change the subject Megan says, "Kevin and I are going to work down at the shelter…."

In the middle of Megan's stories about her current boyfriend Kevin, Catherine begins to mentally fade away. Her jumbled emotions are muffling Megan's voice: her own internal screams of pain are simply too loud.

The lunch ends on a good note though, and they embrace in the parking lot before heading to their respective cars. While driving away, Megan resolves to pray harder for Catherine, and Catherine resolves to stay more in touch with Megan. But neither is really sure it'll help.

Chapter Sixteen

Driving to her mandatory counseling session, Catherine squeezes the steering wheel and clenches her jaw, tensing all the muscles in her neck. Almost involuntarily she raises her defenses just thinking about facing her counselor. She wants to get better, but she thinks there has to be a better way. Walking into that office makes her feel incredibly vulnerable, so she instinctively tries to protect herself; protect herself from what, she's not exactly sure. She believes her walls are protecting her from further emotional and mental hurt when they're actually keeping her from healing her emotional and mental hurt. She doesn't yet understand that when good can't get in, evil never gets exposed, and the soul never gets healed.

Elizabeth glances at the clock on her desk and mentally assesses how much time she has to prepare for her next session. Her appointment book lists one last client today. Without wasting another minute she grabs a book off her shelf: *Alcoholics Anonymous*. All AA's call the book, *Alcoholics Anonymous,* the Big Book.

Flipping through her well-used Big Book, she stops at page thirty. The chapter "More About Alcoholism" has always been a helpful resource when working with clients still unsure about their illness. Elizabeth believes alcoholism is an illness, but a unique illness. It's a three-fold sickness: physical, mental, and spiritual. In this office, she primarily treats the mental obsession, but she usually finds ways to address the spiritual problem if the client is open to it.

Thinking about Catherine now, she reads the top of page thirty. "The idea that somehow, someday he will control and enjoy his drinking is the great obsession of every abnormal drinker. The persistence of this illusion is astonishing. Many pursue it into the gates of insanity or death." This is certainly a good description of Catherine she thinks.

Checking her notes from the previous weeks, she recalls how much Catherine has insisted that she could stop drinking anytime she wanted to. In fact, she made a point of saying that she had cut down on her drinking a little, only getting drunk a few times. Elizabeth smiles and remembers being told once that you know you've lost control over your drinking when you start trying to control your drinking. She didn't get it at first, but eventually, it was quite a revelation.

She puts away her Big Book and grabs the equally worn and well-used book right next to it: her Bible. Onc verse has been coming to her mind today, so she looks it up. Romans 7:18 has been one of her favorites over the years; it reminds her of what it was like when she was actively drinking. "I know that nothing good lives in me, that is, in my sinful nature. For I have the desire to do what is good, but I cannot carry it out."

That's what it felt like when she realized she couldn't quit drinking on her own, even when she desperately wanted to. For her and countless others, a spiritual experience was the only solution for the spiritual malady connected with the sins of Alcoholism. Believing that God could help her made all the difference.

Elizabeth puts her Bible back and settles into her chair to listen for a word from the Lord. Today her heart is especially burdened because the darkness surrounding Catherine is heavy. She always asks God for protection against the powers of this dark and evil world, and today is no exception. She silently prays for the ability to stand up against anything that has a hold on Catherine and for the power of God to penetrate Catherine's heart so she can see the truth.

The intercom on her phone comes to life. "Elizabeth, Catherine Ash is here for her 4:00 appointment."

"Ok, I'll be right out. Thanks." She stands up, looks up, and prays, "Guide me in this session, Father. Help me to be your instrument of healing. Amen."

Catherine enters the office, sits down in her usual chair, and sighs heavily. It's been three days since she's had a drink and she's feeling it.

"You seem a little down. What's going on?" Elizabeth asks.

"Nothing. I'm just tired."

"Tired huh? Okay. Tired in what way?"

"Tired of being here for one thing," she says impulsively.

Elizabeth smiles. "What's so bad about coming here?"

Catherine thinks for a minute. "You always end up making me talk about drinking and stuff. Maybe I don't want to talk about that."

"Okay." Elizabeth lays her notepad down and puts her hands in her lap. "What *do* you want to talk about?"

Catherine eyes Elizabeth suspiciously. "What do you mean?"

"I mean just what I said. This is your time. What do you want to talk about?"

Catherine looks down, trying to think of something to talk about: something besides how awful she feels. "I had lunch with my sister today. We could talk about that," she says expectantly.

"Okay. How was lunch with your sister?"

"Good."

Elizabeth's shoulders sag slightly. *This could be a long session if Catherine doesn't open up.* "Just good? This is your topic. Can you elaborate a little?"

Catherine shrugs and starts to feel anxious. "I don't know what else to tell you. We had a good lunch. We had good food. Mmm….it was crowded. But, overall, it was a good time."

"Okay. I'm glad you had a good time with your sister. Anything else about your lunch you want to talk about?"

Catherine leans forward, puts her elbows on her knees, and rests her chin in her hands. "Ummm…well…not really."

"Okay. Then it's my turn to come up with a topic. Have you thought any more about checking out an A.A. meeting with me?"

Catherine crosses her arms. "No."

"Why?"

"'cause I don't see the need to go to some stupid A.A. meeting."

"Have you ever been to one?"

"No, but I remember when my mom was in treatment. We had to go to family sessions and groups with other family members who had someone in treatment. They sucked so bad. I hated 'em, so I just stopped going. So, no, I am not going to go to an A.A. meeting." She sits back, crosses her arms, and stares at Elizabeth.

"A.A. is quite a bit different from meetings in treatment. Why did you stop going to the family meetings when your mom was in treatment?"

Catherine looks at her in disbelief. "I just told you why. I hated 'em."

"Why did you hate them?"

Catherine hesitates. "'cause they kept asking me about stuff I didn't want to talk about. My mom had the problem not me."

"What do you mean they were asking you questions? What kind of questions?"

"What does this have to do with anything?" Catherine demands.

"I want to know what stuff they were asking you, because it seems to me, they should have been focusing on your mom.

Did they ask you about your drinking?" Elizabeth's hunch is that Catherine displayed some alcoholic behavior and was called on it by the staff.

Catherine just sits and glares at Elizabeth. "Maybe. They did an assessment, and said that I was only a problem drinker. See, so there's no problem with drinking." She smiles smugly.

"What about now? Have you been able to go even one week without drinking?"

Catherine says nothing.

"I'll take that as a no. Okay, next topic. Your turn."

Catherine sits up. "Okay." She thinks for a minute and then asks, "Did you really stop drinking when you were only twenty-eight?"

"Yes." Elizabeth doesn't say anything more, and Catherine is intrigued. Smiling Elizabeth says, "All right, my turn again. How's work going?"

"Okay I guess."

"What about the meeting you had with your boss this week? Can you tell me what happened?"

Catherine quickly holds her hand up. "Wait a minute. Isn't it my turn now to ask the question?"

Good. I've got her participating. Thank you, God. "Yep, sorry. You're right. It's your turn."

"Do you want to drink now after all these years?" Catherine wonders.

"No, the desire to drink left me very early in sobriety."

Catherine doesn't react.

"Okay, my turn again. What happened at the meeting you had with your boss this week?"

"The meeting was kind of a downer."

Elizabeth waits for more and then realizes she's going to have to dig a little. "Why was it a downer?"

Looking away she says, "My boss is not happy with my attitude. She says some customers have complained about it. Whatever. I'm getting sick of that place anyway."

"Mmmm...seems like they have been pretty gracious keeping you employed based on how drunk you were when you showed up that day." Elizabeth knows a little more of the true story since Catherine finally admitted to being drunk that day she went into work. "Okay, so you're sick of that place. Can you tell me why?"

"It just seems like they're picking on me all because of that one day. Every week I have to show that I've been to counseling, and I have to meet with Vickie. I'm tired of all the things I have to do just to stay working there. I wish I had never gone into work that day. I never should have gone into work that day. That's the cause of all my problems."

She pauses and looks up. "Hey, wait a minute. I missed my turn asking the question. My turn now." She pauses to think and then asks, "If the desire to drink went away, why do you still go to those A.A. meetings?"

Elizabeth raises her eyebrows. "Good question. Because helping other alcoholics is the best way to ensure that I will continue to stay sober. Also, being in the fellowship is a great place to meet some incredible people. As a matter of fact, my best friends are all in A.A. And last but not least, I continue to go to A.A. because only there am I reminded of what it was like, what happened, and who got me there. I thank God everyday for bringing me to the fellowship of Alcoholics Anonymous. With A.A., I have God in my life, sobriety, love, and serenity. Without God and A.A., I would either be in jail, in a mental hospital, or dead."

Elizabeth lets her comment hang in the air for a minute. Catherine looks down at her shoes and says nothing, but her actions speak volumes.

Elizabeth finally speaks. "Okay my turn again. You keep saying that the only thing that you did wrong with the situation at work was going into work that day." She waits and then says softly, "Look at me, Catherine." Catherine raises her head and looks at Elizabeth with moist eyes. "Has it ever occurred to you that you shouldn't have been drinking the way you did that day?"

Catherine's head drops. One tear falls to the floor. Slowly, she shakes her head back and forth. No. She never thought about that. Not once.

Elizabeth waits to see if Catherine wants to talk, but only silence fills the room. Glancing at the clock, she realizes time is up. "Okay, well time's up for today." In a soft tone she adds, "My door is always open for you. If you decide at any point in the next week you want to meet me at an A.A. meeting just call the office. I'll be there for you. I know this isn't an easy decision, so I'll be praying for you."

Catherine looks up for a second, nods her head, and manages to say weakly, "Okay."

Elizabeth stands up. "See you next week." Smiling she adds, "if not sooner. Take care."

Catherine walks out the door more hopeful than she's ever been, and more scared than she'd ever admit.

Chapter Seventeen

Several days later, Catherine finds herself sitting across the desk from Vickie Reed answering questions about her attitude again. In her own distorted way, Catherine's trying to do her best at work. However, the energy it takes fighting off the desire to drink is filling every space in her brain. She can't think of work because she's thinking of drinking or not drinking or a combination of the two, sometimes in the same minute. The battle is exhausting, and she's not coping well. Without drinking for six days, all her pent up emotions and thoughts are bubbling to the surface, and she has no idea what to do with them. The answer was always to get drunk and silence the emotional noise. But, she's beginning to believe that drinking is the problem, not the solution. That thought almost paralyzes her.

"...was reported to me yesterday," Vickie says. "Can you address that issue for me?"

"Umm...sorry...can you repeat that?" Catherine says weakly.

Vickie pauses and takes a deep breath. "Do you think you're doing a good job here?"

Uh, oh. That's loaded question. "I'm doing the best I can."

Vickie puts her finger on her mouth, pondering what to say next, and then finally says, "Sarah, your immediate supervisor, says she hasn't seen significant improvement in your attitude since we talked several weeks ago. How is your counseling going?"

"Good. I've been going every week like I'm supposed to," Catherine says wearily.

Vickie puts her hands on her lap and looks at Catherine. "I'm not sure how much more I can help you. This is the last conversation I want to have with you about your behavior at work. This is a hotel. We cater to our guests. We smile for them. We help them with whatever they need. We do not argue with them or suggest they go see the supervisor if they are that dissatisfied with the quality of service. Do you understand?"

"Yes. I'll do better. I promise."

"Okay," Vickie sighs.

Leaning on her desk, she says with some concern, "I put my neck out for you because I believed in you, but I have to admit, I'm starting to wonder if I made a big mistake." She holds her gaze with Catherine. Catherine uses all her strength to maintain eye contact. "I've thought about this quite a bit, even prayed about it several times. I'm willing to give you one more chance. Listen, it's not so much *what* you're doing; it's *how* you're doing it. I suggest you do whatever you need in order to fix what's going on inside you, because it's spilling out all over the place and jeopardizing your position here. I'll give you two more weeks, and then we'll meet again. Okay, that's all for now." Vickie sits back in her chair; Catherine rises to leave.

"One more thing, I still believe you're worth helping, but nothing's going to change until *you* believe that."

Catherine nods and turns toward the door, not sure what she believes anymore.

• • •

Pexov knows Sarephah's protective aura around Catherine is still strong enough to withstand his flaming arrows. A direct attack is not possible right now, so he simply changes tactics:

he'll use her inner turmoil to his advantage. He gets excited just thinking about spewing wicked and disturbing thoughts into her already confused mind. "How delightful it will be to squash her little attempts at changing."

Looking at Catherine as she pulls away from the hotel parking lot he sneers, "We can have an intimate moment when my mind touches your sick little mortal mind, *Catherine*. Yes, how special it will be once we are connected again. You will know me, and I will bind you forever."

Slamming her fist on the steering wheel and wiping back the tears are visible indications of Catherine's state of mind. She's angry because she's crying. She's crying because she's scared. She scared because she can't stop crying, and angry because she can't keep it together anymore.

"What's wrong with me?" she yells in the privacy of her car. "I just don't know what to do. I'm losing it. This feeling inside me is horrible," she cries harder. "What should I do?" she whimpers. She angrily wipes the tears off her already tear stained face.

At the next stop light she catches a glimpse of her bloodshot eyes in her rearview mirror: eyes red and swollen from her unwanted tears. "I feel lost. Where did you go Catherine?" she mumbles to her reflection.

Pexov springs into action. His time has come. Thoughts fill Catherine's mind. *A drink will make you feel better. You're worth it. You deserve to feel better. The only thing that can make you feel good is a drink.*

"NO!" Catherine yells and grips the steering wheel tighter.

Pexov continues unfazed. *Why deny yourself something that is so good and will make you feel better? Get something for yourself. You will feel better. Don't you want to feel better? Don't you want to get better? You can feel better. You can be better.*

Catherine can't stop the barrage of thoughts coming at her. They are too strong and too appealing. She sees a drive-through a couple blocks ahead. "Maybe one drink will help. I'll have just one, no more. I've got to do something or I'll explode."

Stopping at the red light, she stares at the entrance of the drive-through. "Yeah, I'll get something to make me feel better, and then I'll figure out what to do next. I know a drink will take away this pain."

After she enters the drive-through, the sound of her own voice ordering a six-pack of beer drowns out the last thought that comes to her: *call Elizabeth.*

• • •

When Catherine gets homes, she paces back and forth in her apartment, pondering her next move. Suddenly, Pip gets tangled up in her feet. "Whoa, watch out, Pip."

Meowing incessantly, Pip runs in circles around her legs. He's agitated about something. Catherine isn't sure what's gotten him so riled up.

Pexov sits in the corner, keeping his distance from Pip while sending distorted thoughts into Catherine's mind.

"What's wrong with you? Do you need fed? Okay."

Pip's odd behavior momentarily distracts her from the beer waiting for her and the thoughts telling her to drink. She opens a can of whitefish and tuna supreme and scoops out the runny, molded gelatin-like meal into Pip's dish. Pip just looks at her when she sets it on the floor.

"What? I thought that's what you wanted?"

Pip looks toward the other room, meows loudly, and rubs up against Catherine.

Catherine looks into the other room and then back at Pip. "What? You're driving me crazy tonight. Well, you got your food. Have at it." But Pip just sits there looking at Catherine.

"I don't know what you want, but I know what I need."

She opens the refrigerator and grabs one beer. She stares at the bottle for several seconds, opens the top, and stands there.

Several thoughts come. *Yes, this will make you happy, very happy. You are worth it. You don't need to stop drinking.*

Moving to the couch in the other room, she sits, puts the bottle down on the table in front of her, and sighs. *You need to stop drinking. This will not make you happy. Have you thought about going to A.A.? Call Elizabeth. I still believe you are worth it. The shepherd seeks his sheep.*

"I'm not one of his sheep. God doesn't even know I exist. And even if he does, he sure hasn't done anything to help me."

She grabs the bottle and takes a gulp. Pexov roars with delight.

Catherine takes another gulp. Pip meows loudly.

Catherine takes one more gulp.

Then, she starts to cry. The pain is not going away; it's getting stronger.

She cries harder. Despair presses down on her.

She begins to sob. Blackness fills her.

She sobs uncontrollably. "I can't do this anymore. I need help," she says between sobs.

Pexov growls. Pip hisses.

Catherine barely notices what's going on around her because a strange feeling comes over her. She gets up, walks to the sink, and stands there with the half empty bottle. Deep within her, she finds the strength to do something she's never done before. Lifting the bottle, she tips it over, and pours out the rest of the beer into the sink as tears stream uncontrollably down her face.

She turns, swings open the refrigerator door, and brings out the rest of the beer. One by one, she opens them and pours all the beer into the sink. While watching the alcohol swirl down the drain, Catherine wonders how she'll ever survive. In her distorted mind, alcohol had always come to her rescue, but by her actions this evening, she just eliminated that option. "What will save me now? *Who* will save me now?"

After pouring out all the alcohol in the house, she lays down on the couch, and Pip curls up with her. The emptiness she feels is almost refreshing compared to the terror that engulfs her. Exhausted, sleep comes quickly, but not peacefully. Evil enters Catherine's dream and turns it into a nightmare.

• • •

Catherine's swimming alone in a lake. The only source of light is the moon casting a long reflection on the water. She's bobbing up and down in the cold water. Shivering, she moves her eyes from side to side trying to get her bearings. Suddenly, someone pops up out of the water. Catherine swirls around and sees Vickie Reed. "I'm willing to give you a chance. I think you're worth it." Vickie reaches out her hand and Catherine reaches to grab it. Suddenly, Vickie's dragged under the water. Catherine screams and hits the top of the water searching for her.

Another head pops up out of the water. It's her mom. "I believe God is pursuing you right now. I've been praying for you." Catherine begins to cry and swims toward her mom. Just as she gets close enough to grab her hand, her mom is sucked under the water. She splashes the water to find her, and then another person appears.

Catherine turns and sees Elizabeth. "Come to A.A. Or you'll be locked up, crazy, or dead." Suddenly, Elizabeth disappears beneath the water. Catherine frantically looks around for her when she feels something touch her legs. She screams. Megan yells for her from behind. "Are you okay? I'm a good listener." Just as she turns, Megan disappears below the water.

Catherine twirls around and around in the water. "Help! Somebody help me! Mom, Megan, Elizabeth," she screams, but nobody hears her.

A strong hand grabs her leg and pulls her under. She's surrounded by cold blackness. Kicking frantically, she finally frees her leg and shoots up out of the water. Taking in a deep breath, she coughs and wipes her eyes.

Again, a hand grabs her leg and pulls her under.

She can't breathe. It's so cold. It's so dark.

Out of nowhere, Sarephah sweeps in, lifts Pexov off Catherine, and hurls him across the room. Pexov scrambles to his feet, glares at Sarephah, and disappears into the heavenlies.

Catherine sits up panting. She holds her hand against her chest, trying to catch her breath. She's disoriented, covered in sweat, and scared. "I can't breathe."

Sarephah looks over at Catherine and sends out her aura of peace to help her get back to sleep and to comfort her through the night. Then, she decides to follow Pexov to keep him as far away from Catherine tonight as possible.

Catherine focuses on slowing her breathing and eventually begins to calm. Shivering, she grabs a blanket off the back of the couch and wraps it around her. She curls up on the couch, looks around the room, and sees the clock. She stares at the second hand slowly clicking around the numbers and settles in for what she knows will be a very long night. She just made a decision, and can hardly wait for the morning to come.

Chapter Eighteen

The first light of morning awakens the day and ends the long black night for Catherine. The warmth of the sun, the song of the birds, and the newness of the day strengthen her resolve to follow through on the decision she made last night. Breathing in courage for the day and breathing out fear from the night, she picks up the phone and sets in motion a whole new set of possibilities.

Pexov glares at Catherine with his red, glowing eyes and quivers with hatred because this mortal just neutralized his power. Her decision last night didn't stop him, but the action accompanying her decision this morning did. When Catherine picked up the phone, Pexov knew he failed to infiltrate Catherine's nature with his lies and hatred. He shudders in horror, realizing he did not sufficiently break her will enough for her to be consumed by the desire for every kind of wickedness and evil.

He turns away from the image of his loathing and failure to consider what he must do next. Without much thought, he quickly realizes there really is only one thing to do. He knows the only way to get back what he lost and to alter the future possibilities for this wretched soul is to go before the one who will either consume him by his rage or assist him with his power. With a shriek filled with knowledge of the terror that awaits him, he moves into the darkness and into unknown possibilities.

• • •

Sarephah is extremely pleased with Catherine. She can't wait to tell the Divine Three, even though she supposes they already know. Her excitement is almost uncontainable. Twirling around and around excitedly, she thinks the possibilities are endless both for her and Catherine. Raising her arms in victory, she praises the Divine Three because she's sure that the battle is over: good triumphed over evil. Wondering what her next assignment will be, she practically skips into the presence of the Divine Three.

Laughing heartily, the Divine Three send their aura out and welcome Sarephah into their presence. "Hello Sarephah. We are very pleased to see you. We must talk about Catherine because the time is coming when we can begin our work with her."

Sarephah stops cold in her tracks and frowns. "Umm…what do you mean, the time is coming when we can *begin* our work with Catherine? I thought we were already working with Catherine. In fact, I thought we were almost done. Did you see what she did this morning?" she says while pointing excitedly toward the image of Catherine.

"Yes, we see everything that happens with our children." The Word steps forward and speaks for the three. "Right now, Catherine is scared and confused, and therefore, willing to find a different way. She's puzzled because her nature is hungry for sin but, at the same time, repulsed by that same sin. Her will has been awakened to new possibilities and she's willing to explore them. She desires something better; however, she's being driven by fear and desperation not by our grace and love. Unfortunately, the fear that drives her now can easily pull her back toward even greater sin, given the right circumstances."

Sarephah puts her hand to her head and sits down slowly. "I don't understand," she says with a sigh.

The Word, now the only visible representation of the Divine Three, sits down next to Sarephah. They both remain silent for several minutes. Finally, the Word turns to Sarephah and says, "Sarephah, I want to tell you a story."

Sarephah turns toward the Word and smiles because she loves the stories of the Divine Three. Knowing that their stories always contains nuggets of wisdom, she can't wait to learn something new. "Oh, good, I love your stories. Will this have something to do with Catherine?" she asks expectantly.

"I'll let you be the judge of that," he says with a teasing smile, thoroughly enjoying his time with Sarephah.

"There was a woman who sat on a beach and watched the beauty and power of the water as it roared in and out of the shore. She sat in awe of the sound and majesty of the crashing waves. She was told once not to enter or swim in the water, because those who do, rarely make it back to shore safely; the few who do make it back, are never quite the same."

"Day after day, she sat on the shore and watched as others swam out. They looked like they were having fun or at least more fun than she was having. One day, she was invited to swim out to join the others. Nothing on the shore seemed pleasing to her, so she stepped into the water and began to swim out to sea. At first, she enjoyed her time in the water. It was new and exciting. She wondered why she was ever told not to enter the water, and soon began to believe that those on the shore lied to her."

"However, eventually, life in the water took its toll on her. She finally realized how powerful the water was when she was tossed and turned violently during many, many storms. She tried to hold on to the others in the water with her, but they were too busy trying to stay above water themselves to care about her struggles."

"After riding out several horrible storms and nearly drowning, she looks for a way out of the water. On the horizon a boat appears. Near death, she manages to swim to the boat and get in. At first, she is relieved simply because she is out of the water. Taking the oars of the boat, she starts to row.

But where will she go she wonders? If I go the wrong way and row further out to sea, I will die. If I just keep rowing around in this boat, another storm will come, and I will be in just as bad of shape as I would have been in the water. As a matter of fact, if that happened, I'm sure I would jump back in the water. If I row to the shore from which I came, I will have to sit glumly and watch the water with envious eyes. Plus, I can't go to the shore I left because everyone there will judge me for going into the water in the first place. She sits and ponders what to do. She simply doesn't know which way to go."

The Word stops and smiles at Sarephah. Sarephah sits up and says, "This is about Catherine! Can I tell you what I think it means?" she asks exuberantly.

"Yes, Sarephah. Tell me what you think it means."

"The woman is Catherine. The water is sin, or I suppose, evil. The boat is only a temporary means of escaping the water. Am I right so far?"

"Yes, very good. Go on."

"Catherine's in the boat right now, but she needs help deciding which way to row. If she is left on her own, she will either die in the water, or in her sins, since the water means sin, remain miserably wondering around in the water, or find the shore and be delivered from the water. I'm glad she finally got in the boat, but I see now how she is still in danger. So I guess our work with Catherine is just beginning. She needs to know which way to go."

The Word pats Sarephah on the knee and with joy in his eyes says, "Sarephah you are becoming a very wise angel. We are pleased with you."

Sarephah bows her head and allows the praise to enter and refresh her spirit. "Thank you."

"Many will get in the boat with Catherine without being invited, and she will allow them because she is desperate. A few will ask to enter the boat, and Catherine will have to make a choice. However, only one belongs in the boat with her, but he must be invited by Catherine. Only one can show her the way to go."

"That would be you right?" Sarephah asks.

The Word looks over at the image of Catherine and declares, "Yes, I am the way, the truth, and the life. I am the only way for Catherine to be fully released from the evil that holds her nature captive. My truth will guide her will, and my life will energize her soul."

Turning back to Sarephah, he says, "In order to help Catherine, I must get in the boat with her. She still has a choice to make, because the one who seeks to hold her captive will also want in the boat. And he won't wait for an invitation."

Sarephah nods. "I better get back to Catherine because, knowing Pexov, he won't only get in the boat, he'll try to capsize it."

• • •

Pexov trembles uncontrollably standing before his Master, Satan. He just spent countless hours in the gathering room with other demons, loathing every single minute and every single one of them. Now that he is before the one who holds his life in his slimy hands, he is overwhelmed with an equal measure of hatred and fear.

"EXPLAIN YOURSELF!" Satan roars.

Pexov drops to his knees and covers his ears with his hands. The sound of his master's voice is deafening. Slowly he lifts he head and raises his eyes to the hideous throne. "I...I...she…she…"

"Stop your stammering! Stand before me and answer me! What kind of a demon are you?"

Suddenly, the hand of a huge sentinel demon grabs Pexov by the neck and lifts him up. The demon holds him slightly above the ground and sneers at him before letting his feet touch the ground. Pexov steadies himself and tries to stand tall while returning the sneer of the demon that just touched him. Finally, he faces Satan and says, "That mortal is resilient and crafty. Other mortals have been interceding for her, and the angels are protecting her."

"SHUT UP!" Satan growls and rises from his throne. The creatures surrounding the throne quickly slither down the steps and circle the room.

"Pexov, Pexov, Pexov. You worthless servant. What am I going to do with you?" He turns his head from side to side and up and down, sizing up Pexov. Finally, he shouts, "What *am* I going to do with such a failure?"

He walks down from the throne, pausing deliberately on each step. When he reaches the bottom step, all the slithering creatures move in closer.

Pexov begins to sweat uncontrollably. "Let me explain."

"SILENCE!" Satan roars.

Walking behind Pexov, he moves in closer and whispers in his ear, "You have failed me. You are a failure." Pexov is paralyzed by fear. Satan walks back around to face Pexov. "But *I* will not fail. Nothing and no one will ever defeat me." He slaps Pexov so hard he falls to his knees again.

"GET UP!"

Pexov scrambles to his feet and tries not to show the fear in his eyes.

Satan begins to pace back and forth in front of Pexov. "Right now, the Divine Three are probably telling that idiot angel a stupid story, attempting to illustrate some lesson or to give her some valuable piece of wisdom. How ridiculous. I don't have time for storytelling. I have planning and strategizing to do. I'm not concerned at all by the actions of our precious Catherine. Let her make a phone call. Wherever she goes and whatever she does, I will be right there with her. I will be there whether she wants me there or not. That is my advantage. I don't need an invitation. I am always around."

Satan stops right in front of Pexov. "YOU…if you can handle the assignment…will be there for Catherine. You will help her get new friends; friends that will want to help her. Yes, new friends for our scared and lonely little mortal who seeks help is a brilliant idea. If she wants help, we've got just what she's looking for. Go get Catherine a few friends to help her, Pexov. And you may just save your own neck in the process."

Satan turns and climbs back up to his throne. The creatures quickly slither up the steps and return to their resting places. Pexov bows, turns, and walks out of that horror chamber with more hate in his heart than even he thought possible.

• • •

Catherine's been anxiously pacing back and forth in front of the phone for the past two hours. "What is taking so long?" she yells in frustration. She looks at the clock for the thousandth time and then looks back at the phone. "Why won't you ring?" Seconds later, as if on cue, the phone rings. She lunges for it, but knocks it off the table. One ring, two rings, three rings. Dropping to her knees, she reaches under the table searching frantically for the phone. Four rings. Finally, she gets a hold of it and hits the answer button.

"Hello," she says out of breath.

"Hello. May I speak with Catherine?" the caller asks.

"This is Catherine."

"Oh, hi, Catherine. That didn't sound like you when you answered. This is Elizabeth. I got a message saying you called. Is everything okay?"

"No. No, everything is not okay," she admits. "I drank again last night. I just can't stop. I don't know why. I poured it out, but now I want to go get more. It's so crazy. I feel crazy." The words come quickly, and Catherine feels some relief with her confession.

"I'm so glad you called, Catherine. That took a tremendous amount of courage. Did you pour out everything you have in the house?"

"Yes. That's why I feel like I'm going crazy because I want to go get more, even after all the crap I've been through."

"Would you be willing to go to an A.A. meeting with me tonight?"

Catherine is expecting this question, but it still sends shivers down her spine. She pauses.

"Catherine, are you there?" Elizabeth asks when Catherine doesn't respond.

"Yes, I'm here."

"The meeting is at 8:00 at the Methodist church on the corner of King and Grant. I can meet you there at 7:45. I'd like you to meet some people who know exactly how you are feeling right now. They can tell you how they got sober. We can help you get through this." She waits for a response. Nothing. "You'll never know until you try."

Something stirs in Catherine. Hope washes over her like a cool breeze. *I've got to try something. Maybe this is it.* "Okay. I'll meet you at the meeting."

Elizabeth smiles. "Great! In the meantime, do your best to stay sober. Just take it one hour or even one minute at a time. You can do this. I'm proud of you. I know this isn't easy. Hang in there."

One tear drops from Catherine's eye. "Okay. I will. Thanks."

Catherine hangs up the phone, looks at the clock and wonders how in the world she's going to make it till 7:45 without completely losing it.

Elizabeth hangs up the phone, mutters a quick prayer, picks up the phone again, and calls in reinforcements for the meeting tonight.

Catherine sits down on the couch and stares blankly.
Pexov settles in the corner and stares at Sarephah.
Sarephah stands by Catherine and stares at Pexov.
Satan scans the horizon and dispatches several demons.
The Divine Three scan eternity and smile.

Chapter Nineteen

The mid-afternoon sun moves across the room and settles on the two forms sleeping on the couch. Catherine stirs after dozing on and off for most of the day. Blinking rapidly, she tries to adjust herself to the glare of the sun. Yawning, she rubs her eyes and stretches. Pip meows and stretches along with her.

The only sound in the room is thc ticking of the second hand on the clock across the room. Tick, tock; tick, tock. The sound begins to lull her back to sleep. Pip repositions himself. Catherine opens one eye and peers at the clock. "5:40, Okay, only about two more hours. I can make it," she says groggily. Closing her eyes again, she hopes to sleep away the time to avoid thinking or drinking.

"Ring! Ring!" The sound of the phone startles Pip and he jumps off Catherine. "Ugh…What the…" Looking at the caller- ID screen sends a chill up her spine. "Ring! Ring!" She hesitates. Finally, she picks up the phone and hits the answer button.

"Hey, Kelly," is all she manages to choke out with her dry throat.

"Hey, Girl. What's up? You sound funny. What's wrong?" Kelly asks curiously.

Catherine sits up, clears her throat, and tries to sound more awake than she feels. "Nothing. What do you want?" she asks wearily.

"I want to tell you about the events for the evening since I'm still your entertainment director, even though you blew me off last time I suggested a party. Listen, there's an awesome party going on tonight, girl. We can't miss it. You know Jake and Sunshine. Well, they're having a huge blowout tonight. It'll probably last the whole weekend. Remember the last time they threw a party? Ooohhweee was that fun or what?" Kelly laughs. "Anyway, you're going right?"

Catherine sighs heavily. She closes her eyes and says, "I…ummm…can't go tonight. I…have…other plans."

"WHAT? You have got to be kidding me. What other plans?" Kelly practically screams.

Catherine starts to get anxious. Her hands are sweating and her breathing accelerates. "I just have other plans, plus I'm sure Mark will be there with what's her name."

"You can't stop going to all the good parties just 'cause Mark might be there. Come on…you don't have other plans."

"I do have other plans."

"Then what are they?"

"Maybe it's none of your business. Can't I do something other than going out to parties," Catherine says angrily. Secretly she's hoping to make Kelly angry enough to hang up on her. It's happened plenty of times before.

"You know, you have been acting so strange lately. I can't figure out what's wrong with you. You never miss a party, but lately, I just don't know."

"Nothing is wrong. I just have other plans."

"Who are you going out with?"

Catherine puts her head in her hand. "Kelly, I've got to go. Maybe I'll stop by the party later tonight…or Saturday…or something."

"Okay, you better. I'm going to check in with you later. You know the saying, 'Friends don't let friends stay home on the weekend when there's partying to do,'" Kelly laughs.

Catherine shakes her head and says, "Right. Well, gotta go, bye." Catherine hangs up before Kelly can respond. *This A.A. meeting better be worth it, or I may just head over to that party.*

After hanging up the phone, she glances at the clock and quickly assesses how much time she has before she needs to leave for the meeting. Feeling confident that she has plenty of time, she decides take a shower and then grab a little something to eat.

Pip, as if reading her mind about the food, meows when Catherine stands up. Reaching down, she rubs Pip's head, "I won't forget to feed you today, honey. Give me a couple minutes." Pip rubs against her leg, jumps back onto the couch, and curls up for a short snooze before dinner time.

Revived from the shower, Catherine fixes a bite to eat after feeding Pip. However, the butterflies in her stomach prevent her from eating much of anything. She dumps the food in the trash and begins pacing to relieve some of the anxiety. *What have I gotten myself into? I wonder what this is going to be like. Hopefully, there won't be too many people.*

Stopping mid-step, it suddenly occurs to her that she might see someone she knows. *What if my mom is there? Oh, no I never thought of that.*

She glances at the clock. "6:15. Crap! I can't go if she's going to be there. This just isn't going to work." She continues pacing frantically, trying to think of she should do.

Seemingly out of the blue, a thought comes. *I'll call mom and see what she's doing tonight. If she's not going to a meeting I'm safe.* Strengthened by her idea, she grabs the phone and dials home.

"Hello," says a male voice.

Not expecting her dad to answer, Catherine cringes and almost hangs up. Recovering quickly, she says in the best happy voice she can muster, “Hi Dad! What’s up?”

“Catherine?” her dad says curiously.

Irritation bubbles up, but she pushes it back. “Yeah. It’s me. Hey…is Mom there?”

“Yes…hey…umm…how are you?”

“Good, real good. Things are good. How ‘bout you?” she says while glancing at the clock.

“Things are good here, too.”

Silence.

“Umm…dad…can I talk with mom? I’m kinda in a hurry.”

“Oh, yeah. Okay. It was good talking with you.” He pauses. “I’ll get your mom.”

Catherine isn’t completely sure why she feels so irritated with her dad. He never abused her in any way. Matter of fact, she loved the times they used to spend together. It just seemed like it all went bad somewhere along the line. Oh well, she thinks, I have too many other things on my mind to think about him.

“Hi Cath. What’s up?” her mom’s voice fills the air.

Catherine sighs in relief. “Hey mom. What’s ya doing?” she asks quickly.

“Fixing dinner for your father and I. Wanna join us?”

“No thanks. I have some plans tonight.” She hesitates, wondering how to broach the topic of her mom going to a meeting without being too obvious.

Her mom’s voice breaks into her musing. “Okay. Your father and I thought we would go to a movie tonight. What are your plans tonight?” she asks suspiciously.

Catherine, although relieved to know she’s safe to go to the meeting, is immediately irritated by the tone of her mom’s voice. “I’m not drinking,” she says more angrily than she intended.

“I didn’t say anything about drinking.”

"It was your tone," Catherine snaps.

Silence is heavy on the other end.

Catherine puts her hand to her forehead and closes her eyes. "Well, I'm not drinking, so you can quit worrying," she says with a slightly calmer tone. Glancing at the ever advancing time, she says hastily, "Listen, I gotta go. Have fun tonight."

"Okay. Well, have fun whatever you're doing tonight. Love you honey," Nancy says genuinely but wearily.

"Okay. Bye." Catherine hangs up and whispers "love you too," as a tear forms in her eye. After hastily wiping her eyes, she picks up her keys and heads for her car.

As she pulls out of the apartment parking lot, one more thought comes. *A drink would sure make this meeting easier to handle.* Using every ounce of her will power, she pushes that last thought out of her head. Determined to drive straight to the meeting, she grips the steering wheel so hard her knuckles turn white.

Just as she turns into the parking lot of the church, she remembers what Elizabeth said this morning. *I'd like you to meet some people who know exactly how you are feeling right now. They can tell you how they got sober. We can help you get through this.* "I sure hope you're right," she mutters to herself while catching a glimpse of several people standing outside the church doors smoking.

Pexov sneers, knowing that he has a few friends waiting to meet Catherine.

Sarephah smiles, knowing that there are true friends waiting to help Catherine.

Chapter Twenty

In her rush to leave her apartment, Catherine arrives several minutes early for the A.A. meeting. The idea of meeting Elizabeth before the allotted time is unthinkable to her, so she decides to wait in her car and take in her surroundings. Slouching down in her seat to avoid any unwanted notice, she secretly observes everyone entering the church. The mix of age, race, and gender of the people going into the meeting surprises her. They look so normal. She wonders if they're actually going to some Bible study or something because they sure don't look like her idea of an alcoholic, which is ironic since her own mother suffers from the same disease.

Catherine is startled when someone knocks on her window. Sitting up quickly, she sees a smiling Elizabeth bending down, looking into the window, and motioning for her to come out. She fumbles with the door handle and practically falls out of the car when the door opens. Standing up outside the car, she's greeted by two overly enthusiastic women: her counselor and a stranger.

"Hi Catherine. I'm so glad you made it! This is Hannah, a friend of mine. Hannah, this is Catherine." Hannah reaches out to shake Catherine's hand, "Welcome. This is your first meeting, right?" she says a little too loud and with a little too much enthusiasm for Catherine's liking.

"Yes," she says uncomfortably.

"Well, Welcome. It's very nice to meet you."

"Hannah and I got sober together. Been quite a journey, huh" she says looking at her friend.

"Yeah, but worth every minute of it."

Elizabeth puts her arm around Catherine and starts to lead her toward the doors. "Catherine, you'll find that AA's like to shake hands and hug a lot, which might be a little overwhelming for you at your first meeting. So when we get in I'll find us a seat. There are a couple more people I would like you to meet. Okay?'

Catherine is not okay with any of this, but responds with a muted okay.

The voices, the laughter, the smell of coffee and donuts all assault her senses the minute she crosses the threshold into her first meeting of Alcoholics Anonymous. Everyone is either hugging or shaking hands or both. Catherine stops and stares wide-eyed at all the commotion when they first enter the room. Several people notice Elizabeth, smile broadly, and wave a greeting. Some who are closer reach out for a hug.

Catherine is paralyzed. Someone grabs her hand and shakes it vigorously. "Hi, I'm Samuel." Catherine shakes his old, withered hand, but says nothing.

"Are you new?" her new friend Samuel asks through his toothless grin.

"Umm…yes," she says while looking for an escape. Thankfully, Elizabeth frees herself from her love fest to rescue her. "Hey, Samuel, this is Catherine. This is her first meeting."

"I thought so. Welcome, welcome. What a wonderful thing. Some never make it here and you being so young. It's a wonderful thing all right." Then he takes both her hands, looks her square in the eye, and says seriously, "Don't let anyone tell you you're too young to be here."

Catherine just looks at him expressionless, unsure how to respond.

"Samuel has forty years of continuous sobriety. If he says something, you should listen. Good to see you, Samuel."

Elizabeth leads Catherine to an empty chair. "Okay. Why don't you sit here. I'll be right back. Want any coffee?" Unable to speak, Catherine simply shakes her head no.

Elizabeth disappears into the sea of laughing, hugging people, and Catherine suddenly feels very claustrophobic. One by one, as each person passes by, they hold out their hand and introduce themselves. "Hi, I'm Joe. Hi, I'm Lisa. Hi, I'm Rich." Like an assembly line, she simply takes each hand and states her name quietly. She makes sure to avoid any eye contact and all unnecessary conversation.

Why are these people so freaking happy she wonders, and why in the world do they have to hug each other so much? She's beginning to regret ever coming to this freak show when a young, cute guy reaches out and offers his hand.

"Hi, I'm Tyler."

Catherine breaks her one rule and makes eye contact. "Hi, I'm Catherine."

"Are you new? I haven't seen you around before," mister young and cute alcoholic says.

Maybe A.A. isn't so bad after all. "Yeah, it's my first meeting," she announces as if this should earn her some prize.

Before Tyler can respond, Elizabeth returns, notices Tyler, and quickly sits next to Catherine. "Hey, Tyler. How are you doing?"

"Hey, Elizabeth. Good. I just met Catherine."

"That's good. It's her first meeting," she says with the same intensity of a mother bear protecting her cub. Tyler gets the message.

"Yes, I know," he says with a smile. Turning to Catherine, he says, "It was nice to meet you. Maybe I'll see you around."

Elizabeth watches Catherine watching Tyler and frowns. "Listen, Catherine, it's suggested that you don't get into a relationship during your first year. Tyler is a good guy, but it's better to focus on getting sober first." Before she can respond, Catherine is saved by another hand shake, and the topic is never mentioned again that night.

A few minutes later, Hannah joins them along with a very elegant looking lady of about seventy, Catherine guesses. The elegant lady gracefully extends her hand to Catherine, "Hello young lady. My name is Valerie. It is a pleasure to meet you."

Catherine shakes her hand and soaks in Valerie's calming presence.

"Elizabeth tells me this is your first meeting." Patting her on the back, she leans over and whispers, "We all survive our first meeting, honey. Relax, I pretty sure you'll make it through your first one." With one encouraging wink from Valerie, Catherine decides that indeed she just might.

Suddenly the room gets quiet as someone steps up to the podium at the front of the room.

"Hello, everyone. My name is Herb and I'm your alcoholic chairman for this month," says the energetic man at the microphone.

"Hi HERB!" shouts the crowd. Catherine slumps slightly in her chair.

"Welcome to the 'Friday Night Grace for the Journey Group.' I have only one announcement tonight. There will be a potluck dinner for the First Things First group next Saturday. The speaker will be Pete R." The crowd starts mumbling encouragement. Pete waves his hand in acknowledgement.

"Okay. Are there any anniversaries of a year or more?" the guy at the podium asks.

Someone to the right of Catherine stands up. "Hi, my name is Sally. And today, by the grace of God and with the help of my sponsor, I have two years." The crowd goes wild with shouts of congratulations and applause. Catherine looks around at the scene and claps her hand weakly, wondering what all the fuss is about.

"Great! Congratulations, Sally. There will be cake after the meeting to celebrate, so make sure you stick around for the meeting after the meeting. Is there anyone here for their first time?"

Several heads turn in her direction and Catherine suddenly feels the urge to crawl under the table. She looks at Elizabeth with fear in her eyes, petrified at the prospect of standing up in front of people she doesn't know.

"It's okay. You don't have to stand up if you don't want to," Elizabeth whispers.

Relieved, Catherine looks down at the table and barely hears the names of several others who stand up and announce that they are alcoholic and at their first meeting. She can't imagine what would possess someone to stand up and introduce themselves in front of a bunch of complete strangers. She's absolutely sure that's something she'll never do, ever.

After a round of applause for each new member, the chairman continues. "Welcome. We don't do that to embarrass you, even though it does." Sympathetic laughter breaks out from the more seasoned members. "We do that so we can get to know you. You are the most important people in this room tonight. Make sure to get a meeting schedule and a few numbers before you leave. There's lots of sobriety in this room and people ready and willing to help."

While the chairman is still talking, several latecomers walk into the meeting and sit in the back. Distracted by the commotion, Catherine turns to look. She notices how young they look, and is immediately intrigued. The group is laughing and being a little too noisy, but what catches her attention the most is that they're having fun, which she didn't think was possible in A.A. Finally, after several minutes of loud whispers and muffled laughter, the rowdy group is hushed by others around them.

Catherine discreetly watches the group out of the corner of her eye and smiles internally at the possibility that she may indeed meet some new friends tonight.

Chapter Twenty-One

Catherine's fixation on the group of young people in the back of the room is interrupted by the applause for the main speaker of the meeting. What Catherine doesn't hear since she's so distracted is the gut-retching story of the speaker's descent into the hell of alcoholism, the event that brought him to A.A., and the joys of a redeemed life. Unfortunately, everyting Catherine does manage to hear goes through her filter of denial, and she fails to see her story in his story.

What she doesn't yet know is that the power of recovery is connecting with other members through shared stories. In fact, it is when an alcoholic sees herself in the story of another alcoholic that the wall of denial starts to crumble; this can be both enlightening and frightening. Sadly, Catherine is focusing more on the differences between his story and hers rather than on the similarities they share. Frankly, she's beginning to wonder why she's even here at all.

After the applause dies down, the chairman steps back up to the podium. "Thanks, Mitchell. That was a great lead." Catherine learns later that a "lead" is simply telling your story. The chairman continues, "I would like to open the meeting for comments," then sits down.

To Catherine's astonishment, person after person stands up, thanks the speaker, and describes the ways in which his story connects with theirs. Tears are shed, laughter is shared, and love is displayed with each new comment. The acceptance and gratitude in the room is undeniable, even to Catherine. Something stirs deep inside her, but she refuses to acknowledge the feeling because it's so foreign and uncomfortable. Even though she successfully shoves the feeling aside, the memory of this night will linger long after the feeling fades.

Catherine fidgets in her seat and wonders when this freaking meeting is ever going end. She steals one more look at the group in the back and makes eye contact with one of them. She's relieved when the chairman steps back up to the podium as the comments end. Turning to the speaker, he says, "Thanks again Mitchell. Would you help us close this meeting with the Lord's Prayer?"

The sound of fifty people pushing back their chairs and standing up startles Catherine. She stands slowly and watches in angst as a circle begins to form when everyone takes the hand of the person next to them. Tentatively, she takes the hand of Elizabeth on her right and Valerie on her left.

With heads bowed, they begin, "Our Father…" The power of fifty people holding hands and praying out loud almost brings Catherine to tears, but fear and anxiety simply won't give up their control of her. Standing there with so many conflicting emotions makes her feel vulnerable and out of control: two things she fights hard to avoid.

With a bounce of their hands emphasizing each word, everyone shouts, "Keep coming back!" at the end of the prayer. The laughter, hugging, and conversations begin immediately after the collective rally cry, and the noise of all the commotion starts to calm Catherine.

Elizabeth and Valerie are swept up in the chaos of the crowd, leaving Catherine standing alone for a moment. Turning to find the group of young alcoholics brings Catherine face to face with one of them.

"Hi! I'm Courtney. This your first meeting?" says a very petite, blonde haired twenty- something while thrusting out her hand.

"Yeah, this is my first one," Catherine says, shaking Courtney's hand.

"Welcome!" Looking around at the room she adds, "It's not so bad really. You'll get used to it." Grabbing Catherine's arm, Courtney starts walking toward the others in her group. "Come on. I'll introduce you to a few cool people."

Catherine turns back toward Elizabeth, wondering if it's okay to go with Courtney, but Elizabeth's deep in conversation with someone. Oh well, she thinks. The point is to meet new friends anyway, so she goes along with Courtney. To her surprise, Catherine notices that cute guy, Tyler, standing among the group, even though he didn't walk in with them.

"Hey everyone, this is Catherine. It's her first meeting," she says with a little too much fanfare.

"Hi, Catherine," shouts the group. Catherine acknowledges them, but doesn't know what to say.

"So, what'd ya think of your first meeting?" Tyler says with a grin.

"Kinda overwhelming, I guess."

"Yeah, we all felt that way. It's gets easier, really. Did you come with Elizabeth?"

"No, but she met me here," Catherine says while looking down. She's embarrassed that she's seeing a counselor; after all, she doesn't want to appear too sick, which is weird since she is at an A.A. meeting.

"I see," he says without expression.

"Elizabeth is good A.A. Stick with her, and you'll do okay," Courtney interjects herself back into the conversation. Smiling, she adds, "We have a saying here, 'stick with the winners.' Not everyone wants to get better here."

"Okay, I'll keep that in mind."

"Speaking of winners, you want to go out with some of us winners?" Courtney asks excitedly. "We always go out after a meeting and have some fun."

Before Catherine can respond, Elizabeth appears by her side. "I see you're making some new friends. Hi, Courtney." She nods, "Tyler."

Turning Catherine away from the group, she says, "Here, I brought you a meeting schedule. I had a few friends write down their numbers on the back, and I circled a couple good meetings in the area. Are you doing okay?"

"Yeah."

"Good. I am really proud of you for coming tonight." Looking back at the group, "I'm heading out now. Wanna walk out with me?"

Catherine isn't exactly sure what she wants to do. The idea of going with the group is appealing, but she feels safer with Elizabeth. She looks back at the group and then back at Elizabeth. "Okay. I'll walk out with you. Hold on for a minute though."

Stepping back toward the group, she says softly, "It was nice to meet you all. Umm...I don't think I'm up for going out tonight."

"That's cool. Hang in there, Catherine. Maybe we'll see you tomorrow. We all go to the Saturday night 'Weekend Busters' meeting. Check it out on the meeting schedule." Courtney speaks for the group, and they all nod in agreement, except Tyler.

Catherine catches Tyler's expression and wonders where he'll be tomorrow night, but doesn't dare ask.

"Thanks. Maybe I will."

Later, back in her car, Catherine turns on the inside light so she can get a better look at the meeting schedule Elizabeth gave her. Tracing her finger down the list of meetings for tomorrow, she sees two meetings that are circled; Weekend Busters is not one of them. She wonders why. Turning the schedule over, she looks for the names and numbers that Elizabeth got for her. Not recognizing any of the names except Valerie's and Hannah's, she suddenly wishes she'd gotten two other numbers: Courtney's and, of course, Tyler's.

• • •

Pexov turns toward Sarephah. "I see we have a few more players in this game," he says with a wicked grin.

"What makes you think this is a game?" Sarephah asks incredulously.

"I don't *think* it's a game. I *know* it's a game," he spits out angrily. "I find it delightful that more mortals are joining in this little game of ours. It wasn't right to keep her all to ourselves. Though, I do wonder how you'll keep track of the new cast of characters, and more importantly, which side they're on – mine or yours."

Sarephah watches Catherine drive away and then turns back toward Pexov. "First of all, this is *not* a game. Maybe you think this is all a sick game, but the Divine Three don't."

"Oh, please. They love playing with their creation. They find great pleasure letting mortals think they have freewill and then ripping choice right out of their dead, cold fingers. But my master loves playing this game even more, and he hates to lose."

"What are you talking about?"

"You saw what happened tonight at that ridiculous meeting. The best part was all the lovely introductions. It was fun watching that forsaken mortal meet some interesting sickos," he laughs. Then with a snarl, he adds, "You're a fool if you really think she had a choice who she met tonight. This night was carefully arranged. You better stay alert, 'cause the players are in place, and the game is on."

"As always, you distort and exaggerate everything. I know more than you give me credit. I prefer to look at this as an ongoing love story between Catherine and the Divine Three, not a game. As far as the cast of characters, you're wrong. There are several mortals yet to be added to Catherine's story. And you, Pexov, will be surprised who they are and what role they will play. By the way, sometimes characters in a mortal's story are not who they appear to be. And if I have anything to say about it, Catherine will learn this long before you do."

Chapter Twenty-Two

"I need somebody to make sure the room is ready for the Women's club luncheon," yells Sarah Mitchell, Director of Banquet Operations for Holden Suites.

The clank of pots and pans in the busy kitchen almost drowns out her voice. The kitchen staff is busy serving breakfast for the hotel crowd, while at the same time, preparing seventy-five meals for the luncheon scheduled to begin in two hours. Waitresses and waiters move rapidly in and out of the swinging double doors that separate the controlled chaos of the kitchen from the more serene atmosphere of the restaurant.

"I'll do it," someone yells.

Sarah turns around to locate the person attached to the voice. "Catherine?"

"I'll make sure the room's ready," she says while heading to the swinging doors off the main banquet room.

"Wait a minute," Sarah reaches out and grabs Catherine's arm as she passes by. Catherine stops abruptly and turns to face her supervisor. Sarah eyes her suspiciously. She cocks her head in curiosity and smiles. "Okay. We have seventy-five confirmed, but you know how these ladies are, we should expect somewhere around eighty. Check that all the side serving stations are in place, especially the ones farthest away from the main doors. We always get nailed on that. I would add two more tables, fully set, in the far right corner of the room, but cover them. We'll only use them if necessary." She pauses slightly. "Thanks for volunteering. I appreciate your willingness to help."

"Sure."

Catherine turns toward the doors and smiles. This morning she feels better than she has in months, maybe years. Instead of constantly thinking about drinking, the images of last night's meeting are playing in her head. The faces, the laughter, the names, the noise of sobriety don't seem as overwhelming today.

After some deliberation this morning, she's sure she'll go again tonight. Although the thought of walking into a meeting alone is scary, the chance to meet up with Courtney and to go out after the meeting with that fun group is drawing her back. Her motivation is a little skewed, but the results aren't: she's getting to another meeting.

While making sure the banquet room is set up, Catherine's thoughts keep coming back to A.A. She wonders if all meetings are the same, and if she has to go every day. But she quickly pushes those thoughts aside, because she doesn't want to think about what's expected of her in this process of getting sober.

Recovery is not exactly high on her list of reasons for going to meetings. She's all about meeting new friends. But if she's honest about it, there does seem to be something in those rooms, and with those people, that she wants to experience again.

She's slightly intrigued by the acceptance, gratitude, and love that permeated the room last night. The source of the positive vibes has her curious, especially since everyone was sober. She's excited about having something to do and somewhere to go tonight. In fact, just the anticipation of the evening is easing the ache of loneliness and the desire to drink, if only for today.

The Women's Club luncheon is in full swing when Catherine, busy overseeing all the side serving tables, thinks she recognizes someone. She moves to get a better view, but someone moves their head and blocks her. She moves back the other way and the view opens. It can't be she thinks. Not *that* lady. What's she doing here?

Catherine scans her area of responsibility, sees that everything is in order, and grabs a pitcher of water to take to the table as an excuse to get a closer look. Trying not to stare, she moves in and out of the tables and comes up directly behind her target. She picks up the first glass, pours water, sets it down, and moves to the next. She draws in her breath sharply when she makes eye contact with the lady in question.

For a split second, both are wide-eyed in their recognition of each other. Then, with one wink and a sly smile, Catherine knows it's her. Valerie, the elegant lady from last night's meeting, just sent her a secret signal and Catherine nods her head in acknowledgement. She instinctively knows better than to draw attention to the fact that she knows her and leaves the table after filling all the glasses.

Walking back to her station, she remembers she has Valerie's phone number and thinks she just might give her a call sometime.

The rest of Catherine's shift is uneventful, and she's grateful to finally end her shift after a long day on her feet. Driving home, she rehashes the conversation she had with her supervisor just before she left.

"Good job today with the Women's Club luncheon. The side serving stations were well stocked and running smoothly. I was especially impressed that you took some extra initiative and covered the water at table seventeen."

"Thanks," Catherine smiles inwardly.

"I'd like you to take the lead tomorrow morning during the breakfast buffet and organize the staff. Think you can handle it?" she asks.

"Okay. Yeah, I can handle it," Catherine says without copping an attitude. She hasn't forgotten her last meeting with Vickie and knows she needs to be on her best behavior.

"Good. Nice job today. Keep it up," Sarah says over her shoulder as she hurries off to her office.

Catherine hasn't been asked to take on extra responsibility since she was suspended, and secretly wonders if she can really handle it. Her confidence and energy level are still extremely low and the thought of added duties suddenly makes her very anxious.

A couple days ago she knew of only one way to handle these feelings: drink. But today, even though she wants to drink badly, she stores those desires in the far corner of her soul. Gripping the steering wheel tighter, she refocuses on the meeting she's going to tonight. All she needs to do is go straight home, clean up, feed Pip, take a nap, and then go straight to the meeting. What could possibly go wrong with that plan?

• • •

Pip is waiting right at the door when Catherine gets home. She can barely get in the apartment with him rubbing up against her legs with each step. Excitedly, he lets out a long meow.

"Hello to you too, Pip. Did you miss me today?"

Pip responds by promptly rolling over on his back.

"I knew it. Well, either that or you're hungry. But I prefer to think that you missed me dearly," she says while squatting down and rubbing his now exposed belly.

Standing up, she puts her keys on the counter after pushing away the dirty dishes that cover every inch of the counter top. She'd put the dishes in the sink, but that's full too. "I really should do some dishes sometime."

Back in the bedroom, she glances at the message machine. No messages. At first she's disappointed, but dismisses the thought almost as quickly as it comes. Turning around in the room, she looks for the meeting schedule she got last night. "Where did I put that schedule?"

She bends over and rummages through the piles of clothes on the floor. Falling to her knees, clothes start flying as her search intensifies. Catherine begins to panic. "Where did I put it?" She sits back on her heels and thinks.

Next to her, Pip starts playing in the discarded clothes. Catherine manages a slight smile as he hides completely under a pair of jeans, and then starts dragging them on his back. The jeans look like they're moving on their own. A memory stirs. The jeans!!

"Hold on, Pip!"

She lunges forward and grabs the pair of jeans. Pip stops and swirls around, wondering what just happened. Catherine shoves her hand in the left pocket: nothing. She switches to the other side and shoves her hand in the right pocket. Her fingers touch paper; she withdraws her hand, and waves the schedule in victory.

Grabbing Pip and giving him a big kiss, she says, "Thanks, Pip. What would I do without you?" Pip squirms out of his master's arms and shoots toward the door. He looks back and meows once before heading out into the other room.

Sarephah smiles at her new furry friend and decides that cats are all right.

Clutching the new found treasure, she returns to the kitchen to check the location and time of the meeting tonight. Furrowing her brow in concentration, she can't remember the name of the meeting that Courtney told her about. To make matters worse, it wasn't one of the circled meetings. Her eyes move rapidly over the list, but nothing triggers her memory. She sits back in frustration and slams her fist on the edge of the table. "You've got to be kidding me. Why didn't I get her number?"

In the middle of her ranting, the door bell rings. Startled, she sits up. "Who could that be?"

Angry that she's missing some precious nap time, she stomps through the hallway to the front door and peers out the peep hole. Her eyes grow wide. The doorbell rings again. She backs away from the door as if it's on fire.

"Hey, girl, open it up. I know you're home 'cause your car's in the parking lot." The pounding on the door sounds as loud as the pounding of her heart.

The door flies open. "Kelly! What are you doing here?"

Kelly puts one hand on her hip and frowns. "Is that a way to greet your best friend, especially on a Saturday night when I'm here to help you get your evening started?"

Smiling wide, she produces a six-pack of wine coolers from behind her back and holds them up like an athlete showing off the winning trophy.

Before Catherine can respond, Kelly pushes her way into the apartment, moves down the hallway, and sets the wine coolers down on the kitchen table.

"Don't you ever clean this place?" she yells back to Catherine as she clears papers off a chair before sitting down.

Catherine shuts the door and strides slowly down the hallway.

Spitz!

The sound of a wine cooler being opened causes her to hesitate before she enters the kitchen. She takes a deep breath and sits down across from Kelly. Taking a long swig of her wine cooler, Kelly looks at Catherine out of the corner of her eye. "Come on girl. Let's get the party started," she says with her usual enthusiasm. Catherine just sits there, unsure how to respond.

Kelly shrugs, opens another wine cooler, and places it forcefully on the table in front of Catherine. She doesn't react. They eye each other for several seconds. Then, almost instantaneously, they both catch sight of a piece of paper in the middle of the table. With amazing speed, Kelly snatches up the paper before Catherine can get to it.

"What in the hell is this?" she says in complete shock.

Leaning over, Catherine grabs the paper out of Kelly's hand and quickly puts the evidence in her pocket. "That is none of your business," Catherine says angrily.

"I know what that was. It's was a freaking A.A. meeting schedule. Oh, my God, girl! What would ever posses you to go to A.A?"

"I'm not going to any stupid A.A. meetings. Have you lost your mind? That's one of my mom's schedules. I'm no alcoholic."

Rising to her feet, she tries to get as far away from the smell of the wine cooler as possible. She leans against the wall and crosses her arms. "I'm not really in the mood for wine coolers tonight." Coughing to emphasize her point, she adds, "I don't feel very well."

Kelly takes a couple more swigs and drains the bottle. Quickly opening another, she eyes Catherine and says, "Fine. All the more for me I guess. These were just appetizers anyway. Okay, here are the plans for the evening. First, we're going to Crazy Eights and then…"

Catherine puts up her hand to silence Kelly. "Apparently, you didn't hear me. I don't feel well." She coughs a little harder this time.

"Since when has being sick ever stopped you from going out? What's really going on? You never did tell me what you did last night. You and your big plans are getting on my nerves," Kelly says in frustration. Only on her second wine cooler, Catherine suspects that Kelly had her very own six-pack before coming over.

Sitting back down, Catherine pushes the wine cooler away from her and sighs. "I'm just not up for going out." Eyeing the open wine cooler, she suddenly feels thirsty and the frustration begins to come out in the tone of her voice.

"What's the big deal anyway? You'll end up ditching me tonight when Justin comes along anyway. So get off my back and stop your whining."

"I am not whining, and I don't just dump you when Justin comes. Hey, maybe you can meet someone tonight," she says with renewed enthusiasm about the evening festivities.

"No!" Catherine slams her fist on the table.

The force of the strike shakes the table, knocks the wine cooler over, and it splashes all over Kelly. She jumps up and cusses like a drunken sailor. "Hey, this is a new outfit." She looks back at Catherine, who is too stunned to react to the puddle of sweet smelling wine that's forming on the floor from the spill running off the table.

"Sorry, Kelly," Catherine rushes to get a towel.

"Man. This just sucks. I gotta go change. I can't go out looking like this."

"Sorry, Kelly," Catherine says again while wiping the floor with a wet rag.

Kelly whirls around, picks up the last of the wine coolers, and heads toward the door, clicking loudly on her heels. "If you change your mind about tonight, I'll be at Crazy Eights till midnight." The door slams. Silence.

After cleaning up the mess and shooing Pip away several times, she sits back down at the kitchen table. The lingering smell of the wine cooler is both nauseating and appealing. She digs in her pocket and pulls out the meeting schedule. Running her finger down the list, she lands on the first circled meeting: Saturday Serenity Seekers. *Catchy name.* "I need some serenity, and it is Saturday. Looks like I'm heading to that meeting."

She stands up, surveys the messy kitchen, scrunches her nose at the smell, and sighs. "This evening is not going exactly like I planned."

Chapter Twenty-Three

The glare of the headlights coming straight at her is blinding. She frantically grabs the steering wheel and swerves sharply back into her lane. Whizzing by her, the other driver lays on the horn, and Catherine cringes. Safely back in her lane, she slows down and tries to read the road signs, but the pelting rain is making vision nearly impossible. The rhythmic thump of the windshield wipers and their lack of ability to actually clean her windshield are beginning to irritate her. Afraid to take her eyes off the road again, she rehearses in her mind the directions she wrote down earlier, which have since fallen on the passenger seat. Leaning forward and straining to see the white lines on the road, Catherine mutters, “This just sucks!”

While keeping one hand on the steering wheel and both eyes on the road, she reaches over to the passenger side. Moving her hand across the seat, her fingers find the directions, but as she attempts to pick them up, she knocks them off the seat, and the paper falls to the floor. “Crap!” she yells in frustration.

Putting both hands back on the steering wheel again, she contemplates just turning back around and going home. After several more minutes driving down the deserted stretch of road, anger and frustration get the better of her.

The combination of the unfamiliar road, heavy rain, ineffective windshield wipers, and the rising fear that she's getting lost, force Catherine to pull off the road and into the nearest parking lot. Once the car comes to a screeching stop, she bends over and stretches to reach the fallen directions. Unable to reach them, she sits back up and angrily removes her seatbelt. Freed, she reaches back down on the floorboard of the passenger side and retrieves the blasted piece of paper.

Wondering if she took a wrong turn, she turns on the overhead light and studies the directions. She glances out the front window, and with the help of the headlights, the road sign comes into view. "I must have passed it." Sighing, she says, "Maybe I should just go home. I can't even see the road with this rain."

She sits for a minute, fighting between the strong urge to head home and the crazy desire to go to the meeting. The easier thing, she thinks, would be to just head home. Yet, the idea of spending the evening alone in that apartment is unsettling, because she knows she most likely won't stay home for long. Deciding that going home might not be a good decision, she pushes the thought out of her mind for the moment. In contrast, the desire to go to the meeting is gaining strength, which surprises her. She has to admit last night's meeting made an impact on her, and wonders what's drawing her back. However, looking out the window at the pouring rain, she figures she's not going anywhere in this weather. Slamming her fist on the steering wheel, she looks up and yells, "Rain would you stop already!" Almost as if on cue, the rain begins to let up.

Amused by the idea that she somehow stopped the rain, she takes one more look at the directions, puts them back on the passenger seat, and pulls out of the parking lot. With visibility restored, she easily finds the meeting place and pulls into the crowded parking lot of the Arid club – a dry club for Alcoholics. Scanning the parking lot for her mom's car, she pulls into a space and takes a deep breath to shake off her nerves. After getting a better look at the area, she's pretty darn sure there's no danger of her mom being here: the neighborhood isn't exactly the type she would frequent sober or drunk.

Several rough looking people walk into the building, and Catherine suddenly wonders if she made a big mistake. Out of the corner of her eye she sees Samuel, who was the old guy who shook her hand and told her not to let anyone tell her she was too young to get sober, walking toward the door. The relief of seeing a familiar face gives her courage to forge ahead. She steps up to the large, heavy doors and pulls them open. The same laughter and noise she heard the night before comes rushing at her. She steps tentatively into the room, wondering what in the world she's doing here.

The first thing that catches her attention is the fact that the room is set up different than the meeting last night: everyone is sitting in a circle. This unnerves her, and she stops to survey the room. She sees only one open chair, and it happens to be right next to Samuel. Reassured, she heads directly toward the empty chair before anyone else gets the seat. The moment she reaches the seat, Samuel turns and acknowledges her.

"Hello, young lady!" Samuel says with genuine enthusiasm. Motioning toward the empty chair, he says, "Sit. Sit." Catherine sits down awkwardly and clutches her purse to her chest.

"How delightful that you came back; some don't ever come back you know," he says with a serious expression. Leaning forward to gesture around her to the older gentleman on Catherine's other side, he introduces her to Paul. "Paul…Paul…Paul!" he yells louder to get Paul's attention. Catherine slumps slightly in her chair.

"What!" Paul says gruffly.

"This is Catherine. She's new."

Paul turns to get a better look. "Aren't you a little young to be here?"

"See, what did I tell you, Catherine. Don't let anyone tell you you're too young. Be nice Paul," Samuel says with a grin.

"So what brings you to a meeting of Alcoholic Anonymous on a Saturday night? You one of those college students who needs to observe us sick and depraved alcoholics for a school assignment?" he asks harshly, and then raises his eyebrows, crosses his arms, and waits for her answer.

Flustered by his abruptness, she looks at the ground and says quietly, "No."

"Good, 'cause this meeting is closed. That means only alcoholics can attend." Looking directly in her eyes, he continues more softly, "If you have an honest desire to stop drinking, then I guess you're in the right place." Smiling warmly, he extends his hand. "Welcome."

Taking a deep breath, she accepts his hand. "Thanks."

"How much time you got?"

Catherine looks confused, so he rephrases the question. "How long since your last drink?"

"Oh, umm…two days, counting today," she says quietly.

"Probably still feeling pretty lousy I bet. Hang in there. It does get better. This your first discussion meeting?"

"It's only my second meeting. Last night someone stood up and talked the whole time."

"Well, this is different. A topic will be given, and then people just jump in and make comments. You'll see."

During the entire conversation with Paul, people were shaking her hand and introducing themselves. The constant noise and interruptions are nerve racking, and Catherine's head is spinning by the time the meeting starts.

"Hello, everyone. Welcome to the Saturday Serenity Seekers' meeting. My name is Betty, and I'm your alcoholic chairperson for this month."

"Hi Betty," shouts the group of about twenty souls.

Catherine misses most of the rest of what the chairperson has to say; she's too busy glancing around the room. She fixes her gaze on a group of six women sitting next to each other. They stand out because they're the only women in the room besides her. They obviously know each other well, and she can't help notice the peaceful way they carry themselves. One of them catches her eye and smiles warmly. Catherine quickly looks away.

"Okay. Let's go around the room and introduce ourselves. Like I said, I'm Betty, and I'm an alcoholic."

One by one, each person states their name and announces their alcoholism. Catherine squirms in her seat, knowing she'll eventually have to say her name and add the word "alcoholic" like it's her surname. This is definitely not something she bargained for when she picked this meeting. For several brief moments, she contemplates racing out the door and never coming back. She even turns her head toward the door and mentally calculates the amount of time it would take to jump up, run out the doors, get in her car, and drive to Crazy Eights. But before she can even attempt to get out of her chair and escape this madness, it's her turn.

Everyone's eyes turn to her; she freezes. Paul gently nudges her with his elbow.

"Umm...Catherine...alalalic..." is all she can manage to say. No one seems to notice her incoherent babbling, and they all shout, "Hi Catherine," with great enthusiasm. Several smile at her with compassion, but she doesn't notice since she refuses to look up until the introductions are finished. When she does look up again, she notices the women staring at her, and she suddenly feels like throwing up.

"All right, before I pick a topic for tonight's meeting, I want to open the floor to see if anyone has anything they want to talk about?" She pauses and looks around the room. After what seems like an eternity of silence to Catherine, someone says, "I'm Calvin, alcoholic." Everyone says hi and he continues.

"I'm kinda new at this stuff, and I was readin' in the Big Book last night about the second step. You know, the one about coming to 'believe that a power greater than ourselves can restore us to sanity.' Well, I'm having trouble with the whole God thing, and was wondering how I can accept spiritual help like it says I need to do there on page twenty-five. I mean, it's bad enough you all are telling me I'm insane but, well, this God stuff is really getting to me."

Everyone's silent. Finally, Betty asks kindly, "So, what exactly is your topic, Calvin?"

"I guess it's how to accept all this God stuff and how to accept spiritual help. I guess," he says quietly.

"Okay. Great topic. I'll open the meeting for comments."

God? What does God have to do with getting sober? What does God have to do with anything? Catherine rolls her eyes at the idea of sitting around with a bunch of losers talking about God. As far as she's concerned, God's in heaven, she's down here, and neither one has anything to do with the other, which is just fine with her. *I don't need help from anyone, especially a distant, unavailable God.* Her mind snaps shut. Not much gets through to her, except later in the meeting when Paul starts talking.

"Paul, alcoholic."

"Hi Paul!" the crowd shouts. To Catherine's ears, it seems like the crowd's a little extra enthusiastic when Paul speaks up. She senses that he's admired by the group, so she attempts to listen with at least one ear open.

"Before I got sober, I had no need for God in my life. I didn't know how to pray, and didn't want to know, frankly. What was the point I figured. God was in heaven, and I was down here. I had to take care of myself 'cause no one was gonna look out for me."

Catherine looks over at him, curious to hear what else he has to say.

"I didn't need God, and I wasn't going to ask for help from him or nobody. Then I got a nudge from the Judge to attend my first meeting." Several laugh at his comment about the Judge. "I thought I could stay sober on my own. Boy was I wrong! After several relapses, my sponsor sat my butt down, and we did step one, again. Then he talked to me about God. At first, I didn't want to hear it. But then he told me that I had two choices: 1) keep on doing what I was doing and try to blot out the misery I felt until I eventually died, went crazy, or got locked up; or 2) accept spiritual help. You'd think it'd be a no brainer and I'd pick accepting spiritual help. But it wasn't that easy. I didn't even know what I believed about God. How am I going to accept help from something or someone I didn't know or trust?"

"That's when he told me I needed to find a power greater than myself who could help me. He said God could be whatever I wanted God to be. Ain't that beat all? I could make up my own conception of God. Well, I wasn't sure if I totally liked that idea, but it did give me the freedom to search and find out what I believed about God. For the first time in my life, I wasn't forced to accept someone else's idea or belief about God."

"Ya know, it's the best thing that ever happened to me. The minute I opened myself up to learning about God, he revealed himself to me, and I was eventually able to accept help from him. The best thing you can do is just be willing to open yourself to the concept of a Higher Power, and then let him do the rest. That's all I got. I'll pass."

Catherine settles back in her chair and begins to ponder what Paul said. She's never heard anything like it before, and is not sure what to do with this new revelation. She believes in God thanks to spending her childhood in church, but ever since walking away from Church and God, she hasn't thought about anything religious or spiritual in a decade or more. Can she really make God be whatever she wants him to be? Cynically, she thinks maybe he'll be a God who doesn't mind if people get drunk. *Now that's a concept of God I could support.*

After several more comments, the meeting ends and everyone stands to hold hands and say the Lord's Prayer. Catherine, a veteran of one meeting, knows the drill and stands with the rest. Grabbing the hands of Paul and Samuel, she bows her head, but says nothing. During the prayer, anxiety returns with a vengeance; she begins feeling trapped and vulnerable. When the prayer is concluded and chants of "keep coming back" are shouted, she drops the hands of Samuel and Paul. The chaos of multiple conversations and genuine laughter begin immediately, but Catherine stands alone and silent. She looks toward the exit ready to escape, but something holds her feet firmly in place.

In the midst of her indecision, she looks over toward the group of women. They are laughing and hugging each other, but one woman turns from the group, looks at her, smiles, and with determination in her eyes, begins to walk across the room toward her.

Catherine's first instinct is to run. It's too late. What has been set in motion cannot be stopped. The only question now is whether Catherine can determine the real motivation behind the people she will meet before it's too late. She'll soon learn that sometimes good and evil are hard to distinguish.

Chapter Twenty-Four

"Hi, my name's Jane," she says, looking directly into Catherine's eyes. Her gaze is so penetrating that Catherine looks away uncomfortably. Jane smiles and asks, "What's your name?"

Still looking down, she says quietly, "Catherine."

Extending her hand, Jane says, "Welcome. It's nice to meet you."

Catherine shakes her hand weakly. "Thanks." Dropping her hand quickly, she looks down again and shuffles her feet.

"What brings you to the meeting tonight?"

Catherine looks up confused by the question. "Umm…well, I got into some trouble at work, and well, now I'm here just to see what this is all about. I'm not really sure what to think. It's all so different. Part of me isn't sure why I'm here, and whether I belong or what to expect." Embarrassed by her rambling, she stops abruptly and crosses her arms.

"I understand. It's not easy coming to an A.A. meeting. This your first meeting?"

"No, I went to one last night."

Jane looks at her for a moment. Sizing her up, she tilts her head from side to side and then asks, "Do you think you have a problem with alcohol?"

Catherine thinks for a moment. “I’m not sure.”

Jane smiles. “Well, then you’re in the right place to find out. Do you have a meeting schedule?”

“Yes.” Catherine grabs it out of her purse and shows it to her.

“Good.” Jane takes the paper, turns it over, and adds her name and phone number to the list. Handing the schedule back to Catherine, she says, “I wasn’t sure if I had a problem with alcohol either when I got here. But I stuck around long enough to find out the truth. If you ever want to talk, I’d be happy to share with you how I got sober and stayed sober.”

They lock eyes for a brief moment; Catherine turns away. There’s something about Jane that baffles Catherine. Her presence is peaceful, yet powerful, which Catherine finds both calming and intimidating. Frankly, she’s just not sure what to make of Jane. Jane, on the other hand, knows exactly what to make of Catherine.

Finally, Jane turns toward the group of women and calls a couple of the others to come over. Immediately, several walk toward them and extend their hands in fellowship. After all the introductions, Catherine is invited out for coffee and ice cream with the group. Not wanting to pass up another invitation, she accepts this time. After all, she sure doesn’t want to go home too early on a Saturday night. Yes, the thought of going out with the group feels right to her.

As Catherine turns to leave, Paul gently grabs her arm. “Hey, young lady. What’d you think of the meeting? Did all the God-talk scare you off?” he asks with a disarming grin.

Catherine can’t help but return his smile. “No, well, not yet at least.”

“Ummm…good…’cause God isn’t scared off by you either,” he says with a hearty laugh. “Take care, young lady. I’ll see you next week,” he says with a nod and handshake. Hesitating, he turns back and looks her straight in the eye. “Watch out for wolves among the flock. You’re not strong enough to fight them off alone." Without another word, he turns back and heads toward the door and into the night.

Catherine stands there puzzled by his cryptic message. What was that all about, she wonders? Shaking her head, she grabs her purse, and heads out the door. Thankfully, the night sky is clear and dry, unlike the downpour she drove through earlier. A full moon, the only source of light in this dark parking lot, helps her locate her car. Fumbling through her purse to find her keys, she's unaware that someone's approached her from behind.

"Hi, Catherine."

Letting out a muffled scream, she jumps, drops her keys, whirls around, and sees the outline of shadowy face.

Reaching down to pick up her keys, the stranger says, "Sorry. I didn't mean to scare you. I'm Kaleb," he says while handing Catherine her keys.

Snatching the keys out of his hand, she glares at him, "Well, you did scare me." Trying to get a better look at him and at the same time backing away slightly, she asks suspiciously, "How do you know my name."

"From the meeting," he says, smiling broadly.

"Oh, yeah." She suddenly understands Paul's warning about the wolves.

"I hope all the talk about God didn't upset you." She looks at him funny, so he adds with a shrug, "I saw how you reacted when the topic came up."

"Right. Okay, nice talking with you, umm…Kaleb was it? But I got go."

"Wait. Are you heading to Mama's Cafe with the group?"

"Yeah."

"Good. I'll save you a seat."

Catherine turns away, rolls her eyes, and climbs into her car. He waves enthusiastically to her as she starts her car. She wiggles her fingers in his direction and watches him walk away. *Note to self: stay away from that dude.*

When Catherine enters the coffee shop, she can't hide the disappointment on her face when the only seat left at the table is right next to the creepy guy from the parking lot. He smiles, points to the empty chair, and waves her over. She does a quick scan of the others at the table and notices that Jane occupies the seat on the other side of the empty chair; not totally comforting, but it will have to do. Sighing, she moves slowly to the table. Several people shout out their hellos, welcoming her warmly.

"We meet again," he says with a wide grin.

"Yes, we do." In the light of the restaurant she gets a better look at her parking lot bandit. Disheveled dark hair, brown eyes, and a shiny white row of teeth don't impress. His enthusiasm is annoying. She wonders how anyone can be so freaking happy and sober.

"Since we didn't have a proper introduction," he extends his hand, "My name is Kaleb."

Catherine grabs it, "My name is Catherine, but I guess you already know that."

"How much time you got?"

"Two days."

"Oh. I knew you were new, but not quite that new. I have nine months. As a matter of fact, today is my ninth month anniversary," he says, beaming from ear to ear.

"Congratulations," Catherine says with little enthusiasm.

"What'd you think of the meeting topic?"

Catherine thinks for a minute. "Well. I really haven't thought much about God or a Higher Power or whatever you want to call him…her… it."

"Hmm…I never thought much about God either until I got sober. Now, he's one of my favorite topics."

Catherine cringes. *Great, this creepy guy is also a religious fanatic.*

"Finding God made all the difference in my life. I don't think I'd be sober today if I didn't find God. You really need to find God to stay sober just like they said in the meeting. You need to be able to accept spiritual help."

"Kaleb, don't scare the poor thing off with all your God-talk. She's barely sober for goodness sake," Jane interjects.

He raises his hands in surrender. "You're right. I just get carried away sometimes."

Jane turns to Catherine, "God, or a higher power if you prefer, is a big part of the program of Alcoholics Anonymous, but the first step is all about you. Admitting powerlessness and unmanageability is the key that will eventually unlock the door to more talk of God or whatever you want to call him, her, or it. But, in the meantime, focus on step one, don't drink, and go to lots of meetings," she says with a serious expression.

Catherine nods, but doesn't reply. She has some questions, but dares not ask less Kaleb jumps back into the conversation and starts talking about God again.

"Jane's right. Get to lots of meetings. You got a meeting schedule?"

"Yeah."

Putting his hand out, he says, "Good. Let me see it for a minute."

Catherine looks at him suspiciously.

"What? I just want to circle a couple good meetings."

"I already have some meetings circled."

"Good. Did you pick a home group yet?"

"A home what?" she furrows her brow in confusion.

"Kaleb, this is her second meeting," Jane shakes her head and laughs.

"Yeah. Right. Sorry."

"Catherine, is the Monday night 'How it Works' Big Book meeting circled on your schedule?"

Shuffling through her purse, she withdraws the schedule in question and scans the Monday meetings. "Yes."

"Good. That's my home group. Having a home group basically just means that you make an extra commitment to the group to show up each week, make coffee, chair, and do whatever it takes to keep the meeting going. I'm there every Monday and, unfortunately, so is Kaleb," she says while throwing him a teasing smile.

"Hey! I heard that," Kaleb yells with mock indignation.

Catherine smiles at their easy bantering, but keeps her distance. She's not sure about either of them, but thinks that a Big Book, whatever that is, meeting might be okay. At least she'll know two people there, and who knows, maybe Courtney or Tyler will be there too.

Heading home later that evening, Catherine reflects on how many people she's met in the past forty-eight hours. What an interesting group she thinks. There's fun Courtney, cute Tyler, elegant Valerie, old Samuel, mysterious Paul, creepy Kaleb, and of course, penetrating eyes Jane. She smiles at all the nicknames she's given them. *That meeting on Monday ought to be interesting. I wonder who'll show up there.*

• • •

Pexov laughs hysterically. "That stupid mortal has no clue what's going on. This is going to be so easy."

Sarephah grimaces because she knows Pexov's right: Catherine doesn't have a clue.

The problem is that Catherine's nature is still drawn to that which is most like her. She wants to be around people who act and think like she does, and anyone who contradicts her or tries to show her a different way will be viewed suspiciously. She knows it won't be easy convincing Catherine that what she thinks is good is really bad, and what she thinks is wrong is really right. Sarephah needs to teach Catherine how to sift the wheat from the chafe, and do it quickly. The consequences of not doing so will cost her dearly.

Chapter Twenty-Five

Catherine can hardly believe she's been sober four days now. It's Monday night and she's heading to her third meeting. Life is good she thinks. Work went well on Sunday when she took the responsibility to lead the staff during the breakfast buffet. Except for one slightly irritating customer, the morning went smoothly. The cravings for alcohol have lessened, and thankfully, Kelly hasn't called or stopped over since Saturday. Chuckling, Catherine's pretty sure Kelly's battling a monster hangover, and doesn't envy her one bit. Yes, today she feels good, real good.

In her mind, the only cloud on the horizon is that her thoughts have turned to God several times over the past few days. She hasn't thought about anything religious since she was thirteen and doesn't see the point in starting now. No, thinking about God or whatever spiritual being might be out there, isn't sitting well with her. She basically just wants to avoid the whole topic.

She remembers Paul saying that a person just needs to be willing to think about the concept of God, but her mind snaps shut at the idea of God or accepting any sort of help from him or anyone else for that matter. She just wants to meet a few new friends, get out of trouble at work, feel better, and have some fun. God doesn't figure in to that picture at all.

• • •

Catherine's so busy staring at the entrance of the meeting that when she steps out of her car she practically runs right into Kaleb. Startled, she gasps, backs up, and drops her keys.

"Kaleb, why do you keep sneaking up on me!?"

They both reach down at the same time to pick up her keys and bump heads. "Ouch!" they cry while grabbing their heads. Standing up quickly, they stare at each other for a moment. "Here, let me," Kaleb says as he bends over, scoops up the keys, and then drops them into her outstretched hand. "Sorry," he says with a sheepish grin. Rubbing his head, he adds, "Are you all right?"

"Yeah, I'll live."

"I'm glad we, umm, ran into each other," he says with a slight chuckle. "I wasn't sure if you were going to come tonight. I think you'll like this Big Book meeting."

When she turns to walk toward the door, Kaleb follows behind. Realizing she can't get away from him, she asks over her shoulder, "What's a Big Book anyway?"

Stopping, Kaleb looks at her funny. Catherine senses he's not following her anymore, stops and turns around. "What?"

"You don't know what the Big Book is?"

Turning back around frustrated, she yells over her shoulder, "Forget it. I'll ask someone else."

Running to catch up with her, Kaleb puts his hand on her shoulder and turns her around. Catherine pulls away angrily. "Don't touch me!"

Kaleb snatches his hand away quickly. "Sorry. Really, I meant nothing by it." Looking down at the ground and shuffling his feet, he mumbles, "Oh, this is going all wrong. I'm sorry. I keep forgetting that this is only your second or third meeting, and that you would not possibly know what the Big

Book is. I didn't mean to question you, and I certainly didn't mean to touch you. Well, I did mean to touch you, but not like you think…" His voice trails off, and Catherine can't help but feel some empathy for him. He seems harmless enough.

"It's okay. I didn't mean to react so strongly. It's just that I don't know you and well, guys at the bars can be a little aggressive. It was just a reflex. Don't worry about it."

"Okay, but I really am sorry."

They turn toward the doors and walk a few steps in silence. Finally, Catherine turns to a now very contrite Kaleb and asks softly, "What is a Big Book?"

Smiling, he replies, "It's the main text of Alcoholic Anonymous. Bill Wilson, one of our founders, wrote it to show other alcoholics more about this disease and to help them find a power greater than themselves who will solve their problem. At this meeting, we read a portion of the book, usually each person reads one paragraph, and then we discuss what we've read. Tonight, we're in the chapter called 'More About Alcoholism.'"

"Oh, okay." Catherine could really care less about learning more about alcoholism, but doesn't voice her opinion. Kaleb might give her a lecture.

Catherine is unexpectedly comforted when she sees Paul heading toward the doors.

"Hey, young lady. You made it to another meeting! I guess all the God-talk didn't scare you away after all," he says with an easy smile.

She grabs his extended hand and smiles. "Hi Paul."

Paul and Kaleb enter the church through the main entrance and lead Catherine to where the meeting is located. She's actually grateful to have them with her since she doesn't think she would have found the room in the labyrinth of hallways. Opening the doors at the end of the hall releases the now familiar sounds of an A.A. meeting into the hallway. Catherine tenses slightly but follows Kaleb and Paul in without hesitation. Over the din of the noise, she hears her name loud and clear.

"Catherine! Catherine! Over here."

Catherine turns toward the sound of her name and immediately sees Courtney waving both her hands over her head like an air traffic controller guiding a plane onto the runway. Smiling, she moves quickly toward Courtney. Kaleb glares at Courtney as Catherine walks away. Eventually, he moves to the other side of the room to meet up with several friends.

"Hey, how are you?"

"Hi, Catherine. I'm great! I'm so glad to see you. We missed you at the Saturday 'Weekend Busters' meeting," she says with a pout. "But, you're here now. This is so cool. Sit here next to me."

"Okay." Catherine is a little overwhelmed by Courtney's exuberance, but it feels good to have someone actually excited to see her. She thinks Courtney could be a really good A.A. friend.

"You probably don't have a Big Book do you?"

"No. I just learned tonight what it was. Where do I get one?"

Pointing to the literature table, Courtney says, "Go up there. You can get one tonight. Don't worry if you don't have the money. You can pay for it later."

Catherine looks over in the direction that Courtney points. However, she doesn't see the literature table right away because her eyes come to rest on the person standing behind the literature table. "Tyler's here," she whispers to herself.

"What?" Courtney asks.

"Nothing. I'll be right back." Standing, Catherine smoothes out her shirt and wishes she had worn different jeans. Walking with more confidence than she feels, she heads toward the table ready to buy whatever Tyler is selling.

"Hey, Catherine! Good to see you again."

Catherine stops in her tracks. She turns to see Jane standing there. "Oh, yeah. Hi," she says, looking back toward the literature table.

"Are you going to get a Big Book?" she says as she follows the direction of Catherine's stare and sees the look in her eyes. "Or are you going to say hi to Tyler?"

Catherine whips her head back to a now smiling Jane. "Umm…no. I mean, yes. Wait. I mean, no. Are you kidding me, Tyler? No, I was just going to get a Big Book."

Jane stares at her for a moment, smiles, and turns away. "Okay. But, once you have a Big Book, make sure you read it, especially the first hundred and sixty-four pages. You might learn something about yourself," she says over her shoulder.

Catherine rolls her eyes in irritation. *Whatever. That Jane is a little too outspoken for her own good. Who does she think she is anyway?* Undaunted, she heads to the literature table to buy a Big Book and to buy a few minutes with Tyler.

"Hi, Catherine! I saw you talking with Jane. She's good A.A."

Catherine tries not to roll her eyes. "Yeah. I'm sure she is. It's nice to see you again."

Tyler smiles. "Are you here with Elizabeth again?"

"No. Came by myself this time."

"Getting out on your own," he says with a crooked smile. "That shows real progress."

"Yeah. I'm progressing all right. I have four days of sobriety today," she says with a little laugh.

"Are you looking to make a purchase?"

"I sure am," she says with a flirty smile.

Tyler pulls back, raises his eyebrows, and looks at her curiously. Smiling, he gestures toward the table. "What would you like to purchase *on this table*?" The emphasis on the last few words, "on this table," doesn't go unnoticed by either of them. Tyler gently and skillfully puts Catherine in her place without embarrassing her.

Slightly flustered, she quickly recovers and snatches up a Big Book. "I'll take one of these," she says without making eye contact. They exchange money, and Catherine turns to leave.

"Hey, Catherine. It *is* nice to see you. And congrats on your four days." His smile eases her earlier embarrassment.

"Thanks."

Catherine rejoins Courtney and Jane, who sat in the seat next to Catherine's while she was at the literature table.

"Good! You got your very own Big Book," Courtney exclaims. Grabbing it out of Catherine's hand, she flips through the pages, stops, and with her finger on a page she says, "We're starting here tonight."

Catherine takes the book back and sighs. *I sure hope we go out after this meeting.*

"Um…do people usually go out after this meeting?" Catherine asks hopefully.

"Yeah, we go out all the time. We call it the 'meeting after the meeting.' It's actually very helpful. A big part of recovery is the fellowship time."

"The fellowship time is a companion to actually working the program and doing the steps," Jane interjects. Catherine isn't sure if she's speaking to Courtney or to her.

"Right. That's what I was going to say. Hey, Catherine have you met Jane?"

"Yes."

Courtney leans over and whispers to Catherine. "She can be a little rough, but I think she means well. Don't let her get to you."

Before Catherine can respond, the meeting starts. After general announcements, they bow their heads for the serenity prayer. For the first time, she tenses during this part of the meeting and wishes there wasn't so much prayer and talk of God. She still doesn't announce that she's new, but does better during the introductions. She actually spits out the word alcoholic without much effort; after all, it doesn't really mean anything to her. She says it mainly so she doesn't draw any attention to herself. She's already learning how to play the game.

As the reading begins, Catherine mentally calculates how many people are between her and the person currently reading. Then, counting the paragraphs, she figures out which part she will eventually have to read. She hears little of what's being read because she's too worried about messing up when it's her turn. Sweating, she thinks this type of meeting is way too stressful. Her heart starts racing when Jane begins reading her section: Catherine knows she's next. Finally, it's her turn and she reads without making any glaring mistakes. But as her eyes flow over the words she reads, something catches her attention; her blood runs cold.

The rest of the meeting is a blur in Catherine's mind. The words she just read keep ringing in her ears. She's confused and wonders who she can talk to about it. Jane's abrupt, but she does seem to have some wisdom. Tyler's distant, but she's thinks he might help her, even though she practically threw herself at him. Kaleb's creepy, but he's harmless and does like to help. Courtney's excitable, but she's easy to talk with. Paul's mysterious, but his comments were good the other night. She sighs and thinks harder about which one to talk with.

Sarephah sends a wave of calm in Catherine's direction. When she sees her visibly relax, Sarephah speaks truth into the air.

Catherine's head snaps up. She slowly turns her head to look at the person whose name she clearly heard in her head. Looking away quickly so she doesn't catch their eye, she lowers her head again. *Hmm...not exactly who I would have chosen.*

At the same time, Pexov is whispering near the ear of someone in the room; they look over at Catherine. Slyly, they watch her for a moment, and then drop their eyes.

Once the messages are sent, Pexov and Sarephah glare at each other across the room.

Pexov's eyes blaze red. He nods in Sarephah's direction, throws his head back, laughs wickedly, and moves into the corner

Sarephah's eyes shine brightly. She flashes her sword at Pexov and moves behind Catherine to stand guard.

Chapter Twenty-Six

"Keep coming back!" shouts the group; their hands dancing to the beat of their collective voices. The minute Catherine releases the hands of those on either side she turns toward the person whose name popped into her head a few minutes ago. But before she can speak, someone comes up behind her.

"Hey! Wasn't that a great meeting?" Kaleb yells from behind, careful not to touch her this time: he learned his lesson earlier.

Catherine swirls around and sighs. "Yeah. I guess."

"I thought it was a great meeting, too." Catherine twirls back around and sees Courtney.

"Hey, who wants to go out to Mamma's Cafe?" Courtney yells to no one in particular.

Catherine tries to speak, but Jane puts her hand on her shoulder. "You seemed a little upset during the meeting. Wanna talk?" she asks softly.

Catherine's eyes grow wide. She looks back at Courtney and Kaleb. She feels a strong urge to meet up with the group, but Jane's question makes her hesitate.

Suddenly, Courtney grabs a hold of Catherine in a half-hug and begins dragging her toward the door. "Come on. We're all going to Mamma's."

Catherine manages to squirm out of Courtney's grip just in time to see Jane walking away. A flicker of regret stirs within her. Oh, well she thinks. *I'll talk to her another time.*

The sound of her name jolts her back to the present. "Catherine! Come on. Hurry up!" Courtney yells.

She pushes back the thoughts of talking with Jane and turns toward the group waiting for her.

As Catherine walks toward the impatient Courtney, Jane watches from a distance. When the group is finally out the room, she shakes her head and looks at Paul.

Putting on his jacket, Paul grumbles, "I warned her, but she's new." Shaking his head, "I think this one's gonna have to learn the hard way."

"Yeah, I tried to talk with her after the meeting." Turning back toward the door where Catherine just exited, she adds, "I sense that I'm supposed to keep a close eyes on that one," Jane says.

"Really? Hmm…I got that same feeling."

They look at each other and smile. "Great minds think alike," Paul laughs and gives Jane a hug. "See ya later. Come on, Tyler. Let's go get some coffee."

"Okay. See ya later. Bye Tyler."

• • •

Mamma's Café is a quaint restaurant owned by a local couple who bought it as a retirement project. Papa cooks all the food, but Mama makes sure everything is running smooth. Mama, a sweet looking elderly lady, always wears comfortable tennis shoes and a white apron to cover her checkered dress. If you have a problem with anything, you talk with Mama. And if anyone *causes* problems, they talk with Mama. Nothing goes on in Mama's Café without Mama knowing about it.

"Hello dear. Are you here alone?" Mama asks gently.

Seeing the group in the corner, she points in their direction, "No. I'm with that group."

"Hey, Catherine!" yells Courtney.

Catherine's beginning to wonder if Courtney's on something. She's just a little too excited about everything. Shrugging off the thought, she takes a seat between Courtney and Kaleb.

The table is actually several tables pushed together. Catherine counts fifteen people from the meeting gathered around for fellowship. She recognizes a few from the other two meetings, but can't remember all their names. Paul and Tyler show up a little later, but sit by themselves. Catherine wonders what they're talking about. She glances over several times, but eventually focuses on those sitting around her.

Kaleb on her left is chatting non-stop about something. Courtney on her right is laughing hysterically about something she just heard. The guy directly across from her seems nice, but he's busy talking about something with the younger guy next to him. Catherine suddenly feels unsettled and restless. She's kicking herself for not staying and talking with Jane.

Just when she's ready to call it a night, Courtney leans over and starts a one-sided conversation.

"I'm so glad you came to the meeting tonight. I'm even more glad you decided to come out to Mama's with us. I've been coming to Mama's with the group since I got sober. I got three months right now, but really I should have one year and six months. I slipped a couple times and drank. I always come back into A.A. though, which is really important. Relapsing is part of recovery after all. Just 'cause you drink again doesn't mean you don't want to get sober. I want to get sober. In fact, I have three months. Oh, I already said that. So, how much time do you have?"

"Four days, including today."

"Hey! That's great. I remember when I first came in. I mean the first, first time. 'Cause I came back in after each relapse."

Catherine's head is spinning.

"When I first came in and was brand spanking new, that was a trip. I was so scared. But, just like you, I met some really great people who showed me the way. I got a sponsor. Do you have a sponsor yet?" Courtney continues on before Catherine can respond.

"My sponsor didn't work out. She didn't understand me. Actually, I've had several sponsors. I got a new one each time I came back. But this is my last time. I mean last time to come back after a relapse. I am done drinking. I can't take anymore blackouts. It's awful waking up and not knowing what you did the night before or who you talked to. Ugh...I am so done with all of that. Did you have blackouts?"

Catherine doesn't respond at first, figuring that Courtney's just going to keep rambling on. When Courtney asks her again, she answers, "I guess I had blackouts based on what you just described." Catherine's never heard anyone talk about blackouts before.

"Well I had lots of blackouts. Man, one time, I found out that I threw up on a bunch of my buddies at a party. They were so pissed at me. I just laughed when I found out, but then I realized that wasn't cool."

Catherine is amazed to hear that someone else did something like she did in a blackout. "Yeah, that's not cool at all."

Gathering her courage, Catherine asks, "Hey, I was wondering about something we read tonight. When we read that an alcoholic won't be able to stop drinking based on self-knowledge, what did that mean? 'Cause I thought that all you had to do was say that you were an alcoholic and then you could stop. Isn't knowing the truth about yourself enough?"

Courtney thinks for a minute. "Here's my take on it. You do have to admit that you have a problem with alcohol. I did that a hundred times, but I never stopped drinking. I just kept relapsing. So there's more than just admitting you're an alcoholic, you have to accept spiritual help. The Big Book says that you have to find a power greater than yourself who will solve your problem."

Catherine looks confused, so Courtney adds, "It's all about finding a Higher Power or God. I can help you find a Higher Power. The best part is that your Higher Power can be anything you want it to be. Mine is so wonderful. He loves me no matter what."

"Really? You just make something up?"

"Well, kinda. I listened to a lot of people in the program and then just started praying about it. It's not hard."

"I don't know. It seems weird to me to just make something up."

"Well, you won't know until you try. I bet your beliefs about God come from your parents or church or something. Make it real for yourself. Don't just cling on to the ideas of someone else."

"But you used ideas from others when you decided what your Higher Power would look like?"

"No. I threw out all my old concepts of God and started with fresh ideas: ideas that were my own. Yeah, some people gave me ideas, but I took only those ideas I liked."

"Hmm…sounds interesting," Catherine is intrigued.

"I used the Bible to discover more about God," interrupts Kaleb.

"Yeah, you can use the Bible, but you shouldn't limit yourself to only one way to understand who God is," Courtney retorts.

"Well, I think the Bible is the best way to know something about God. I think going back to church was what really helped me," Kaleb proclaims.

"Church! Are you kidding me? You don't have to go to church to know about God," says the unknown man sitting across from Catherine. "I've never stepped foot in a church, and I have a better understanding about God than any of those church people. I've been to hell, so I know there's a heaven.

Church didn't have to teach me that. All I know is that God loves me. I don't need church to tell me anything about God 'cause I've experienced God."

"I agree. I use crystals and do yoga at the local center, New Spirit Power, to help me get centered and connect with my Higher Power," announces the soft-spoken lady a couple seats down.

"That is so cool," exclaims Courtney. "See Catherine, you have so many options to find a Higher Power. Seek and you will find." Smiling, "I heard that once somewhere. I believe it. Just open yourself up to finding a Higher Power. It'll make all the difference."

Catherine's head is spinning. Who knew there were so many options?

• • •

Pexov smirks at all the talk about a Higher Power. "Higher Power! What a great way to describe *powers* that can both kill and give life." Looking back at the group, "Who do you think they were talking about: The Divine Three or the Ruler of the Kingdom of the Air? Personally, I don't think they have any clue which one they were talking about." Laughing, he adds, "Coming up with your own concept of God is brilliant, brilliant! I think that's my Master's greatest contribution to the world."

Sarephah is concerned for Catherine. "At least she's thinking about God," she says feebly, wishing the talk of God at the table was more fruitful.

"HA! Yes, our precious mortal is thinking about God all right. She'll think her way right into utter confusion and despair. Then I'll show her the real Higher Power: a power that lives to kill her, unlike the one who died to save her."

Sarephah tilts her head to listen for the voice calling her.

"Sarephah, come."

Sarephah rises up, hovers over Pexov, and flashes her sword. "There is power in truth. My side has the ultimate Truth."

She raises her sword toward the heavenlies. Flash! Crack! In an instant, she disappears when a surge of light from the heavenlies touches her sword.

The explosion of sound and light knocks Pexov across the room. Slamming into the counter, cups and plates go flying. Mama runs out from the kitchen to survey the mess. She looks around, but no one is left in the restaurant.

She squints her eyes, lifts her hand, and shouts, "In the name of Jesus Christ, I command you to leave." Pexov cringes as pain shoots into his flesh. He rises with great effort, glares at the woman, and then silently retreats to safety.

Chapter Twenty-Seven

The Word, the current visible representation of the Divine Three, walks with Sarephah toward the outer rim of Nede. The calming presence of the Word is comforting, yet Sarephah is still extremely upset about Catherine.

Sarephah can't stand the silence any longer. She stops, turns to the Word, and puts her hands on her hips. "I'm not sure you understand the danger Catherine's in. She's being corrupted by this, this crazy concept of making up your own God," she sputters out, waving her arms in the air in frustration.

The Word stops and looks at Sarephah. "Is that what's really going on?"

"Yes! I was right there. I heard everything."

The Word smiles, puts his hands behind his back, and continues walking slowly. Actually, he's not walking as much as he's gliding over the ground. Sarephah sighs and rushes back up to walk by his side. They walk in silence for what seems like an eternity to the agitated Sarephah.

Surging ahead of the Word, she turns around and glides backward so she can see his face. "Okay. Then what's really going on?"

The Word stops and smiles broadly. "I thought you would never ask." Taking Sarephah's hand, he rises in the air and glides to the edge of the crystal blue lake. They land softly on the sand, and then the Word continues onto the water. Sarephah watches from the shore as the Word skips and dances upon the water.

He picks a fish out of the water and yells, "Sarephah, are you hungry?" She laughs at his silliness and shakes her head. Angels don't eat food like mortals.

"No?" He bends down and releases the fish into the deep blue water. When several fish leap in the air, he swirls around catching each one. He raises each one to his eyes as if inspecting them, laughs heartily, and then releases them gently back in the water. Eventually, he glides back to the shore.

Sitting on the sand, he laughs. "That was fun! Sarephah, don't ever forget to enjoy life."

Sarephah looks down, embarrassed by her earlier outburst. When she looks up, the Word looks at her with a love that surpasses all understanding. No words are needed; this love is experienced.

"I need to tell you another story, my beloved. Come, sit with me."

When Sarephah sits down, a large oak tree appears behind them to supply shade. They both lean back against the newly grown tree. After a few moments, the Word puts his head back on the tree trunk, closes his eyes for a moment, opens them, and begins the story of the rare, beautiful gem and the empty canvas.

"There once was a rare and beautiful gem. In fact, no gem before or since this one has ever been as stunning or as coveted. Many admired the gem from a distance, but a few studied the gem closely. They held it and touched it, noting all its angles, shapes, and colors. They spent time discussing its qualities and markings. These few knew the gem like no other.

Then one day the gem was taken from them. They grieved the loss of such a precious stone. Talking among themselves, they decided to paint a picture of this very rare and beautiful gem so that all future generations would know of its existence. In order to preserve the accuracy of their remembrance, they worked together to create one true masterpiece that depicted the gem just as they knew it to be."

Once the masterpiece was created, they each devoted their lives to telling people about the gem and to preserving the integrity of their original masterpiece. Master painters were trained by the original painters to teach others. The master painters carefully passed along all their knowledge in order that all subsequent paintings of the original gem would be identical in size, shape, color, and splendor. In fact, no one ever painted the gem without help from one of the master painters.

One day, a master painter walks by a woman standing at a canvas that is cluttered with images of gems of various shapes, sizes and colors. The woman looks confused and distraught. The master painter asks her what's wrong. The woman says, "I heard about the one rare and beautiful gem and wanted to know what it looked like since I had never seen it with my own eyes. I asked someone about the gem, and they painted me a picture of the gem the way they believed it looked. Then another person added more brushes strokes to the picture using their own ideas. Then another person did the same until the canvas looks like what you see before you: a cluttered and confusing mess. I am beginning to think that I will never know what the original gem looked like."

The master painter studies the woman for a moment and then says, "Do you really want to know what the original rare and beautiful gem looked like?"

"Yes, but this canvas is a mess and I don't know how I can fix it. I don't know which gem is accurate and which one isn't from all the images that are painted. You're a master painter. Can't you just paint the picture of the gem for me?" she asks expectantly.

"Why don't you paint your own picture?" Handing her a blank canvas, he says eagerly, "Just throw out that cluttered canvas and start with this blank canvas."

"You mean I can draw my own picture of the gem?"

"Yes!"

Excited about the prospect of drawing her own picture, the woman thinks for a moment, and then dips her brush in the paint and raises it to the empty canvas.

"However," the master holds up his hand to stop her, "if you want to draw the exact replica of the original rare and beautiful gem, you must be willing to do one thing."

Putting down her brush, the woman asks, "What must I do?"

"You must be willing to study everything you can about this particular gem before you begin to paint your own picture. Read what has been said about the gem and talk with others who have studied the gem. I will help you in the same way I was helped. Finally, if you are diligent in your research and have opened your heart to the truth about this gem, when you are done, you will have created an accurate masterpiece."

So the woman sets out to learn everything she can about this special gem. Starting from a blank canvas was intimidating, yet exhilarating. There were days when she wished someone or, at least, the master painter would just tell her what to draw or draw it for her. However, it isn't long before she adds the first brush strokes to the empty canvas and begins her masterpiece. She faithfully studies and paints without missing a single day.

Finally, she proudly displays her masterpiece to the master painter. When he sees the woman's painting of the gem, he uncovers his canvas and says, "Come and see what the original gem looked like."

Nervously, the woman moves over to see the master painter's picture and gasps. "My picture looks exactly like yours, except for a few minor personal touches that I added."

"Well done, good and faithful painter. You have painted the perfect picture of the original rare and beautiful gem. You are now a master painter. Go and tell others how to paint the same picture from their own empty canvas. And never again let someone paint your picture, or you paint theirs."

The Word stands and offers his hand to Sarephah. She takes it, and he pulls her to her feet. They begin to walk slowly around the blue lake. "There's no danger starting from an empty canvas as long as the painter is willing to study the subject of their painting. Give Catherine an empty canvas so she can study the subject of her painting without the clutter of another's paint strokes."

Stopping to admire the surroundings, he draws in a deep breath. Exhaling, he adds, "Of course, many will try to paint the picture for her, but Catherine must paint her own picture. And, if she's willing to study, touch, hold, and experience the true gem, she will paint a masterpiece."

Sarephah smiles at the idea of Catherine painting a masterpiece. "How do I give Catherine a blank canvas when everyone is already painting on it?" Sarephah wonders.

"Encourage her to ask her own questions and to experience her own feelings. Don't let anyone stifle her desire or thirst for knowledge, even if it gets uncomfortable. She will be angry at times; she will be confused at times; she will be wrong at times; she will be right at times. We will send master painters alongside her on this journey of discovery. An image always takes shape on the empty canvas of a diligent painter."

"What if the image doesn't look like you?"

The Word stops, turns, and smiles at Sarephah. "Within each mortal is knowledge of Our image in all its fullness. Catherine has suppressed that knowledge by pulling away from Us. But in seeking to know Us, she will be drawn to Us. Images get distorted and indistinct the farther one moves away from them; images get clearer and more defined the closer one gets to them. Sarephah, bring Catherine near to Us and We will draw near to her. Then she will know Us fully, even as she is fully known."

• • •

"I know all there is to know about that ignorant mortal," growls Satan at Pexov. "She's falling hard for the idea of making up her own God 'cause she's never bothered to learn anything about him in the first place. Her ignorance is like putty in my hands. We can shape and mold her ideas to fit our needs."

Turning quickly, he grabs Pexov's arm and drags him through the inner court into the chamber of ignorance and confusion.

The chamber is full of the fruit from the tree of the knowledge of good and evil. The fruit is colorful and pleasing to the eye. There are two primary colors of fruit that represent either good or evil with a million shades in between to indicate degrees of each. The closer the color gets to the primary color of evil, the sweeter the taste, but the bitter the effect. On the other hand, the closer the color gets to the primary color of good, the sweeter the taste *and* the sweeter the effect.

Everyone in this chamber believes the lies of Satan that all fruit is essentially the same. They're ignorant about the fact that the color of the fruit represents its true value, and are therefore utterly confused when the sweet taste turns bitter.

Pexov sees a mortal doubled over in excruciating pain. The wretched soul reaches for the same piece of fruit he's been eating day after day, a piece colored evil, and says out loud, "It will be different this time. The sweet taste will not turn bitter."

Another pathetic soul cries out, "It doesn't matter what piece of fruit I eat, they are all the same." She picks fruits of all colors and takes a bite out of each one. They all taste sweet, but when the bitter effects surface later, she is confused. "Which one caused the bitter taste?" Reaching for another piece of fruit, she sighs, "It doesn't matter what piece of fruit I eat, they are all the same."

Satan turns to Pexov, "Make sure our ignorant Catherine believes that all fruit is the same. Give her many, many options of fruit to choose from. Let her see the bright colors and taste the sweetness of each. When she has had her fill, she will be so full of bitterness she'll beg to know which fruit only contains the sweetest taste. Then I will personally feed her one of the sweetest, yet most bitter fruit of all: tolerance without conviction."

Chapter Twenty-Eight

"I am so confused. I just can't decide," yells a frustrated Catherine.

"What does it matter anyway? Just pick one," says an equally frustrated Courtney.

"But I want to look nice for the meeting tonight, and my best jeans are a mess." Catherine stands with her hands on her hips, surveying the clothes hanging in her closet.

Shaking her head, Courtney plops on the bed. "Those other jeans are just as good. Just pick something already," she mumbles.

Grabbing a pair of jeans, Catherine turns toward Courtney. "What's wrong with you? You've been dragging for a week now. Have you talked with your sponsor?"

Courtney reaches for Pip, but he hisses and jumps off the bed. "You're cat doesn't like me. He's always running away from me," she whines.

"He likes you. He's just moody sometimes. Like you," she says with a teasing laugh, hoping to bring Courtney out of her dark mood. Over the past several weeks, Courtney's moods have been swinging between over exuberance and a deep, dark depression. Today is one of her dark days.

"Well, what did your sponsor say?"

She shrugs. "Nothing new; I've heard it all before anyway."

Catherine's not sure what to say, nothing seems to get Courtney out of one of her dark moods. She's learned just to ride it out. For the most part, they've been having lots of fun over the past six weeks, so she takes the good with the bad. It's nice to have a buddy at the meetings.

"How's it working out with Jane?" Courtney asks. Sitting up on the bed, she adds, "I still can't believe you asked her to be your sponsor. She's hard core."

"Yeah, well, I really didn't have a choice. My mandatory counseling *counselor* said I had to get a sponsor. I think she's in cahoots with my boss. Anyway, Jane's not so bad. I don't really use her much. But, I have to say, she does feel free to tell me what's on her mind, even when I don't ask."

Courtney rolls her eyes, "That's my point exactly."

"Hey, we better get to the meeting. I've been told that if I'm not a half hour early, I'm late. Let's go!" she yells, slapping Courtney's feet.

"You're killing me here."

"Move it! We're gonna be late. Hey, I think Kyle and Pete are coming tonight."

"Now you're talking." Jumping off the bed, Courtney races past Catherine. When she reaches the front door, she calls over her shoulder, "Come on, we don't want to be late."

• • •

Jane sees Catherine and Courtney talking with several new guys as she walks up to the doors of the meeting. After shaking hands with the guys, Jane says, "Hey, Ladies. Don't be late for the meeting."

"What do you mean? We're here aren't we?" Catherine responds.

"The meeting's *inside*," she says over her shoulder just before disappearing into the meeting room.

Courtney and Catherine look at each other and roll their eyes. "I told you she was hard core," Courtney mumbles as they turn to follow Jane into the meeting room.

Jane begins greeting people the minute she walks into the room. Several people reach out to her and receive warm, heartfelt hugs. She moves intentionally around the room shaking everyone's hand, looking them in the eyes, and spreading hope that recovery works.

Catherine and Courtney, on the other hand, move quickly to empty chairs, sit down, and begin laughing and chatting with each other; they're in the meeting, but not part of the meeting. Several others join them at the table, and the laughter and rowdiness escalates.

Catherine's too busy having a good time with her friends to notice Jane talking with someone near the entrance of the meeting. Catherine's fixated on her small group of peers and can't be bothered by anything else going on at the meeting. Her selfishness and self-centered focus is blinding her from the real help she needs, the real needs in the room, and the real problem in her own soul.

"Catherine, I'd like you to meet Shelly. This is her first meeting." Catherine turns and sees a pitiful looking creature standing before her. Only a few years older than Catherine, Shelly carries in her slumping shoulders the heavy weight of shame and despair. Her hair and clothes are neat but unkempt; she's shaking and staring at her shuffling feet, unable to make eye contact with Catherine.

Catherine looks at Jane curiously, unsure exactly what to do. Jane raises her eyebrows and tilts her head in Shelly's direction, silently telling Catherine to acknowledge the new girl.

"Uh…Hi, I'm Catherine." Catherine hesitates, and then slowly extends her hand. Tentatively, Shelly reaches up and shakes Catherine's hand. They drop hands quickly, and Shelly sneaks a quick peek at Catherine. Not knowing what else to do or say, Catherine looks down uncomfortably, wishing she could get back to her friends.

"Shelly, why don't you sit here with us?" Jane urges, pointing to the chair next to her.

"Okay," she says, barely above a whisper.

Catherine turns back toward her friends, but before she enters back into their conversation, Jane taps her shoulder.

"Did you go around the room and shake hands?"

"No. I'd rather sit here and wave at people," she says flippantly.

"Okay. Go ahead and stay sick," Jane says calmly and turns her attention back to Shelly.

Catherine is stunned by Jane's words, mainly because they cut deeper than she's willing to admit. She's been told several times about the importance of shaking hands after entering a meeting. No one knows exactly how the tradition started, but the practice is widely accepted and practiced as a way to create a special bond of unity between members. By extending your hand in fellowship, you're extending hope to the newcomer and the old timer alike, acknowledging that by this handshake we've made it to another meeting, and by God's grace, made it through another day sober.

The thought of actually getting up and shaking hands is terrifying, but the thought of drinking again is just as terrifying. Although not totally convinced of the efficacy of shaking hands, she stands up slowly, moves to the next table, and shakes everyone's hand. A few are surprised to see Catherine initiating the handshake and gently tease her about it. Not wanting to overdo it, she quickly takes her seat after shaking only a few hands. Taking a deep breath, she thinks that wasn't so bad after all.

Jane watches, smiles, but says nothing.

After the meeting, Catherine is immediately caught up in conversation with Kyle. Soon, the others gather around to discuss what's going on tonight. Several want to go for coffee but others petition for getting ice cream. With more fanfare than necessary, they decide they'll do both. Next on their important lists of decisions for the evening is where to go. "Mama's Café" is shouted simultaneously, which they find extremely hilarious, even though no one else around them does. Catherine can't remember when she's had so much fun sober.

Walking toward the door with her group, Catherine sees Jane and Shelly embrace. Shelly wipes away a tear before heading out the door. Jane turns and looks directly at Catherine. Her look is neither condescending nor judging, yet a twinge of guilt runs through Catherine. She quickly dismisses it.

Grabbing Courtney, Catherine says quietly, "I'm gonna talk to Jane for a second. I'll be right out."

"Really? Okay. Well, hurry up. You don't want to miss anything," Courtney calls over her shoulder.

Catherine walks up to Jane and waits until she's finished talking with someone else. Finally, Jane shifts her attention to Catherine. "Are you heading out with Courtney and gang?"

"Yeah. We're heading to Mama's Café?"

"Mmm. How come you guys didn't invite Shelly? Matter of fact, I don't think I saw any of you guys even talk with her. Did you notice that she was new?"

Shuffling her feet, she says, "No. Not until you brought her over," she says quietly.

Sighing, Jane sits down and Catherine joins her. "I know you like to have fun, and fun does have its place in A.A. The Big Book even says that we are not a glum lot. We do like to have fun, and I have no problem with that as long as your fun does not get in the way of sobriety: yours or someone else's."

"The fellowship can be fun, and you will make many wonderful friends, but the program of A.A. is serious. Meetings are a time to work the program of Alcoholics Anonymous, not cluster with your own special group. This disease is serious, deadly, and needs to be treated as such. That means working the twelve steps."

"I know."

"No, I don't think you do know." Jane looks hard at Catherine, and then asks, "Are you working tomorrow morning?"

"No, I'm off tomorrow."

"Good. I'm picking you up at 10:30 a.m."

"What are we gonna do at that hour of the morning?" whines Catherine.

"We're going on a twelve step call."

Catherine learns later from Courtney and the others that a twelve step call is when you carry the message of recovery to another suffering alcoholic. None of her new group has ever been on a twelve step call, and Catherine's not sure what to expect. No one seems too interested in talking about recovery, so the evening's conversation moves to more interesting topics such as who's relapsing, who's staying sober, who's dating who, and other general gossip.

The fun runs into the wee hours of the morning, and Catherine doesn't get to bed until well after 4:00 a.m. Throughout the evening, she soaks in all the camaraderie she can get. Being with this group doesn't feel much different than her life of drinking. Recovery, working the steps of A.A., is far from her mind. Yet, in spite of all the fun and ambivalence about her own alcoholism, Catherine can't get one image out of her mind: Shelly leaving the meeting last night.

• • •

Pip jumps onto the bed, onto Catherine's stomach, and then meows loudly.

Startled, she jerks awake. Popping her eyelids open, she looks directly into two green eyes inches from her own eyes.

"Good morning, Pip." Catherine groans under the weight of her cat.

Pip howls impatiently.

"Pip, hush. It's too early to get up."

Catherine closes her eyes and reaches up to pet Pip. He lowers his head and receives her strokes while playfully pushing against her hand. Catherine begins to doze off again. Suddenly, Pip stops, perks up his ears, turns his head toward the door, and stares at the empty space. Then just as quickly, he turns back to Catherine, meows loudly, and starts pawing at her cheek.

Catherine opens her eyes again. "You're awfully persistent this morning. Okay, I'm getting up." Sitting up, she yawns, stretches, throws off the covers, and climbs out of bed.

Pip jumps off the bed, walks toward the door, and stops abruptly. Catherine watches as he flops over on his back and starts wiggling back and forth. Catherine laughs and shakes her head. What a funny cat, she thinks.

Sarephah smiles at her furry friend as she bends over to rub Pip's belly. Sarephah knows Catherine must meet with Jane this morning, and Pip was just a fun way to accomplish her goal. Actually, using Pip was the Divine Three's idea. Each one of their creation has a purpose, and they love using them in their plans.

Tired and grumpy this morning, Catherine is not at all thrilled at the prospect of going on some lousy twelve step call. She's all about sleeping in, doing her own thing, and going out tonight with her new A.A. friends. Except for some talk about a Higher Power, she's enjoying her life of sobriety. She figures all she needs to do is just get through this thing she's being forced to do, and then she can get on with her day.

Hearing Jane honking her horn, Catherine grabs her purse and heads toward the door. As she reaches for the doorknob, she mumbles, "this better not take too long." The door slams behind her. She moves slowly down the steps to Jane's car.

Surprisingly, a growing sense of fear and trepidation begins to well up inside her. Taken off guard by this sudden surge of emotions, she's suddenly not sure if she's ready for this. The next emotion she feels is anger at Jane for making her do this.

She decides that after this little fiasco is over she's getting a new sponsor.

Catherine opens the door, slides in the passenger side, and slams the door. She grabs her seatbelt and puts it on with one swift motion. Sitting back, she finally looks at Jane with irritation; her angry eyes speak words her mouth isn't willing to voice.

"Well, I see you're in a good mood today. Good morning!" Jane grins, amused at Catherine's attitude.

"Morning," Catherine mumbles.

Jane puts the car in gear and pulls out of the parking lot. They drive for several minutes in silence. The air is heavy with tension. Catherine's tense because she doesn't want to be here. Jane's tense because she doesn't want to go there: the house of a dear friend who's slowly killing herself.

"Today, you get the honor and privilege of sharing your experience, strength, and hope with a struggling alcoholic, who unfortunately, is beginning to lose hope. The twelfth step says, 'Having had a spiritual awakening as a result of these steps, we tried to carry this message to alcoholics, and to practice these principles in all our affairs.' So, this morning, we are going to carry the message of recovery."

Catherine shifts uncomfortably in her seat.

"And the message of recovery is a message of hope. In the Big Book, it says that there is a solution for our alcoholism: accepting spiritual help. We just need to pick up the kit of spiritual tools laid at our feet. That's page twenty-five in the Big Book, if you want to look it up later," she adds with a smile.

Catherine slumps slightly in her seat.

"Did you notice Shelly's eyes last night?"

Catherine wrestles with her memories. "Not really," Catherine admits.

"She had the eyes of someone whose shame and guilt are robbing her of hope. They were the eyes of someone who doesn't want to live, but is too afraid to die. She had the eyes of a lost child who is wondering what will become of her if she quits drinking, or what will become of her if she doesn't." Turning to look at Catherine, "She saw hope in your eyes, you know."

Catherine lifts her head and looks at Jane. "Really?"

"Yes, I saw her look at you, and for one brief moment, she saw hope. It was a glimmer, but it was there."

Catherine's not sure what to think. Would someone new like that really look at her for hope?

"I want you to pay close attention to what goes on this morning. This may be a real battle, because some don't want to accept help, even in the face of incredible misery and pain. This woman in particular is confused by what she believes to be true and what she actually experiences as true. I'll explain more about that later."

"I can do most of the talking, but feel free to encourage her anyway you can. Look in her eyes and offer her hope; extend your hand and offer her acceptance; listen to her story and offer her love."

Catherine's palms are sweaty by the time Jane pulls into the driveway of a large Victorian home complete with a manicured lawn and beautiful landscaping. Confused, Catherine wonders who lives here and how they can possibly be an alcoholic. She's not sure what she expected to find at their destination, but this sure wasn't the picture she had in mind.

Jane parks the car and takes a deep breath. "Are you ready?"

Catherine is definitely not ready. "Yeah, I guess."

"Okay. Let's go."

They both climb out of the car and shut their doors. Catherine stops and waits while Jane opens the door to the backseat to grab her Big Book. Armed and ready for action, they proceed to the front door.

They ring the doorbell, back away from the door slightly, and wait in silence. Then, just as Jane reaches up to ring the doorbell again, they hear the doorknob rattle and an indistinct voice yelling for them to wait.

The door flies open and a disheveled elderly lady appears. She stands unsteadily before them and smiles wide. She's wearing a pearl necklace around her neck, an exquisitely cut diamond on her finger, and an equally beautiful diamond bracelet. To compliment the attire, she has on a bright pink bathrobe, tattered slippers, and curlers dangling from her stringy hair. Her eyes are glassy and red; her skin has a yellowish cast.

"Well, hello ladies," she slurs, drawing out each word. She waves them into to the house. "Come in…come in."

Catherine can hardly breathe. She's stunned by what she sees. Standing before her is one of the first people to greet her in a meeting and to make her feel welcome. A tear comes to her eye as she remembers the elegant lady who winked and told her she would indeed make it through her first meeting.

Catherine steps wide-eyed into the house and wonders, what happened to Valerie?

Chapter Twenty-Nine

The contrast between the immaculate outside of the house and the dark, cluttered inside of the house is striking. The first thing Catherine notices is the smell of alcohol mixed with an odor she can't quite identify. The only things she can compare them with are the smells of a bar at closing time and a badly managed nursing home. She stifles the urge to cover her nose, but can't control the involuntary coughs as her throat constricts from the rancid odor.

Catherine follows closely behind Jane as Valerie leads them down a long hallway to a sitting room. Valerie enters the room at the end of the hallway and moves slowly to the chair next to the picture window. She hesitates in front of the chair, turns slowly in an attempt to keep her balance, and then sits down heavily. Jane and Catherine glance at each other after watching Valerie struggle with a simple task like sitting down. Catherine is momentarily unsure of what to do. After signaling to Catherine to sit in the other chair, Jane steps over to the love seat.

It's hot and stuffy in the room due to the lack of fresh air and ventilation. Dust particles dance in the little crease of sunlight that breaks through the closed blinds. For a brief moment, time seems to stand still for everyone in the room. The pictures on the wall tell a story of a young, vibrant Valerie. She's smiling with friends, hugging children, playing tennis, sitting with her husband. The images, captured during better days, seem to mock the woman who now sits enslaved by alcohol.

"What brings you ladies to my home today?" Valerie asks, emphasizing each word. Her smile is engaging, but her eyes betray distrust of her visitors.

Jane's shoulders slump slightly. "You called me yesterday and asked if I would come over to talk with you."

Valerie's eyes grow wide. "Oh, yes, yes. I remember now. Well, I do say I must have had a senior moment. Oh, well, it happens." She clasps her fingers together in her lap and sighs. "I have trouble remembering things these days. But I do remember now." Looking at Catherine, she smiles. "I see you brought a friend. Catherine, it is good to see you dear."

"Thank you. It's umm…good…to see you, too." Catherine manages to sputter out; not at all sure she believes it.

"Valerie, do you remember what you wanted to talk with me about?" Jane asks gently.

"Well, now let's not jump into all that so quickly. What can I get you ladies to drink?"

"Nothing, were fine, really." Jane answers for the both of them.

Frowning, Valerie waves her hand, dismissing her answer. "Nonsense. I can't have guests in my house and not offer them some of my wonderful iced tea." Standing up slowly, she adds, "Come now; let's get some refreshments before we began our little talk."

Jane and Catherine look at each other and shrug. They rise, follow Valerie back down the hallway, and turn into a large kitchen. The smell of alcohol in the kitchen is unmistakable. Valerie is not even attempting to hide her drinking. Catherine just hopes the iced tea isn't spiked with anything.

After grabbing several tall glasses from the cupboard, Valerie places them on a platter. She brings out the pitcher of iced tea that's been cooling in the refrigerator and pours drinks for everyone. She is shaking slightly, but manages to fill each glass without incident. Finally, she places a small bowl of lemon slices and a bowl of sugar next to the pitcher on the platter. Catherine and Jane watch intently, fascinated by her attempt to maintain dignity even in the grips of active alcoholism.

"Catherine, dear, can you carry this platter?"

Catherine picks up the platter and moves back toward the sitting room.

"Wait." Catherine and Jane stop and turn back toward Valerie. Holding her hand to her chin thinking, she states, "I believe we will move to the larger room off the patio. Come this way."

Jane and Catherine look at each other and shake their heads. They follow Valerie through the kitchen into a spacious family room. At the end of a short hallway, they walk into a room full of windows that run from the ceiling to the floor. The view would be gorgeous if the blinds were open.

Catherine sets the platter of drinks on the glass-topped coffee table, grabs a glass, smells it discreetly, sighs in relief, and sits down. Jane smiles at Catherine, grabs a glass, and also checks it out for any trace of alcohol before she sits down. Finally, Valerie sits, leans over, and picks up a glass with two hands in an attempt to still the shaking. It doesn't work. Tea spills on her bathrobe, but she doesn't seem to notice.

"Now we can have a proper conversation," she announces. "I called you Jane because frankly I am concerned about something. I have been praying for deliverance from this issue about drinking, or spirit of addiction, or whatever you want to call it, and nothing has happened. I find it quite maddening that God has not delivered me after all my prayers." Valerie's tone is calm, but her anger is revealed in her narrowed brows and pursed lips.

Jane is not all surprised by this frustration and anger toward God. Unfortunately, Valerie's been indoctrinated into the "name it and claim it" gospel of the new mega church on the west side: Faith Fellowship.

Church members are told that God will heal or deliver them and even give them riches beyond measure if they simply have enough faith. They just need to name the problem and claim the healing without any further action on their part. It's as if God is just the vehicle by which their personal desires are fulfilled. What they fail to tell these poor souls is that sometimes, well often times, God likes to use others in the process of healing, that he expects obedience and personal responsibility of his followers, and that healing doesn't always happen in the way humans expect.

Jane thinks that what that church should be telling their members is that when we name our sin or addiction and claim our helplessness to save ourselves, God will absolutely show us the way to His healing, but in His time and in His way.

Jane calms herself and focuses back on Valerie. "Prayer is a good thing. I'm glad to hear that you are praying to God. What else have you been doing in addition to praying for deliverance from alcoholism?"

Valerie looks up in deep concentration. "Well, let me think for a minute." She sighs heavily. "Hmm…I have been attending all the deliverance services at Faith Fellowship. I have been reading my Bible every day. I go to church faithfully each Sunday."

"Again, those are good things, but you still haven't told me what you have been doing specifically to treat your alcoholism."

"I am doing something *specifically* to treat my issue with drinking." Jane notices that Valerie refuses to call herself an alcoholic. "I'm praying specifically about this issue, but God isn't answering. In my mind, that means God is not as powerful as he claims to be, and well, I wonder if he even really exists." Valerie states in a huff.

"Maybe God is answering your prayers." Jane smiles at Valerie.

"What makes you think that?"

"You called me last night. Catherine and I are here to talk with you. I'd say God is answering your prayer. What were you expecting?"

Valerie is surprised at this idea that God just might be answering her prayers. "Well, I guess I expected to be delivered from this issue with drinking."

"What would that look like? I mean, how would you know you are delivered from alcoholism?" Jane uses the word alcoholism purposely, even though Valerie practically squirms out of her pink bathrobe when she hears the word.

"I would be free from this problem." Stumbling for the right words, she gets frustrated. "I don't know what freedom or deliverance from an addiction looks like, but I know what bondage to disease looks like," she says angrily. "I don't want to think about drinking all day. I don't want to finally give in and drink until I blackout or pass out. I don't want to feel sick in the morning and shake in the afternoon." Looking down, she says softly, "I don't want to lose my husband, my family, or my life." She straightens up in her chair, draws in a deep breath, and looks at Jane with a combination of fear, anger, and sorrow.

Jane waits for a moment, looks at Catherine to make sure she's paying attention, and then asks, "Why did you stop going to meetings?"

"Oh, those meetings were nice. In fact, I had fun going to A.A., but the meetings weren't keeping me sober. And then once I started going to Faith Fellowship, I began to think that going to meetings was unnecessary. After all, I was praying and seeking God, which is part of steps three and eleven. I was told over and over again that all I needed was to pray and God would heal me. Now I don't know what to believe. I tried A.A. meetings, I tried God, and I tried church and none of it worked."

"Actually, Valerie, all you've done is put your foot in the water of A.A., God, and church. You haven't really tried anything. You should also know that most of what you have been told in your church and believe to be true about recovery from alcoholism is faulty." Pausing, she adds, "Do you really want deliverance from alcoholism?"

Valerie looks at her hands in her lap for several seconds. Finally, she looks first at Catherine and then at Jane. "Jane, one thing that I have always admired about you is how straight forward you are. I don't know what I believe any more about church, A.A., or God, but yes, I believe that I do want deliverance from…alcoholism."

"Many die from this disease because of their inability or unwillingness to see the truth about themselves. Do you believe that you are powerless over alcohol and that your life is unmanageable?"

Valerie's eyes fill with tears. "Yes," she says softly.

Smiling Jane asks, "Are you willing to take some suggestions from me?"

"Yes," she sighs.

"The steps are written in the order that they are to be taken. You don't get to pick and choose the steps you want to work. We will start with step one and work our way to step twelve. Next, I would like to ask you to open your heart and mind to a new understanding of God, based on your own diligent search of him. You will seek to know Him through the fellowship of A.A., the Big Book and the Bible, if you are willing. Finally, I believe that God has established the program of Alcoholics Anonymous specifically so we drunks can get sober and help each other. I would like you to attend an A.A. meeting everyday for the next few months to immerse yourself in the solution to a problem that is greater than you can handle on your own. The Big Book tells me that the plan I have outlined rarely fails for those who completely give themselves to the A.A. program. It's up to you now. Are you ready to get started?"

"Yes," Valerie says with more fear than conviction, but it's a start.

Glancing at the clock, Catherine wonders when this is going to end.

As the conversation between Valerie and Jane continues, Catherine gets lost in her own world of confusion and denial. The questions about God and church are disconcerting to Catherine. She secretly agrees with Valerie that God appears to be limited in his ability since he doesn't heal those who, like Valerie, pray earnestly for help.

Jane's answers are not very satisfying either. Although Catherine has never really bothered praying, she's pretty sure God should be answering prayers for healing. What kind of a God doesn't answer prayers?

Catherine wonders if Valerie needs a better concept of God. After all, she's been hearing that you can make up anything you want about God. She also wonders why someone needs to go to A.A. meetings and do all those twelve steps. God…church...meetings…steps. Seems like a lot of work with little reward.

A thought comes out of her confusion: *maybe there are other ways to get a handle on the problems in my life.* She decides to ask Courtney about that tonight.

Pexov is utterly pleased with himself for sending confusion into Catherine's consciousness. He knows that her confusion is growing and becoming more troublesome, even overriding the original problem that sent her to A.A. in the first place. Confusion along with many options will be his greatest allies. Before Pexov slithers back into the darkness he so loves, he throws more confusing thoughts at Catherine.

Jane and Valerie finish their conversation, stand up and embrace, and interrupt Catherine's musing. Catherine stands and sighs in relief at the thought that the long morning is almost over.

"So, I'll see you at the meeting tonight?" Jane inquires.

"Yes, I'll be there. I'll call Hannah like you suggested. I'm not sure I'm able to drive tonight," admits Valerie.

"Good idea." Looking at Catherine, Jane confirms more than asks, "You'll be at the meeting tonight, right?"

"Yep, I wouldn't miss it." She smiles internally, knowing she's mainly going to the meeting so she doesn't miss going out after the meeting.

Valerie hugs Jane again. "Thank you, Jane." Catherine watches the two hug, wondering what effect this meeting will have on Valerie. Mostly, she wonders if God is watching, and if he even cares.

Next, Valerie turns to look at Catherine. "And thank you, Catherine." Catherine stiffens when Valerie draws her into a hug. They hug just long enough for Catherine to become self-conscious and uncomfortable with such intimate physical contact between virtual strangers. When Catherine is finally released by Valerie, she steps back slightly embarrassed by all the emotions surging in the room and in her soul.

Sarephah removes her hands from Catherine's shoulder and returns to hover in the corner of the room.

As if suddenly aware of her disheveled appearance, Valerie uses one hand to smooth out the wrinkles in her pink bathrobe and the other hand to fiddle with the curlers randomly placed in her hair. She looks down at her tattered slippers, and says softly, "Your visit today has encouraged me more than you know."

Jane and Catherine wave to Valerie as they pull out of the driveway. Valerie waves back while wiping away several tears.

They drive in silence for several moments. Jane's silently praying for Valerie. Catherine's stewing in her raging emotions. What did she feel in that house? Was it love, pity, compassion? She's not sure what she's feeling at the moment, but it's uncomfortable whatever it is. And the whole conversation about God and church is weighing heavily on her mind.

With a frustrated huff, she finally blurts "I don't see what God has to do with getting sober. I'm not drinking, and God had nothing to do with it. I quit on my own, and I am staying sober on my own. So what's the point of God or church anyway? Valerie prayed, and God didn't answer her. I just don't get all this stuff about God, or a higher power, or whatever you want to call it."

Jane smiles wide and chuckles, "I think that's the first honest words I have heard you say since I met you a couple months ago."

Catherine crosses her arms, looks out the passenger side window, and rolls her eyes.

"Okay." Glancing quickly at her watch, she asks, "Do you want to talk? Mama's Café is just around the corner."

Catherine bites her lower lip, calculating the cost of talking this out or just keeping it all inside. Neither seems like a good choice. In the midst of her internal struggle, she slowly senses a strong desire to know more about Jane's version of God. After all, she can talk with Courtney later tonight about her ideas.

Without turning away from the window, Catherine mutters, "Yeah, okay. Let's go talk."

"Yeah, let's talk." In her heart, Jane utters a silent prayer of thanks. She glances in her side mirror, shifts lanes, and accelerates in the direction of Mama's, knowing she'll have lots of prayer cover.

Catherine suddenly wants to run for cover. This morning was nothing like she expected. Valerie thanked her; she's not exactly sure why. God keeps coming up in conversations; she's not exactly sure why. She's going to talk with Jane about God; she's not exactly sure why.

Why is she thinking about God anyway? She's so confused. How in the world is any of this happening? She clenches her teeth, concerned that the direction of her thoughts and even the direction of her life seem out of her control. She's beginning to wonder if there's something directing all of this; even more concerning, whether that something is good for her or not. And how would she even know?

Sarephah releases her grip on Catherine and moves swiftly to position herself at the entrance of Mama's Café. She needs to survey the battlefield, assess Pexov's strength, and make sure her primary main spiritual warrior is armed and ready for the fight.

Chapter Thirty

There is a certain rhythm created in the hustle and bustle of a busy restaurant. The dance of the wait staff with the customer is a delicate balance of attentive interaction to meet current wants and the patient observance of anticipated needs. This morning the dance is going well. Mama is pleased with the atmosphere of joyful celebration of food and fellowship. She's grateful that peace has settled on this place by the blessings of God.

A wave of cold air rushes past mama, disturbing her musing about the blessings from God, when Pexov glides into the restaurant, circles once, and then hovers over an empty table. Mama looks up quickly from the stack of menus she's arranging at the cash register. The faint odor of evil alerts her to the spiritual danger that has just shattered her peaceful world. Slowly, she scans the restaurant searching for the source of the strong presence she feels.

Pexov sees mama looking in his direction. His eyes grow red with anger at the presence of one of the Divine Three's agents. He won't admit it, but he fears this one. She can strike him with the power of the Word.

The presence invading her space is dark and powerful, raising the hairs on the back of Mama's neck; she begins praying.

She intuitively knows whatever demonic entity just entered her restaurant is transitory. This can only mean one thing: this powerful demon is tracking someone.

In the middle of praying fervently against the entity she sees with her spiritual eyes, several more demons enter the restaurant. Mama stops praying and draws in a deep breath. "Uh, oh. This is *not* going to be good."

Several other demons answer Pexov's call for support, and the unwelcome attention of the lone mortal is momentarily halted. Pexov hisses at her, and then calls the demonic powers and authorities over to the empty table. The demons slither past table after table, leaving a trail of stone cold fear in their wake.

Mama, keeping her eye on the empty table in the far corner where the demons are gathering, reaches under the counter for some protection. "Come on, where are you?" she mutters in frustration. Frantically, she stretches out her arm, pushes aside several menus, and reaches as far as she can under the counter without taking her eyes off the empty table. Her fingers touch the edge of something. Wiggling her fingers to gain a better grasp, she finally gains a firm hold of her most precious and powerful possession: her Bible. Pulling the Bible out from under the counter, she holds it to her chest. She glares at the empty table and whispers resolutely, "Okay, I've got my sword. Let the battle begin."

Bowing her head in prayer, Mama asks God to send some angels to protect her from the evil in this place and to show her what she is to do.

"Excuse me. Um...can I pay for this?" asks an impatient customer.

Mama looks up and sees a couple looking around the restaurant nervously. "Sure. How was everything?" Feeling anxiety rising, mama glances back at the empty table. The back of the restaurant is starting to clear out.

"The food was good, but... well," the man looks at his wife, and they exchange a worried glance, "we just need to go."

"I understand. Please come back, and may you go with God's blessings."

Several more customers come up to pay, and mama takes care of each one, sending them off with a special blessing.

Sarephah stands at the entrance of Mama's café waiting for Jane and Catherine to arrive. She longs to comfort mama, but there is no time. The gathering of demons has stirred the heavenlies. The surrounding atmosphere is filled with screeching, hissing, and flashes of lightning. Sarephah has already interceded for Mama, Jane, and Catherine; help is on the way. The most powerful angels have been dispatched by the Divine Three, but Sarephah must wait for their arrival. More critical at the moment is Catherine's protection. As the primary target, she is too vulnerable, and the demons are too powerful for her to fight alone.

In a flash of brilliant light, several powerful angels appear before Sarephah. They bow in recognition of each other. Sarephah smiles at her fellow warrior angels, and then raises her sword in the direction of the gathered demons. The demons hiss and screech in defiance of the group of powerful angels.

Sarephah grabs her sword with both hands, points the glowing tip toward the group of demons and a stream of power radiates from her sword. The crackling of power causes the lights of the restaurant to flicker. The surge of power crackles above the heads of the demons. The demons draw their weapons and prepare for battle.

Sarephah points in the direction of a corner as she directs each angel to their post. One by one, they draw their sword and move to the position indicated by Sarephah. With everything in place, Sarephah turns just in time to see Catherine and Jane pull into the parking lot.

Mama shuffles quickly into the kitchen when the lights flicker. She's glad the angels have arrived, but she's scared about what's going on her cafe. It feels like a mini Armageddon to her. "Papa, Papa, hurry, we need to pray. Something big is about to happen!" Mama cries out breathlessly.

Without turning away from the stove, papa flips a burger and yells over his shoulder, "What did you say Mama?"

Mama puts her hands on the counter behind Papa. She looks behind her for a second, then turns back toward Papa and whispers loudly, "I said we need to pray. That demon is back, but this time there are others too. And some angels have come as well. Something big is happening."

Papa stops midway through flipping the next burger. He slowly places the burger back on the grill and hangs up his spatula. "Charlie, come here and watch these," he yells in the direction of his assistant cook. "Mama and I have something to take care of. I'll be back in a few. Don't let these burgers burn." Charlie nods and grabs a spatula.

A bell sounds as the front door opens. The demons begin hissing and screeching wildly. The angels raise their swords and send streams of power at the demons. The demons crouch to dodge the streams and hiss defiantly. Mama and Papa pray earnestly in the back room.

Catherine walks into Mama's and looks for an empty table. Jane follows closely behind, but hesitates at the entrance. She furrows her brow as a sudden wave of anxiety hits her. Noticing that the restaurant is quieter than normal, she wonders where Mama is.

"Look, an empty booth. Wanna sit there?" Catherine asks.

Jane tries to shake off the uncomfortable feeling. "Yeah, okay." Turning and leaning to look into the kitchen, Jane tries to find Mama. "I wonder why Mama's not out here." Shrugging, Jane follows Catherine to the booth.

Catherine slides into the seat and grabs a menu from the holder on the table. Jane slides in slowly and shivers slightly. She senses that something is not quite right, but the source of her foreboding is difficult for her to define. Glancing back at the front counter, Jane absently grabs a menu.

"Hello, ladies." Jane jumps when she sees Mama. Grabbing Jane's cup, she pours some coffee. "Sorry I missed you when you came in. I was…um…busy in the kitchen. It's been an interesting morning, Jane: a morning where prayer is absolutely vital." Jane looks momentarily confused by Mama's comment.

Mama eyes moves nervously from the far corner of the restaurant to the top of the window at the table where Catherine and Jane are sitting. Looking first at Catherine, then at Jane she adds, "Yep, some days it's a real battle, just like the scriptures say in Ephesians chapter six."

Mama points with her eyes toward the top of the window again. "We need the full armor on days like today."

Jane follows the direction that Mama is looking and shivers again. She looks back at Mama, and with a tone that is more of a question than a statement, she says, "I agree. The battle can be fierce some days. We just came from a battle."

Mama looks at Jane with an intensity that sends a chill down Jane's spine. "There are many battles, and sometimes they occur in places you wouldn't expect. Always be on your guard."

Looking in Catherine's eyes, Mama suddenly realizes who the demon is tracking. She draws in a deep breath and lays her hand on Catherine's shoulder. "I'll be praying for you dear." Catherine looks at Mama, but the love and intensity of her gaze causes her to look away. Jane stares at Catherine and says a silent prayer for protection and wisdom.

"Thanks, Mama. I think I understand what you mean about battles raging all around us, even when we least expect it."

A look of understanding passes between Jane and Mama. "I will pray for both of you."

Catherine watches Mama walk back toward the front of the café. "What was *that* all about?" she asks impatiently. "What was all that crazy talk about battles and the…what did she say?...the Parisians?"

Jane chuckles. "Ephesians. She said Ephesians. That's a book in the Bible. Mama's a real spiritual warrior. She sees things spiritually that the rest of us only get glimpses of most of the time."

Catherine shrugs. "Well, that was weird and kinda spooky if you ask me." Catherine raises the menu, avoiding any more conversation on the matter, and tries to decide what to order.

Jane glances up at the top of the window one more time. She doesn't see anything, but she feels something dark and evil. What surprises her is that she also feels something equally good and pure.

Shaking her head, she raises her menu, but peeks at Catherine over the top of her menu. Jane's not at all surprised that an innocent lunch is turning out to be quite the spiritual adventure, because Catherine, whether she knows it or not, is seeking answers about God, and someone or something doesn't want that to happen.

• • •

Sarephah stands at the table protecting Catherine and comforting Jane with a power gained from the prayers of the saints. Pexov spews venomous taunts at Sarephah, trying to break the protective aura surrounding Catherine. However, since Catherine is here by her own freewill, Pexov's power is restrained. Prayer and the willingness of Catherine are more than he can handle.

Dripping with sarcasm, Pexov snarls, "Sarephah, I find your presence here quite disturbing." Waving his hand toward the angels in the corners, he adds, "And why did you feel the need to call in reinforcements? Are you that concerned for this pitiful mortal and your ability to protect her?"

As Pexov moves closer to the table, the other demons begin hissing their encouragement. "Or are you just now realizing *your* lack of influence on this little project? I'm surprised you're just now figuring that out. Your incompetence is astounding. I've known for a long time that you couldn't handle this assignment."

Sarephah raises her sword, and Pexov scampers back a safe distance. Screeching, the other demons crouch low when Pexov retreats. The angels in each corner stand firm, unfazed by the obnoxious display by the demons.

Sarephah looks at Catherine. "I stand in the presence of the Divine Three as a manifestation of their love for Catherine. In fact, all these angels are in service of the Divine Three."

Sarephah observes Pexov crouching low in front of his band of demons. "You have grown weak Pexov. Catherine is opening her mind to God. She is willing to listen; she is willing to ask questions; she is searching. I am here to make sure she gets the answers she seeks. And why exactly are you here?"

"I am here for the same reason. My master, the Ruler of the Kingdom of the Air, also wants this mortal to have all the answers, especially since there are so many valid answers. We want to give her as many options as possible. Unlike you, I am not limiting her options. She is free to believe whatever she wants."

"I think you really believe your own lies." Sarephah moves behind Catherine. "You talk about many valid answers, but the Divine Three are more concerned with questions. In fact, they have only one question to ask all of their children, and there is only one valid answer to this question."

The angels flash their swords. Pexov stands as tall as he dares. His fellow demons hiss. The lights flicker in the restaurant. Jane wraps her arms around herself and shivers. Mama continues praying and reading the Bible.

Catherine shifts uncomfortably in her seat. The atmosphere in the restaurant feels oppressive. An overwhelming sense of impending doom causes her to draw in a deep breath. Her mind is saturated with confusing and conflicting thoughts about drinking, sobriety, a higher power, God, good, and evil. Yet, above all the raging emotions and confusion, comes one steady voice. In her very soul, Catherine hears one question, "Who do you say that I am?"

Chapter Thirty-One

Jane can barely focus on the menu in the midst of her struggles with whatever forces are invading her personal space and disrupting her serenity. She glances at Catherine over the top of her menu and wonders what God has in store for this one. Reflecting back on her own spiritual journey, she remembers the questions, the discoveries, and the experience of release from the things that kept her captive. Her search to understand God using the framework of a higher power in the steps of A.A. provided just what she needed to seek and find God without condemnation or criticism. As others helped her on this journey, her prayer is that she can help Catherine successfully navigate the sometimes treacherous waters of spiritual discovery. Jane knows Catherine's life depends on it.

After ordering their lunch, Catherine sits anxiously awaiting the inevitable conversation about God. Something is stirring in her heart to know more about the God that Jane knows, but the battle in her mind still rages over all the new possibilities of a power greater than herself. And the idea that she can make that higher power anything she wants is appealing.

Before addressing Catherine, Jane silently prays for the courage to battle the unseen forces conspiring against Catherine and for the blessings of God on their conversation.

"I'm glad you have questions and even doubts about God, Catherine. It's a great place to start. Never be afraid to be honest with your feelings about God. Some of my best revelations came to me during my doubts and honest struggles about and with God." Jane smiles slightly, "I was a lot like you when I got sober; I was very confused about God and even a little bit angry about the whole topic. It took some time for me to open up to the possibilities of God." Catherine looks down at the table, feeling awkward at the openness of Jane.

Jane's eyes brighten and her smile widens. "The best thing that ever happened to me after coming to A.A. was the absolute freedom to search out a God of my understanding. I was broken and beaten up by the life I was leading. After my head cleared, I had a longing to get better and have some peace in my life. I was told that peace would come when I surrendered and accepted help: not just human help, but Divine help."

Jane looks closely at Catherine. "You can have that same peace, Catherine. It's your choice whether or not you will continue to wallow in the insanity of alcoholism or accept spiritual help."

Catherine crosses her arms in defiance. "I'm sober now, so how can you say that I am wallowing in the insanity of alcoholism. I already made a choice to stop drinking. I haven't had a drink in almost two months."

"Alcohol is a symptom. Just because you're not drinking right now doesn't mean you've dealt with the real issues in your life. You just eliminated one of the main symptoms without actually treating the disease of alcoholism. The other symptoms include selfishness, self-centeredness, and many other character defects that plague people like us. What you need for lasting peace and serenity is to turn your will and your life over to the care of God. He is the solution to your problem."

Catherine doesn't react, so Jane continues. "The disease of alcoholism is a three-fold disease." Using her fingers to count, she says. "One, it's a physical problem; two, it's a mental obsession; and three, it's a spiritual sickness. You can't just treat one aspect of the disease. Right now, you are basically only treating the physical part of the disease by not drinking."

Pausing for a moment, she puts both elbows on the table, clasps her hands together, and leans forward for emphasis. "I really believe that in order to have a balanced life you need to address the physical, emotional, and spiritual aspects of your life. You have been willing to look at the physical aspects of your life like your excessive drinking. You have even opened up to the emotional aspects by attending counseling, A.A. meetings, and working with me. Are you willing to at least open yourself to the spiritual aspects of life? More importantly, are you willing to open yourself up to the possibility of God in your life?"

• • •

The noise is deafening in the unseen realm just above Catherine and Jane. The demons hiss and snarl at the mention of God. Pexov roars in anger and reaches out for Catherine, but Sarephah pushes him back with a power surge from her sword. The angels in each corner raise their weapons and direct them at the demonic assembly.

Suddenly, a strong wind rushes in from the upper realm of the heavenlies. In seconds, the atmosphere inhabited by the angels and demons is entirely illuminated by flames growing stronger within a tunnel of wind. As the force of the wind increases, the demons struggle to maintain their position over Catherine and Jane.

The wind and fire tunnel travels throughout the room and over the heads of the screeching demons before taking shape next to Catherine and Jane's table. First, the wind and flames rush together, forming a swirling fireball. Then, in an explosion of light, the ball expands and rises over ten feet tall. A single flame is left dancing in the middle of the spiritual tornado formed like a human body. Although the outer part of the form is swirling with incredible force, the flame in the center is strong and steady, barely flickering.

Pexov eyes grow wide in horror as he realizes what has just formed in front on his eyes. Paralyzed for an instant, he stares at the light. The light pulsates twice and then flashes brightly. Pexov raises his arms and closes his eyes as he whirls away from the bright flash in an attempt to protect himself. Screeching in agony, he quickly retreats back into the depth of the heavenlies.

Trembling in utter terror, all the demons begin pushing and shoving each other, trying to get as far away from the presence of the One in Three who can destroy them.

The angels in each corner lower their swords and kneel before their Master. Sarephah, backs away from the form, kneels and bows. Rising again, she is greeted by the one who is now the most visible form of the Divine Three, the Text. "Greetings, Sarephah. I see you are taking good care of our precious ones."

Looking at Jane, the Text announces loudly, "We have heard her prayers. As the Text, I come to bring truth and peace into her continuing story of redemption."

Looking at Catherine, the Text proclaims triumphantly, "For the one who has yet to fully understand, I come to draw her near by the truth and through the story of the one Word given up for her." Whispering in Catherine's ear, the Text adds, "Do not fear the story you do not yet know or understand. Come to the Author of your life and the Word spoken for you so that a new story can be written."

The Text curls back into a ball of fire and wind. Hovering for a moment, light radiates from the Text to surround Catherine and Jane. The ball moves swiftly toward the front of the restaurant and hovers over Mama. The ball dances back and forth in front of Mama, and then a bright light from the center of the ball shines down on her. Mama inhales deeply, drinking in the love of her creator. Then, the Text grows into a tunnel of swirling wind and streams of light and passes under the doors of Mama's Café. The bell sounds as the wind and fire pass under the door.

Catherine looks over toward the door when she hears the bell. No one enters or leaves, but the bell is swinging slightly. She looks back at Jane, who seemingly didn't even hear the bell. Time appears to stand still in this moment of decision. The voices in her head have suddenly quieted. She relaxes her shoulders as a peace washes over her. Curiosity stirs within her as she is irresistibly drawn to know about the God of Jane. With surprising tenacity, she begins to open the door to a faith she abandoned as a child.

"I remember learning some things about God when I was growing up." Looking down at the table, "But I have to admit, none of it really mattered to me at the time. Plus, I was too busy drinking and skipping out of the Sunday school classes to understand God."

Catherine raises her head to look at Jane. A memory stirs of a time when she once longed to know more about God. "I had questions about God when I was a kid. I even remember asking a couple questions, but no one seemed to have the answers." Shrugging, she adds, "Or maybe I just didn't understand the answers."

Her eyes darken slightly, "Then, I started drinking and became resentful about anything connected with religion. Eventually, when I was thirteen, I just walked away from church and God."

Catherine sits back in her seat and sighs heavily. "Now, well…I just don't know what I believe about God. I keep hearing all this talk about a higher power, and how the only way to get sober and have peace in my life is to accept spiritual help." Jane sits quietly, waiting for Catherine to continue.

Catherine tilts her head back, looks up at the ceiling, and sighs again. The struggle in the silence is visible on Catherine's face. Jane wisely remains just as silent in her own struggle to pull Catherine toward God. Lowering her head, Catherine closes her eyes for a moment, then opens them and looks at Jane. Jane's eyes are bright with anticipation and radiate an unspoken encouragement to Catherine. Finally, Catherine whispers, "I just never understood God growing up. I don't understand him now, but," she pauses, clears her throat, and nods her head, "I would like to know more about this God of yours."

Jane claps her hands together and lets out a loud sigh to release all the tension she felt waiting for Catherine's decision. "Amen! I know this decision was not easy for you. I'm proud of you for your willingness to seek after God. Not everyone who gets sober desires to know God."

Sitting back in her seat, Jane smiles, "Well, then let's get started. First, one of the best ways to find out more about God is to hang out with people who have a relationship with him. So, how about joining me at Church some Sunday?"

Catherine's eyes grow wide.

Jane laughs, "Ah, come on. Sounds like the last time you were in a church was when you were thirteen. Trust me, you'll like my church, and I guarantee you'll get more out of it now than you did when you were a kid."

Catherine smiles slightly. "Okay, I'll try it. I think I have a Sunday off in a couple weeks." Scrunching her nose, she asks, "Do have to wear a dress or anything?"

"I don't think God cares what you wear just as long as you show up."

Relieved, Catherine nods her head. "Good, 'cause I don't have any fancy church type dresses."

"Next, I also want to you to pay attention when you hear someone in a meeting talking about God. Listen to what they say, and how they talk about God. Do they name their Higher Power? If so, how do they describe him? Go up and ask them questions about God, and how they came to believe in God. I'm not saying you have to agree with them, but it will beneficial for you to start talking about God."

Catherine sits up and interrupts Jane. “Okay, can I ask you what you believe about God?”

Jane smiles and slowly nods her head, “Sure, I never thought you would ask.”

Reaching for the cross she wears around her neck, she picks it up and fingers it. “Here it is in a nutshell. The God of my understanding is the Christian God I read about in the Bible. I believe that I was created in the image of God, but that through sin, which manifested primarily, but not exclusively under the umbrella of alcoholism, the goodness in me all but disappeared in the wake of the lifestyle I chose to live apart from God. Consequently, the relationship with my creator was damaged. In fact, through this sin or alcoholism, the gap between my creator and I grew to the point where I was incapable *in my own power* to repair that relationship. God then sent his son, Jesus, to repair that relationship. Once I accepted Jesus’ repair work,” Jane uses her first two fingers on both hands to signify a quote for repair work, “God reestablished our relationship and showed me a new way of life through the power and work of the Holy Spirit.”

Catherine looks at Jane with that “deer in the headlights” look.

Jane drops her cross back onto her chest and smiles at Catherine. “I know you probably don’t understand all of that, and I don’t expect you to. What I just told you took time to understand and fully accept. I asked a lot of questions, went to church, read the Bible, and opened my heart to God and…well, God will show you the way.”

“How will he show me the way?”

“Well, one way is through prayer. Prayer is how we communicate with God. It can be as simple as saying ‘please help me today’ at the start of the day and ‘thank you’ at the end of the day. Or it can be more formal like saying the Lord’s Prayer at the end of the meetings. I’d like you to start praying both ways: formally and informally. In your formal prayers, start saying the third step prayer and in your informal prayers just start talking with God."

Catherine tilts her head thinking about these two types of prayer. "I don't know the third step prayer."

"It's in the Big Book on page sixty-three. When you get home write it down and use it as your formal prayer each day. I was told to say it every morning and every night whether I believed it or not. The point is to start establishing a pattern of communication with God."

Catherine nods in understanding.

"If you really want to know God just ask him. I remember at one point in my search just asking God who he was, and he answered me. He used his word, other people, my dreams, and the people I met in church and in meetings."

"What do you mean that he used his word. What word?" Catherine asks.

"Oh, sorry 'bout that. Let's see…um…how can I explain it? The Word, written with a capital letter W, is symbolic for Jesus. In the Gospel of John, Jesus is described as the Word. But, when I said that he uses his word, small letter w, I meant the Bible. So I guess if you want to know about the God I know, you need to know Jesus, and you can do that by reading the Bible."

Catherine's eyebrows narrow in consternation. "I don't have a Bible, and I wouldn't even know where to start if I did have one." Sitting back in her seat, she sighs, "I don't know if I can do all this. Seems like a lot of work."

"It is a lot of work, but it's worth it. You'll see." Jane senses Catherine's wall of resistance building. "Okay, here's what I want you to do. Start saying the third step prayer every morning and every night. Start listening and asking questions when you hear people talk about God. That's enough for now. Think you can do that much?"

Catherine relaxes again. "Yeah, that doesn't seem so bad."

Jane looks at her watch. "Listen, I've got to get going." Picking up the bill, Jane says, "My treat."

Catherine smiles, "Thanks."

"Catherine, I will be praying for you. Remember, God is not far from you, and he longs for a relationship with you. I'm excited to see what God has in store for you." With that, Jane rises from her seat and heads toward the cash register.

Catherine sits a second longer. *How can this God want a relationship with me? I don't even know who he is. I bet if he really knew me, he wouldn't want anything to do with me. Yet, I guess it couldn't hurt to find out more about this God that Jane knows.*

As Catherine rises from her seat one more thought invades her consciousness. *But I better not limit myself to just one idea of God. There are so many other options. I'll ask Courtney about some of the other options for God. She seems like she knows a lot about this sort of stuff.*

Pexov smiles at Sarephah before disappearing back into the dark realm of evil.

Chapter Thirty-Two

Catherine hears the phone ringing as she walks into her apartment. Slamming the door behind her, she races down the hallway. She throws her purse on the couch, pushes away several magazines covering the phone, and then snatches it off the table.

"Hello?"

"Catherine?"

"Hi, mom." Catherine swirls around and plops down on the couch. Taking a deep breath, she asks, "What's up?"

"You sound like you're out of breath. Everything okay?" Nancy asks tentatively.

Ever since Catherine finally admitted to her parents that she's attending A.A. meetings, conversations with her parents have been a little less strained, especially those with her mom. They both respect each other's space. Nancy's learning to let Catherine go through her struggles without constantly fishing for details. Catherine's learning to open up to her mom, even with the walls she's built around herself.

"I ran down the hall trying to get the phone before it stopped ringing. Jane just dropped me off. We went on a twelve step call." Catherine adds with some pride in her voice.

"You did! Wow, I'm impressed. How'd it go?" Nancy asks.

"Okay I guess. I was really surprised who it was. I've seen her in meetings, but I never thought *she* would relapse. You know the…"

Nancy quickly interjects, "Don't tell me who it is. That's not yours to share. Whoever it is will share it at a meeting if she's serious about staying sober."

Catherine nods, "Okay. I won't tell you, but I sure was surprised. She's angry at God. She thinks he didn't answer her prayers. But Jane pointed out that…umm…this nameless person drank because she wasn't doing the things she needed in order to stay sober."

"Jane is a wise woman. I'm glad you asked her to be your sponsor." Nancy pauses, "I've been thinking about you all morning. I just couldn't shake the feeling that something was up. Did anything else happen?"

"Well, Jane and I went to Mama's Café after meeting with that lady and had lunch. You'll be happy to know that we talked about God." Catherine adds more forcefully to keep her mom from starting to preach, "I'm not totally convinced about all the God stuff, but I told Jane I was willing to open myself to the *possibility* of God in my life. Just don't start in on me too."

Nancy pumps her fist in triumph, but reigns in her emotions so Catherine doesn't go ballistic on her. "That's great honey. The spiritual part of the program is important, and I'm glad you're willing to open yourself to God in whatever way you can."

Nancy won't tell Catherine, but this morning she felt strongly that Catherine would be in the midst of a battle today: a spiritual battle. Now Nancy knows how true those feelings were. Relief washes over her as she realizes the importance of her prayer time this morning. She's so grateful she took the extra time to pray and intercede for her daughter.

Catherine's voice interrupts her moment of gratitude. "Hey, have you heard of the third step prayer?"

"Yes, it's a great prayer. Why?"

"Well, Jane wants me to say it every morning and every night. I don't know how long I'm supposed to do it, but I just wondered if you ever heard of it."

"I used to say that prayer every day. Now, I just talk to God from my heart." She adds quickly, "Not that formal prayers aren't good. Actually, saying a written prayer is a good way to start praying. Any prayer is good. God loves it when we pray." Nancy puts her hand to her head, exasperated that she's rambling about prayer. She doesn't want to scare off Catherine.

"Yeah, I guess." Catherine sighs heavily. "Anyway, I'm gonna go find that prayer, and then I'm taking a nap. I'm tired. I got up way too early." Catherine yawns loudly, emphasizing her point.

"Are you going to a meeting tonight?" Nancy wonders.

"Yes, Courtney's picking me up at 7:00."

Nancy cringes when she hears Courtney's name. "Honey, I don't mean to interfere."

"But you're going to anyway," Catherine rolls her eyes and shakes her head.

"Well, it's just that I don't think Courtney is a good influence."

Catherine snaps back. "I like Courtney. She's been a good friend, and I like hanging out with her. Listen, Mom, I gotta go. Thanks for calling." The frustration is evident in Catherine's voice.

Nancy closes her eyes. "Okay. Hey, I love you."

Catherine breathes in deeply. "I know. See ya later."

"Bye Cath."

"Bye Mom."

Catherine throws the phone down on the couch next to her. "Ugh. Why doesn't she just mind her own business? She drives me crazy sometimes."

With a flash, the thought of downing a couple cold beers enters her mind. She freezes. Running her fingers through her hair, she closes her eyes trying to shut out the thoughts. *No. I can't have anything. Just one? No!* Her breathing accelerates. *No! No! No!* She holds her head in both hands and rocks back and forth on the couch.

Sarephah touches Catherine's shoulder. An aura surrounds Catherine. Pexov jumps back from where he had been hovering near his target. He is repelled by the strong aura, and knows he can't get anywhere near Catherine now that Sarephah's interceded. He moves slowly into the corner and crouches, but then sees that mortal's blasted creature. In an instant, he's gone.

After rounding the corner, Pip hesitates for an instant, looks around, and then saunters into the room. He moves deliberately toward the distraught Catherine. Stopping next to Catherine, he tilts his head as if assessing his master's behavior. Moving swiftly, he jumps onto the table and knocks over several books and magazines.

When a book strikes her leg before hitting the floor, Catherine gasps, "Ouch," and then grabs her shin.

Pip jumps from the table onto Catherine's lap, does a couple quick turnarounds, and then leaps back onto the floor before scurrying back into the bedroom.

Catherine sits momentarily stunned by the flurry of activity committed by her sometimes erratic cat. "Pip, what is up with you?"

She reaches down to pick up the book Pip knocked into her leg. She stops, pulls back her hand, and stares at the fallen book. To her surprise, she notices that the book Pip knocked over is her Big Book, and it's now lying open to page sixty-three.

"Hmm. That's weird."

Shrugging her shoulders, she reaches back down and picks up the book. She scans the page and finds the prayer she's been asked to recite twice daily. Reading out loud, she says: "God, I offer myself to thee – to build with me and to do with me as Thou wilt. Relieve me of the bondage of self, that I may better do Thy will. Take away my difficulties, that victory over them may bear witness to those I would help of Thy Power, Thy Love, and Thy Way of life. May I do Thy will always!"

"Hmph, so that's the third step prayer. Sounds so old fashioned. Wow, who says Thy wilt anymore? I'm not really sure what good it's going to do to say this prayer twice a day, but whatever, I'll try it."

She closes the book and lays it back on the table. Puffing out her cheeks, she slowly releases the air out of her mouth and mutters to herself, "Sometimes this A.A. stuff is just plain strange."

Stretching and yawning, Catherine lies down on the couch and settles in for a nap. The day has been exhausting, and Courtney is supposed to arrive in a couple hours. Before sleep overtakes her, she opens her eyes and remembers the other type of prayer: simply talking to God.

Sitting up, 'cause she doesn't think it's proper to pray laying down, Catherine wonders if she has to get on her knees to make her prayer official. Shaking her head, she decides that kneeling is not necessary or Jane would have said to kneel. But, she makes a mental note to ask someone about kneeling to pray in order for the prayer to be official.

Coughing to clear her throat, she closes her eyes and clasps her hands together in the most prayerful manner she can muster. "God? Umm, hello. I really don't know what to say. It's been a long time, and I'm kinda new at this. Sorry for that. Umm…well, anyway, thank you for today." She sits and thinks for a minute. "Oh, yeah, and help Valerie. She really wants you to answer her prayers. Amen."

She slowly opens her eyes and looks around the room. Nothing extraordinary happens, and she wonders if God even heard her. She sighs and shrugs, "Okay, well I prayed." Laying back down, a smile forms when she realizes the crazy thoughts about drinking are gone. She sleeps.

• • •

The aroma that rises through the heavenlies into the presence of the Divine Three is so exquisite everyone in Nede stops for an instant and breathes in the rich fragrance of the prayer of a lost soul. The Divine Three smile as the billows of smoke circle around their feet. Crouching down to lift the wafts of smoke to their nose, they laugh and dance for the one who has prayed to them from her heart. Sarephah dances around the throne in jubilation; the surge of energy she feels is almost intoxicating.

There's nothing so powerful in the realms of the heavenlies as prayer. Sarephah watches excitedly as power is released from the throne. She bows to the Divine Three, raises her sword, and returns to Catherine.

• • •

Pexov jumps to avoid the flaming ball of fire thrown at him by Satan. The second ball of fire sails close to his head and singes his ear. He screams in agony, grabs his ear, and falls to the ground. Curled into a fetal position, Pexov rocks back and forth and moans pitifully. "It's not my fault. Give me more time. Don't banish me."

"ENOUGH!" Satan roars. Torches hanging from the walls in this den of demons provide little light. The walls and floor are wet with the tears of the forgotten. Pexov stops rocking and cries silently, listening to the heavy breathing of the demons confined to this den as punishment for their failure.

"I heard a prayer, Pexov. It was a prayer from one of YOURS!"

Pexov shakes uncontrollably, but manages to squeak out, "It was nothing. She doesn't know what she's doing or who she's praying to." Bolstered by Satan's silence, Pexov rolls over, gets on his hands and knees and begins a slow crawl. "Give me more time, please. I need just a little more time." He stops at Satan's feet and bows so his head is only inches from the floor.

Satan listens to the rejoicing in the heavenlies above him, squeezes his hand into a tight fist and trembles with unimaginable hatred. Clenching his jaw, he closes his eyes and whispers, "If this one whom you have been assigned does not become one of mine, you will regret the day you were ever created. My patience is wearing thin, and I will not give you another chance. Go and take what is rightfully mine."

Squatting down, Satan lifts Pexov's chin and stares into his eyes. Pexov shivers. "Your days are numbered Pexov. I have many who can replace you. DO NOT FAIL ME."

• • •

Her breathing and the ticking clock produce a rhythm of sounds in the room. Footsteps break the rhythm, growing louder and louder. A shadow falls across the face of a sleeping Catherine; she stirs slightly. The shadow moves. A hand reaches out and touches her shoulder.

Catherine's eyes fly open; she jerks awake. Someone is standing over her. Sleepy confusion clouds her thoughts for a moment. Her eyes widen. Breathlessly, Catherine sputters, "What are you doing? How did you get in here?"

Chapter Thirty-Three

Raising her hands in defense and backing away, Courtney says with amusement, “Whoa. Chill out.”

Catherine struggles to push herself into a sitting position on the couch. Rubbing her eyes, she says angrily, “You scared me half to death.”

Catherine runs her fingers through her hair and studies Courtney as she moves to the other end of the couch.

Courtney jumps on the couch and laughs. “You were really out of it girl.”

Turning to face Courtney, Catherine cocks her head and asks suspiciously, “How did you get in here anyway?”

Courtney dangles a key in front on her face and smiles. “Spare key.”

Catherine grimaces when she remembers showing Courtney where to find her spare key. She’s instantly irritated that Courtney would use the key to enter her place. “Why didn’t you just knock? You knew I was home. My car’s in the carport for crying out loud.”

Courtney smiles and shrugs. “I thought it would be fun to surprise you.”

Catherine grabs the key out of Courtney’s hand. “I’ll take that back now.”

She stares at Courtney for a second, gets up abruptly, and stomps into the kitchen. Courtney shrugs again and crosses her arms. After stuffing the key in a drawer, Catherine hesitates as a wave of uneasiness washes over her. A shiver runs up her spine. Something's not right, but she can't figure out what it is. She closes her eyes and takes in a deep breath, trying to shake off the creepy feeling she's getting. *Get a grip Catherine.*

"So are you going to be angry with me all night?" Courtney yells toward the kitchen.

After shutting the kitchen drawer, Catherine walks back to the couch and sits down heavily. Courtney uses her best apologetic look, and Catherine smiles slightly.

"Yes, I am gonna be mad at you the rest of the night."

"Come on…I was just having some fun."

"It wasn't fun for me. Don't ever do that again. Okay?"

Courtney shrugs and rolls her eyes, "Okaaaay."

The Big Book on the table catches Courtney's eye and she picks it up. Flipping through the pages aimlessly, she asks quietly, "How did the twelve step call go?"

"I don't know. It was good, I guess. She was really struggling, but Jane convinced her to go to a meeting tonight."

Courtney closes the Big Book and lays it in her lap. "So who was it? I heard rumors that Claudia, the lady from the Saturday Night meeting, relapsed. Was it her?"

"Sorry, it's not mine to tell." Catherine crosses her arms.

"Whatever." Courtney picks up the Big Book again and starts flipping through the pages.

Catherine watches Courtney playing with her Big Book for a second. Sitting up and crossing her legs, Catherine asks, "Do you ever pray the prayer on page sixty-three?" She continues when Courtney doesn't react. "It's the third step prayer. Jane wants me to say it every morning and every night."

Courtney puts the book down on the couch between herself and Catherine. "Yeah, I've prayed that prayer. It's okay. But, I like doing my own thing more than saying some old fashioned, stuffy prayer."

"Really? What kind of prayers do you say?"

Courtney shrugs her shoulders. With little enthusiasm, she says, "I don't know what kind of prayers they are. I just kinda talk to my Higher Power. Like a conversation or something."

Catherine nods her head in thought. "Hmm…Do you pray a lot?"

"Yeah. At least once or twice a day."

"How do you pray? I mean do you get on your knees?"

"You can pray anyway or anywhere you want. My Higher Power doesn't care. I've also tried chanting, meditation, and other stuff." A dark look crosses her eyes. "One time I even tried talking to the dead during a séance. We were doing this thing called 'Spirit Calling' or something like that. Now that was spooky."

She hesitates slightly. Then looking directly at Catherine, she says, "I think something…entered…umm….well, it was just really scary. I never did that again."

Catherine eyes widen. "Wow. What happened? What do you mean by something entered? Entered what?"

Courtney turns and stares into the distance. Gradually her body tenses and her eyes fill with fear. Looking down at her hands, she shakes her head vigorously. "I don't want to talk about it."

After a moment of silence Courtney relaxes slightly. She looks at Catherine. "I just can't talk about it." With a little more confidence in her voice, she adds, "I know my Higher Power will protect me. I pray to my Higher Power for protection."

"Why do you need protection?" Catherine is confused because nothing Courtney's saying is making any sense.

With shaking hands, Courtney pushes her hair out of her eyes. Looking almost through Catherine, she adds quietly, "Everybody needs protection."

Catherine and Courtney lock eyes. Catherine involuntarily sits back when she gets a long look into Courtney's eyes. They are cold and dark. Fear is evident, but so is anger and hatred. Catherine feels an uneasiness that frightens her. She wants to pull back. Yet, a long, awkward silence holds her captive.

Then, for one brief instant, Courtney looks as if she wants to open up to Catherine. Her eyes fill with tears and she opens her mouth to speak. But she doesn't say anything. Putting her hands on her head, she shakes it slowly back and forth. "No. No. No." She stops abruptly, draws in deep breath, and exhales slowly. After wiping away a stray tear, she sniffles and laughs slightly, "How did we ever get on this topic?"

Catherine smiles weakly. "I was asking about prayer."

The sound of the ticking clock pulls Catherine out of the strange moment with Courtney. Glancing at the clock, Catherine sighs with relief.

"It's getting late. We better get going." Refocusing back on Courtney, Catherine asks softly, "Are you gonna be okay?"

Courtney runs her hands through her hair a couple times and then rubs her eyes. Exhaling, she nods and whispers, "Yeah. I'll be okay." With a smile that doesn't match her demeanor, Courtney stands and mumbles, "Let's go."

During the ride to the meeting Catherine can't shake her uneasy feeling. The mood in the car is somber: Courtney focuses on the road, and Catherine stares out the passenger window. The silence is suffocating. It's not a silence brought on by the easy comfort between friends; it's a silence forced by a power neither understands.

• • •

As the doors open, the laughter and low rumble of multiple conversations rushes toward Catherine. An overwhelming relief washes over her as she steps inside the meeting room. She sees Valerie almost immediately, grins at her and raises her hand in a slight wave. Valerie winks at her and somehow Catherine knows Valerie's going to be all right. She also sees Jane, Hannah, and the new girl, Shelly. Jane waves for Catherine to join them. Catherine turns and sees Courtney talking with someone she doesn't recognize. Figuring Courtney will find her before the meeting starts, she heads over to meet up with Valerie, Jane, Hannah, and Shelly.

After the meeting, Catherine talks with Jane for a minute before saying their goodbyes. As Catherine looks around for Courtney, Valerie walks up and gives Catherine a warm hug.

"Thank you again, dear. You'll never know how much your visit this morning helped me." Leaning in closer, she says, "I've asked Hannah to be my sponsor, and I am ready to get back on track." Drawing in a deep breath of courage, she smiles, "I'm starting back on step one. And I'm starting over with God." Catherine smiles as Valerie walks away.

"Hey, Catherine, how ya doing?"

Turning around, Catherine's smile widens. "Hi, Kaleb. I'm good. How are you?"

"I'm great!"

Catherine is distracted when she spots Courtney talking with a new guy, Jake. Kaleb turns to see Jake put his arm around Courtney's shoulder and whisper something in her ear. He looks back at Catherine.

"That's an interesting couple."

"Interesting is not the word I would use." Crossing her arms and turning back toward Kaleb, she sighs, "I can't keep up with Courtney. Her moods change from minute to minute."

"Yeah, that happens in early sobriety. How are you doing, really," Kaleb asks with an intensity that encourages Catherine to answer with more than a causal response.

Glancing back at Courtney, Catherine shakes her head. She turns back to Kaleb. "Courtney and I were having a conversation about prayer, and she kinda freaked out on me. I have questions about God and prayer, and what it all means for me and for my sobriety. She wasn't very helpful. As a matter of fact, she was pretty vague and less than enthusiastic about the whole topic until she got all weird."

Crossing her arms, she smiles at Kaleb. "What about you Mr. Bible guy. What are your thoughts on prayer? Do you say the third step prayer or some other prayer? Do you get on your knees when you pray? Does God hear everyone's prayer? And what about ..."

Kaleb holds up his hands. "Hold on there, Miss Inquisitive." With an easy smile, he says, "One question at a time. I have lots of thoughts on prayer."

Courtney bounces up to Catherine and interrupts Kaleb. Grabbing Catherine's arm, she says breathlessly, "Catherine! Come here. I need to talk to you." Dragging Catherine away, Courtney yells over her shoulder, "Sorry Kaleb. I just need a minute." Kaleb shakes his head.

"What is so urgent?" Catherine asks with some irritation.

"Listen," She looks back over her shoulder and waves at Jake. "Umm…can you find a ride home from the meeting tonight? I'm…ummm…well…Jake wants to take me out for coffee and talk."

Catherine looks at Jake and then back at Courtney. "Talk? Right. Well, you're a big girl." She looks back at Kaleb. He smiles. "I'll see if Kaleb can drive me home."

Courtney gives Catherine a hug that lasts just a little too long. "You're the best. I'll call you later."

Catherine shivers from an uneasy feeling that assaults her. She wraps her arms around her body and walks back to Kaleb. "Can you drive me home?"

"Yeah. Sure." Smiling, he adds excitedly, "That'll give us more time to talk about God and prayer."

"Let's not go overboard with all this God talk. I just want to know a little more about prayer that's all."

"Okay. No problem. Come on, let's go." Bowing toward the door, Kaleb announces in a teasing tone, "Your chariot awaits."

Catherine rolls her eyes and laughs.

• • •

Sarephah follows Catherine and Kaleb all the way back to Catherine's apartment. Pexov is nowhere to be found, and Sarephah worries slightly that he hasn't made an appearance. She wonders why he was with another mortal earlier in the evening. Demons such as Pexov are usually assigned to torment and destroy one mortal at a time, so this change in tactic is concerning.

Regardless of Pexov's new strategy, Sarephah is pleased that Catherine's moving in the right direction. The choices she's making are starting to reshape her nature. Her will, freed by the Author, is being drawn toward the Word by The Text. Working together, she knows They each want to begin a new story for Catherine, but her new story can only begin when she rejects the old and accepts the new.

And Sarephah knows that Pexov will do everything he can to make sure the ending of Catherine's current story is written before the beginning of her new story can ever take place.

Chapter Thirty-Four

Catherine closes her Big Book and sits back in her chair. Stroking Pip, she smiles at his soft purring and lets the serenity of the moment embrace her. She's been reading the third step prayer faithfully every morning and every night. Although it's become a ritual of sorts, she finds it strangely comforting. But rarely does she stray from this formal prayer and simply have a prayerful conversation with God. In fact, she's still not sure what she believes about God. Praying to something or someone she's not quite sure about feels silly. And she concludes, somewhat pointless. No, prayer is not the highlight of her day. It's just something she's doing because she was told to do it.

Yet, in spite of her less than enthusiastic attitude about prayer, her willingness to know more about God has grown over the past month. To her surprise, she finds herself listening more intently to discussions about God in meetings. Several times after a meeting she's even been bold enough to ask someone to explain their beliefs in more detail. This has not always produced the results she anticipated; it sometimes just led to more questions. However, there have been several times when these discussions about God have touched her deeply. She remembers one in particular.

After one of her favorite meetings, Catherine tentatively approaches Paul because he made a memorable comment about God. Even though her initial encounter with Paul at her second meeting was uncomfortable, she's come to respect his wisdom and to accept his gruff personality. He acts like a crusty old curmudgeon, but she thinks he's really a softy at heart. What she enjoys most is his earthy spirituality. God is not just a concept to Paul: He's a tangible reality in his life.

Paul's holding court with all the guys he's working with, so Catherine waits patiently. Finally, after several minutes, Paul notices Catherine and wraps up his conversation by telling his guys to go help clean up the meeting room. Catherine exchanges hellos with everyone as they leave. Kaleb gives her a supportive smile. They've been talking about the steps, prayer, and God for several weeks now, but he's also repeatedly encouraged her to talk with Jane and with Paul.

"Hello young lady. What do I owe the pleasure of your company?" he says with a broad smile.

"Well, I heard your comments about God during the meeting, and I have a question for you," she says while crossing her arms.

Chuckling, Paul leans back in his chair. "Okay. Shoot."

"Who is your God?"

Paul raises his eyebrows and smiles. "Good question. Not what I was expecting, but a good question."

He grabs a chair and positions it in front on him. Gesturing toward the chair, he says, "Here, sit down. Let's talk"

Catherine moves around the chair and sits down.

"The reason I asked is because you talk so much about a loving God, but I don't know how you can talk about a loving God when there's so much suffering and evil in the world." Looking down at her hands, she adds, "And so many people struggling with staying sober and trying to get their life together. I mean who is this loving God of yours?"

Paul nods his head slowly. "Yes, there are a lot of people struggling to get and stay sober." Paul smiles compassionately at Catherine. "And even when you get sober, life isn't easy, especially when the only thing you know about living is to do it with a drink in your hand and with a wall so big that nobody can get in – not even a *loving* God."

Catherine looks up at Paul and wonders how he knows her so well. It takes all her willpower to hold back the tears that threaten to well up in her eyes. Catherine hasn't cried in front of anyone in a long time, and she's not about to start now.

Steadying herself, she reigns in her emotions and focuses on the objective knowledge she's seeking. For her, this is a fact-finding mission to discover more about this God thing, not something to get all emotional about. However, what she will soon learn is that her emotional wall can't hold firm when the intellectual barricade against God eventually collapses.

"In order to explain who God is, well at least my understanding of God, I need to tell you what God has done for me. Everything I know about God came from watching God change lives in the rooms of A.A., mine included."

Catherine shifts in her seat, intrigued by the direction Paul's taking this conversation.

"I didn't have a healthy or accurate picture of God until I came into the rooms of Alcoholics Anonymous. When I was out drinking, I didn't believe in miracles or a loving God. As a matter of fact, I didn't really believe God cared at all about me or the world he created. I thought God only cared about the "good" people: whoever they were. Nothing in my little world was good or pure, so I was sure God didn't want to have anything to do with me."

"Through a bunch of drunken messes, I got into a series of jackpots: several arrests, a trip to jail and one stint in the mental ward. I was so angry with God because I thought he let all that happen to me. In my mind, He should have stepped in and fixed everything. Eventually, I completely shut myself off to

Him. Of course, I had no idea that God didn't let those things happen as much as my choices allowed them to happen. They were all consequences of my behavior."

"So when I walked into the rooms of A.A. I was irate when anyone talked about a Higher Power or worst yet, about a specific God. I put up a huge wall against anything that was remotely connected with God or spirituality, which is hard to do when two of the first three steps deal directly with God. Finally, after my last relapse I was desperate enough to become willing to do whatever I needed to stay sober. My sponsor suggested that if I truly wanted to stay sober and to live happy, joyous, and free, I needed to find a God of my understanding and then to open myself to the *possibility* that my God would help me."

He pauses briefly, soaking in the memories of his first encounters with God.

"The first thing I did was ask God to reveal himself to me, 'cause if I was gonna turn my will and my life over to His care, I wanted to know who he was first. God didn't speak to me in words; he *showed* me who he was."

"I found out that God accepts all those who seek him. In A.A., we don't turn anyone away. No matter how low you have gone in your drinking, you are welcome here. God is a welcoming God. With the acceptance of all different kinds of people, God showed me that those who would not normally get along find a special friendship and camaraderie in His world."

"I found out that God cares about what happens to us. I have seen countless people get sober and stay sober for a very long time. I have seen sanity return to people who were committed to mental institutions. I have seen people find employment who were previously unemployable. God showed me that he really does care about the real needs we have."

"I found out that God loves us deeply. I have seen families reunited and relationships restored. I have seen one alcoholic reach out to help another alcoholic. I have listened to countless fifth steps where grown men cry like babies when they finally get rid of all their secrets and feel God's love and forgiveness for the very first time. God showed me that his love knows no limits."

"I found out that God has expectations and standards. I have seen people who won't or can't believe in a power greater than themselves go back out into the world and die from this horrible disease. I have seen people entangled with the consequences of their behavior drink again. I have seen people drink, and *then* get entangled with the consequences of their behavior. But I have also seen people live happy lives when they embrace the four absolutes: honesty, purity, unselfishness, and love. God showed me what happens when we stray from His will, *and* what happens when we stay within his will."

"So, young lady, here's the answer to your question: my God is a God who accepts all who seek him, who cares about all our needs, who loves us all deeply, and who expects us all to follow his will for our life. One day I got on my knees and asked that God to accept me with all my faults, to care about all my needs, to love me deeply, and to help me follow his will. With that simple prayer, God's acceptance, love, and power flowed into me and changed the course of my life. I have never been the same."

A tear falls from Paul's eye as he finishes talking. He doesn't bother wiping it away. He feels no shame in his testimony.

"Catherine, stay open to the possibilities of God in your life. Keep searching for Him. He is not far from you. In fact, I believe he is waiting for you right now. And whether you believe it or not, he will accept you with all your faults, care for your every need, love you deeply, and empower you to follow His will."

Catherine sighs, remembering the peace radiating from Paul that day he told her about his God. She could barely breathe when he was finished with his story.

After contemplating the memory of her time with Paul, Catherine shuts her Big Book and puts it away. Pip jumps off her lap and trots happily toward the bedroom. It's been a good day, she thinks.

The ringing of the phone startles Catherine. *Who is calling this late?*

She picks up the receiver. "Hello?"

"Catherine," a female voice says in a frantic whisper, "I don't know what to do. Can you come over?" The caller says each word slowly, but the words are slurred.

"Who is this?" Catherine asks.

"Courtney! I neeth some help. Pleath come over."

Catherine instantly realizes Courtney's drunk. "Crap! What happened Courtney? You sound drunk."

"I neeth you. There's something really wrong. I'm scared."

"Courtney, you're drunk that's what's wrong. You just need to sleep it off. I can talk with you tomorrow."

"NO! It's more than that." Courtney's voice is surprisingly strong and clear. "Something's inside me."

"What!? What's inside you?" Catherine is getting an uneasy feeling again.

"Remember when I told you about the Spirit Calling thing?" Her tone changes to a whisper. "I think something entered me. I feel like there's a demon inside me." Courtney starts to cry. "Help me, Catherine."

Catherine almost drops the phone. A chill runs down her spine. As she runs her hand through her hair, she tries to decide what to do. Pip circles her feet and meows loudly. The room seems to be spinning. She sits down on the bed, trying to clear her head.

Sighing, Catherine whispers, "Okay. I'll be right over."

Chapter Thirty-Five

The atmosphere crackles with the sound of a million demons hissing and chattering in anticipation of the upcoming sacrifice at the altar of Satan in the eternal death. They gather to watch the carnage that will ensue when a mortal succumbs to evil with their rejection of good. What gets the demons even more frenzied is the possibility that they might witness two mortals sacrificed tonight.

• • •

After reading the same sentence three times, Nancy shuts her book in frustration. She was looking forward to reading the latest novel by her favorite author, but she just can't concentrate. Her thoughts keep wandering back to her daughter, Catherine. Deciding that it's too late to call, she heads upstairs to bed. But an unsettling feeling won't give her any peace. She pauses just before getting into bed. With an urgency she doesn't quite understand, she gets on her knees, bows her head and starts to pray.

• • •

Elizabeth bends over and puts her hands on her thighs. Breathing hard, she unlaces her shoes and kicks them into the corner. She heads into the kitchen, opens the door, and grabs a bottle of water. After gulping down almost half the bottle, she wipes the sweat from her forehead. Her late night run was good, but for some reason she can't get one of her patients out of her head. She's hasn't seen Catherine professionally in a month, but sees her in meetings here and there. Pausing while stretching out her legs, she listens for the voice of God, shudders, and then bows her head to pray for Catherine.

• • •

Jane chases her youngest up the stairs. "You can't catch me, mommy," laughs her rambunctious five year old, Timmy. Jane isn't sure when this became their bedtime ritual, but it's the only way to get him to bed at the end of the day. As she rounds the corner to his bedroom, Timmy's already on his knees ready to pray. Jane smiles and kneels beside him – another bedtime ritual. Almost like an electric shock, power surges through her, and she draws in a quick breath when her knees hit the ground. One name flashes in her mind. Confused, she hesitates for a moment. Then, in the midst of Timmy's prayer, Jane bows her head and prays her own prayer. Not knowing exactly why, Jane prays that Catherine is safe from the evil one and that God will send His angels to protect her.

• • •

Sarephah is initially stunned when Catherine heads out the door to meet Courtney. Assessing the situation, she remains motionless pondering her next move. In the stillness of the night, she turns her head to hear the cacophony of sounds coming from the depth of the heavenlies. She suddenly realizes that a sacrifice is being prepared. Flashing her sword, she instantly knows Pexov has something to do with this particular offering. Drawing in strength from the prayers being given for Catherine, Sarephah moves quickly to protect her and to bring a message from the Divine Three, before it's too late.

• • •

Banging on the door, Catherine yells "Courtney! Open the door! It's me, Catherine." Frustrated, she shakes the doorknob one more time. "Where are you?" she says through clenched teeth.

The light outside the apartment door flickers, then burns out. "Great!" A car door shuts. Catherine jumps and turns toward the sound. Dogs bark in the distance. Catherine wraps her arms around her waist to try to stop shivering.

Turning back to the apartment, Catherine raises her hand to pound on the door one more time when she hears the doorknob rattle. The door opens only until it reaches the end of the chain lock.

"Is that you, Catherine?" Courtney whispers with a shaky voice.

"Yes!" Looking behind her, she says nervously, "Hurry up, let me in."

The door shuts momentarily, and then swings open. Catherine is shocked by what she sees. Courtney stands there shaking and staring at Catherine with wild, bloodshot eyes. Mascara is running down her face, her hair is a tangled mess, and her top is torn at the shoulder.

Without a word, Courtney turns and lumbers up the steps to the apartment, stopping a couple times to regain her balance. At the top of the steps, she stops. Before entering, she peeks into her apartment and looks around.

"What are doing?"

"Shhh!" Courtney turns and grabs Catherine. "They might hear you," she whispers loudly.

Catherine smells the alcohol and backs away. Peering over Courtney's shoulder, Catherine asks, "Who might hear me?"

"Shhh!!!" Courtney leans farther into the apartment to get a better look. "Okay, I think it's clear."

Catherine shivers when she walks into the apartment. *Why is it so cold in here?* A chill runs down her spine. The heaviness in the room feels like a physical presence of something dark. An intense fear washes over her when something moves behind her. She freezes. Her eyes dart around the dark, cluttered apartment. "Courtney, where are you?"

Walking toward the sound of bottles rattling, Catherine finds Courtney in the kitchen. A bottle rolls off the counter and shatters on the floor. Courtney falls to her knees, trying to clean up the mess. Blood mixes with the alcohol when she cuts herself on the sharp edges of glass.

"What a mess. My life is a mess. Oh, it's a mess…a mess," Courtney moans as she sits back against the cabinets weeping and bleeding.

Catherine watches in horror, not exactly sure what to do. A thought occurs to her that she should call Jane, but before she can act on her thought Courtney abruptly stands up and staggers back into the family room.

After falling onto the couch, Courtney buries her head in her hands and rocks back and forth. Blood and alcohol drip down her arms. Catherine throws Courtney a towel and then sits in a chair next to her, unable to think clearly enough to do anything more. She's seen hundreds of drunken episodes before, but this feels different.

"Courtney, you need to sleep this off. Why don't you come back to my place? We'll talk in the morning. Maybe Jane can help."

Courtney doesn't respond.

Catherine notices an empty prescription bottle on the table. Picking it up, she reads the label. "Diazepam…hmm?" Turning the bottle a little more, she sees that it's Valium and immediately understands. But confusion crosses her face when she realizes the bottle is for someone named Joey Cutler.

"Courtney, whose prescription is this?" She asks, holding up the empty bottle. "And did you take any?"

Courtney looks up at Catherine. “I took them to make the voices stop. The voices just won’t stop.” She begins crying again.

“How many did you take?” Catherine asks anxiously.

“It doesn’t matter. It’s over. I gave into them. They can have me.” She rolls over and curls into a fetal position. “I’m so tired…sooo tired.”

Catherine jumps up and shakes Courtney. “Oh, no you don’t. You’re not falling asleep now.”

Panicked, she begins looking around for the phone. “Courtney, where’s your phone?” she demands.

“I just want to sleep. Let me sleep.”

“NO! Get up! Tell me how much you took?” Catherine asks frantically.

Courtney blinks her eyes slowly, and then opens them wide. “I don’t feel so good.”

Catherine helps Courtney to her feet. They shuffle to the bathroom. Courtney falls to her knees in front of the toilet and wraps her arms around the bowl. The sounds of her retching makes Catherine gag involuntarily. She backs out of the bathroom and leans against the wall.

A buzzing sound begins to reverberate in Catherine’s ears, rising to a deafening crescendo. She puts her hands on both ears to drown out the noise. Startled, she hears what sounds like laughter. Her breathing accelerates. She looks around for the source of the sound. Then silence. She slowly lowers her hands. The quiet is unsettling. Catherine twists around to look in the bathroom. Courtney’s lying on the floor.

Catherine rushes in and drops to her knees.

Shaking her, she yells, “Courtney! Get up!” Stillness.

“WAKE UP!” Nothing.

Catherine sits back on her heels and puts both hands to her mouth in horror. Courtney’s already turning blue.

Scrambling to her feet, Catherine runs into the family room. She hears muffled laughter and stops cold. Panic seizes her.

Unable to move, she scans the room for movement. Shaking, she whispers, “Oh, God. Help me.” The laughter stops. Her breathing slows.

Deep within her soul she hears a strong, yet compassionate voice: *I am with you.* She pauses to reflect on the reality that something or someone is with her in this horrible mess. Her shoulders relax slightly. Her mind clears enough to continue into the kitchen.

She spots the phone on the counter and grabs it. Shaking visibly, she manages to dial 911.

“911, what’s your emergency?” the caller says in a monotone voice.

“My friend, she needs help! She passed out, and now she’s not breathing. Hurry!” Catherine sputters out.

“Okay, honey. What’s your name?

“Catherine.”

“Where are you right now, Catherine?”

“I’m at her house. I…I…don’t know the address.” She starts pushing papers around trying to find an address.

“That’s okay, honey. Are you calling on her home phone?”

“Yes, yes. It’s her home phone,” Catherine says while walking back toward the bathroom. “Hurry! She’s not breathing.”

“Okay. I already have the address. I’m dispatching an ambulance right now. Hold on, Catherine” There’s a click and then a brief pause. Catherine paces back and forth in front of the bathroom.

The 911 operator comes back on the line. “Okay, Catherine, I’m back. Now are you sure she’s not breathing. Maybe she just passed out. Can you check for me?”

“Okay.” She moves closer and watches Courtney for a moment, trying to see if she’s breathing. Then, she leans down and listens. She stands back up and shakes her head. “I don’t hear anything. I don’t think she’s breathing.”

“Okay, honey. Do you know why she might have passed out?”

"She was drinking and took some pills. Hurry!"

"Have you been drinking?"

"No. No. I haven't had anything. I came over to help."

"Does your friend have any medical issues?"

"I...I...don't know?" Running her hand through her hair, she feels totally helpless.

"Do you know what pills your friend took?" asks the operator.

The sound of banging on the door startles Catherine. "I think they're here now. I have to get the door."

"Okay, Catherine. Show the paramedics the pills your friend took. I'm ending the call now. Hang in there."

Catherine throws the phone on the couch and runs down the steps to open the door. The paramedics follow Catherine back up the steps and then rush past her to enter the apartment. While the paramedics begin working on Courtney, Catherine sits anxiously on the couch. A police officer enters the apartment and begins questioning Catherine.

When the police officer finishes with Catherine, he goes over and checks with one of the paramedics. Catherine wonders why they aren't rushing Courtney off to the hospital. After a few moments, the officer looks back over to Catherine, lowers his head, and takes in a deep breath. But, before the officer can speak, Catherine instinctively knows the truth. Overwhelmed with unspeakable pain and grief, she wraps her arms around herself and watches the paramedics put a white sheet over Courtney.

A scream echoes throughout the heavenlies. Pexov howls in utter delight. Sarephah pushes Pexov away. Positioning herself near Catherine, she delivers a message from the Divine Three. Anger wells up in Catherine. Then she slumps on the couch and begins to sob uncontrollably.

Chapter Thirty-Six

Nothing could prepare Nancy and Scott for the phone call that came about an hour ago. There has been a death, the caller said: an overdose. In a rush of conflicting emotions, fear gave way to relief in a matter of seconds when they were informed that their daughter wasn't the victim. The police offered little information, but assured them Catherine was not involved, only present during the event.

"It was horrible, Mom. Just horrible."

Nancy wraps her arms around Catherine and lets her cry softly on her shoulder. Scott shuts the door after thanking the police officer for all his help. They move into the family room and join Megan.

"Honey, can you tell us what happened?" Scott asks tentatively.

Catherine wipes her eyes with the back of her hands and sniffles. She wonders how much she can tell them. Courtney acted so crazy, and now Catherine's beginning to wonder if her death was due to more than the alcohol and pills. Were there really demons inside her or in that apartment? She's not sure, but the laughter she heard was terrifying. And that voice. How can she explain the voice she heard or what the voice said?

Her frayed nerves are clouding her mind. At this moment, she's not sure what really happened in that apartment.

"I don't know what happened." Putting her head in her hands, she closes her eyes. "Courtney called, and I could tell she was drunk. She wanted me to come over." Shaking her head, she whispers. "I didn't know what to do."

She looks up and reaches for a Kleenex Megan offers her. "She begged me to come over so I did. When I got there I found out she took some pills. Then, she started throwing up, and the next thing I know, she's passed out on the bathroom floor. I thought she just passed out, but she wasn't breathing. That's when I called 911."

"There was nothing I could do. It was horrible," Catherine chokes out between sobs.

Megan reaches over and hugs her sister. "Sounds to me like she was trying to kill herself. You did the best you could under the circumstances," she reassures.

Catherine sits ups, wipes her eyes, and takes in a deep breath. "I don't think she was trying to kill herself," Catherine says softly. "She had...she had...something...there was something...oh, I don't know."

Standing up, Catherine looks at her parents. "I'm really tired. I just want to go to bed."

Nancy jumps up. "Sure, honey. Let me make up the guest room. Give me a minute." She kisses Catherine on the cheek and gives her a hug before leaving the room. Catherine sits back down next to Megan.

Scott clears his throat, "I'm just glad you're safe. That was a really bad situation to be in. I think you handled yourself extremely well." Leaning forward, he adds, "It took a lot of courage to do what you did."

Catherine locks eyes with her father for a moment. His show of emotion and positive words touch her. With a smile that melts some of the icy wall that separates them, she replies, "Thanks, Dad. That means a lot."

Scott smiles back. "You're welcome, sweetie."

• • •

Later that night, Catherine rolls over in bed. Her eyes snap open. The room is dark and quiet. A tear falls down her cheek. Sadness tries to invade, but she pushes it away with anger. *Where were you, God? Why didn't you help Courtney*? More tears come. *Why didn't you help me? What kind of a God let's someone die like that?*

Sarephah remains quietly in the corner. Although it's hard to watch, she needs to allow Catherine the freedom to be angry with the Divine Three. Drawing her sword, she stands guard. Tonight, Catherine must wrestle with God and God alone.

All the pent up anger against God that's simmered for years in Catherine's soul begins to bubble to the surface.

Where have you been all my life God? You've never answered any of my prayers. You just remain silent and uncaring. So many times you could have been there to help me...to protect me. But no, you just sit up in heaven on your throne and remain silent. You're silent and mysterious. I don't have a clue who you are. I thought I knew once as a kid, but now I don't know anything. I'm so confused. Everyone says I need to accept your help, but I don't see you helping anyone, so why would you help me. Why should I offer myself to you like that stupid prayer says? Where are you!? Who are you!? Answer me!

Catherine pauses in the darkness and listens. But the only sound she hears is her own breathing. Frustrated with God's silence, she turns toward the wall, closes her eyes, and tries to fall back to sleep.

Later, Catherine stirs but doesn't wake when a slight breeze brushes past her face. The curtains sway in the window. A soft light surrounds the bed, and then gradually fades till the room is dark once more.

• • •

"What!" Jane exclaims. "And you were there by yourself? Oh, honey, you should never go on a twelve step call alone. How are you doing?"

"I'm not exactly sure how to answer that question. I'm tired. I didn't get much sleep last night," Catherine admits.

With all the weird stuff that happened at Courtney's and with foggy memories of a voice and a light from last night, Catherine feels like she's losing it.

"Some really weird stuff happened last night." She pauses, unsure how to proceed without looking like a lunatic. "I have some questions about God and well...about demons."

Jane raises her eyebrows. "Okay. I'm not sure I can answer them, but I'll do my best."

"Do you believe demons exist?" Catherine asks quickly.

"Absolutely. According to the Bible, demons are actually fallen angels. In fact, a third of the angels who followed Satan at the great rebellion were kicked out of heaven. They now roam the earth along with Satan bringing chaos and discord wherever they go. I believe that where there is evil, you will find some sort of demonic influence or presence. I'm not saying we should blame all our troubles on Satan or demons, but their entire existence is to do everything in their power to lead us into sin and to ultimately destroy us. Unfortunately, they are good at what they do, especially when we don't fight against them. Actually, I think demons prefer that we don't even know they exist. We won't fight against something we don't believe is real."

Catherine is shocked. "Really?" After pondering this disturbing revelation for a moment, she asks quietly, "Well, do demons like...enter people?"

"Well, I guess they could. There are examples of some sort of demonic possession in the Bible. Mostly though, I believe they work through other means than possessing someone. They have a supernatural ability to negatively influence people in order to turn them away from anything good or Godly."

Jane pauses and looks intently at Catherine. "Honey, is all this talk about demons about Courtney or about you?" Jane asks.

Catherine's hands are shaking. "Courtney thought that a demon had entered her. She said she did some sort of Spirit Calling and that a demon entered her." With wide-eyes, she says softly, "I don't think she tried to kill herself."

Jane is starting to realize why she felt such an overwhelming need to pray for Catherine.

"Last night, Courtney said that she gave into *them* and that *they* could have her. I think it might have been something evil. She was so scared. You should have seen her when I went over there. Her eyes were wild looking. She was definitely more scared than drunk."

Hesitating, Catherine wraps her arms around herself. "When I went into her apartment, I felt something. The really creepy thing is that I think I heard laughing right when she died. I know you might think I'm crazy, but I think a demon killed her."

Jane proceeds with caution. "I know that Courtney struggled to stay sober, and she very well may have been influenced by something…demonic. But, I also know that she made very poor choices in her life, which left her open to those negative influences."

In a shaky voice, Catherine admits, "I'm really scared, 'cause if demons are real and God doesn't seem able to stop them or help people fight them off, then what's going to happen to me?"

"Who said God isn't able to stop demons or help us fight them off? In the Bible, James chapter four says that we first need to submit to God. Then, with God's help, we can resist the devil, and he will flee."

"That may be all well and good, but why didn't God protect Courtney? It's like he just left her there to die a horrible death. Courtney was trying to understand God." Catherine asks on the verge of tears and with a twinge of anger.

"Courtney never took her search to find a God of her understanding seriously, so she never had a solid spiritual foundation to help her in her fight against alcohol – and whatever else she struggled against. God never left Courtney. In fact, God will never reject those who seek him. But sadly many reject God or worse yet, never even truly seek him."

Catherine's jaw drops and she sits up rigidly. "What did you just say?"

"I said God never left Courtney."

"No, the last part," she says quickly.

"I said God will never reject those who seek him. But sadly many reject God or worse yet, never even truly seek him." Jane waits a moment. "Are you okay?"

The voice! That's what the voice said last night. Catherine squirms in her seat.

"It's just all so confusing. I've been reading the Bible like you asked, but I don't always get it. And I certainly don't get what happened last night. Demons and angels! It's crazy!" Catherine crosses her arms.

"Who said anything about angels?"

• • •

Catherine arrives home from her A.A. meeting exhausted from answering questions about Courtney and from all the condolences thrust upon her. She heard several people whispering that Courtney committed suicide. A few others thought it was a tragic overdose by someone who just couldn't get sober. A couple people even mentioned that Courtney just needed more spirituality or should have worked the steps better. Catherine doesn't care what they think; she knows differently. Nobody understands what really happened because they weren't there. And she's not about to tell because she's not sure they would believe her.

Curling up in bed with Pip, she opens the Bible Jane gave her after their talk at Mama's Café. Flipping through the pages, she finally finds one of the verses Jane asked her to read: Ephesians 6:12. "For our struggle is not against flesh and blood, but against the rulers, against the authorities, against the powers of this dark world and against the spiritual forces of evil in the heavenly realms."

She shudders at the memory of the presence she felt in Courtney's apartment and the laughter she heard. Terrified, she hopes Courtney's demon stays away from her.

With shaking hands, she turns back to another verse Jane highlighted: Psalm 91:11. "For he will command his angels concerning you to guard you in all your ways."

Still unsure about the voice and message she heard, she silently wonders if an angel was also in that apartment.

As she shuts her Bible, a barrage of emotions assaults her. Overwhelmed by the last twenty-four hours, her shaky faith is even shakier. She's scared about things she can't see and confused by what she does see. She can't believe Courtney's gone, and she's left to figure it all out on her own.

With a heavy heart, she reaches to turn out the light, but stops before hitting the switch. Compelled by a source deep within, she forces herself to climb out of bed, and then slowly sinks to her knees. Before a God she still doesn't understand, she asks Him to send her that angel again. Then shuts her eyes tightly and tries to block out the voices in her head telling her that one drink will take away all this pain.

Chapter Thirty-Seven

"I'm giving you a few days off," Vickie announces. "It's been three weeks since your friend died. I realize what a tough thing you went through, and I'm really sorry it happened." After several reports over the past few days that Catherine's behavior has been erratic, her boss decides to take action.

"There's something tearing you up about this, and I think you need some extra time to deal with whatever it is." Catherine crosses her arms with indifference.

Concerned, Vickie asks, "Have you been drinking?"

"No!" Catherine snaps.

"Okay. Sorry, but I had to ask." Sighing, Vickie signs the Leave of Absence report and slides it over to Catherine. "Take this to Beth in Personnel. I've already spoken with her about this arrangement."

Leaning back in her chair, Vickie studies Catherine for a moment. "Once again I am going out on the limb for you, but this is it, Catherine. I know this is a special circumstance, but I'm running a hotel here. I can't keep you on if your attitude doesn't improve. It's your choice. Either get some help or don't bother coming back, 'cause you won't last long with that attitude of yours."

As Catherine walks out the door, Vickie utters one last prayer for her. Shaking her head, she wonders what choice Catherine will make.

• • •

"Have you made an appointment with your counselor like we talked about?" Jane questions Catherine.

"Yes," she lies.

"Good. Why weren't you at the meeting last night?"

'Cause I didn't feel like going. Running her shaking hand through her hair, she responds, "I didn't feel well. I was tired."

Pexov smiles. He's gaining more influence over Catherine again.

"Well, everyone missed you. I'm worried about you, Catherine. Are you still praying the third step prayer every morning and every night?"

Yeah, but it's not doing any good. "Yes," she says truthfully.

Sarephah smiles. She still has some influence over Catherine.

"Are you going to the meeting tonight?" Jane wonders. "I can pick you up."

I don't know what I'm doing tonight or any night. "Yeah, I'm going. I'll just drive myself, though. Thanks."

"Alright, see you later. Listen, I'm praying for you. Don't you give up on God; God hasn't given up on you." Jane hangs up, closes her eyes, and says a silent prayer.

• • •

Catherine has never felt so tired or so empty. She's weary from the battle raging within her soul. This relentless fight between the good she wants and the evil she still desires is tearing her apart. Over the past several weeks, she's listened to the soothing voices of good, yet stubbornly followed her own will.

She's heard disturbing taunts of evil, but hasn't given in to them.

But today is different. She's tired of fighting. She grabs her purse and car keys and heads out the door. The pain is just too great, and the drink is too appealing.

Pexov knows that evil grows when left unattended. He springs into action and prepares to take Catherine. He laughs, because by her own power, Catherine's powerless to stop him.

Sarephah knows that good grows only when attended. She moves swiftly to protect Catherine and intercede on her behalf. She whispers a reminder to Catherine that God is powerful only in her weakness.

• • •

Pulling into the parking lot of the state liquor store, Catherine drives around to find a spot that gives her the best view of the front door. She turns off the car and searches for anyone who might recognize her. With a million different voices competing to be heard, she closes her eyes and puts her head on the steering wheel. She tries to steady her breathing. Her hands are clammy and her heart is racing.

Do it! Go get a big bottle of liquid comfort. Drink up and forget all your problems. Stop fighting it. Give in to your greatest desire. Come and find peace.

God hasn't given up on you. He accepts all who seek him. He cares what happens to you. He loves you deeply. Come and find real peace.

"STOP!" Catherine puts her hands over her ears. Tears start to flow. She angrily wipes them away. With a poisonous mixture of despair and determination, she grabs her purse off the seat and opens her door.

A coin falls from her purse. She stops and watches it twirl round and round until it finally lays flat. Picking it up, she turns it over and over in her hand. One side shows the symbol of the triangle of Alcoholics Anonymous, which stands for recovery, unity, and service. The other side is the serenity prayer. Through tear filled eyes she looks at the front doors of the liquor store and then back at the coin.

You don't have to feel this pain anymore. You can make all your problems go away with one drink. You need to take care of yourself. You must take charge of your life.

I know your pain. I know your problems. I will take care of you. I will never reject you when you seek me. Let me take charge of your life. I gave my life for you.

With one last look at the coin, she shoves it back in her purse. Starting the car, she mutters to herself, "Today is not a good day to die. I choose to live."

• • •

After arriving back in her apartment, Catherine places her A.A. coin on the kitchen table and stares at it. She remembers when she stood up and announced that she'd been sober for ninety days. The chip they gave her that day didn't have any significance to her then. Today, she believes that chip may have saved her life. With a teary smile, she realizes now how this chip represents all the hope, love and acceptance she's found in the rooms of Alcoholics Anonymous. Holding the A.A. chip in her hand, she finally admits two things to herself: she is powerless over alcohol and she needs God.

Putting down her chip, she picks up her Bible. She's drawn to Psalm 86:5-7. Reading aloud she says: "You are forgiving and good, O Lord, abounding in love to all who call to you. Hear my prayer, O LORD; listen to my cry for mercy. In the day of my trouble I will call to you, for you will answer me."

Turning quickly to Ephesians 1:7-8, she reads, "In him we have redemption through his blood, the forgiveness of sins, in accordance with the riches of God's grace that he lavished on us with all wisdom and understanding."

Pexov howls in anger at the words spoken aloud. He leaps up and reaches toward Catherine. Sarephah draws her sword.

"STAY BACK!"

The power of the sword and the force of the words shove Pexov backward. He shivers and shrieks as he disappears into the blackness.

Pausing for a moment, Catherine shuts her Bible, walks into her bedroom, and gets on her knees.

"God, I don't really know you all that well, and what I do know I don't understand completely. But I want to know you and understand you and your purpose for my life. I've made a mess of my life. I don't know how to fix it."

"I've been told that you accept anyone that seeks you. Well, I'm seeking you right now. I admit all my faults – and they are many. I hope you don't want me to list them all right now." She pauses briefly. "Okay, God I admit that I am an alcoholic and that I need your help."

With her heart fluttering, she looks up. "God, I ask you to have mercy on me and forgive all my sins. I commit my life and my soul to you."

Power instantly streams forth from the throne of the Divine Three and enters Catherine. The Author erases the ink of the old story. The Word confirms the start of a new story. The Text settles on the page to begin writing her story of renewal.

A stream of cool air washes over Catherine. She lifts her head and opens her arms wide, soaking in the warmth of a love she's never before experienced.

In a whirlwind of fire and wind, the Divine Three return to the throne after leaving part of their presence and power with Catherine. A celebration begins in the heavenlies.

From the depth of her soul, Catherine feels the overwhelming sense of complete joy and serenity. With a certainty gained from a simple prayer, she knows she will never be the same.

Chapter Thirty-Eight

"Guess who I'm having dinner with tonight?" Catherine asks while washing out Pip's food bowl.

Kaleb grabs a soda out of the refrigerator and sits down at the kitchen table. "Oh, this oughta be good," he says playfully.

"My whole family! I have been officially invited to an Ash family dinner," Catherine announces triumphantly.

Stopping mid-sip, Kaleb sputters out, "Are you kidding me? That's huge!"

"I know. I'm nervous, but also a little excited about it actually. I never thought that I would be invited to do anything with them again. I still feel awkward around them, especially Nicole, but it's definitely better than it used to be."

"That's what happens when you surrender and let God take over. How long's it been since you did your third step and turned your life over to God?" Soberly, he adds, "Which I never thought would happen after Courtney died. You were really lost there for a while." Pausing to catch Catherine's eye, "I prayed really hard for you."

With a genuine smile, she responds "Thanks, Kaleb. Your prayers must have worked. It's been a little over two months since I got on my knees, asked God for help, and gave him my life to use as He pleases. I was so miserable until that day."

She looks off in the distance and stares for a moment. With a smile, she says softly, "You know, I've never felt such peace and joy before or since that moment. It's something I'll never forget."

A comfortable silence frames the moment. A somber understanding passes between them: one life was lost, but another life was saved.

"Oh, and did I tell you that I was taken off probation at work? I still have a long way to go, but I'm pretty sure they aren't going to fire me."

"Wow, you're just full of surprises today."

"Lately, I feel like my whole life is full of new surprises," Catherine chuckles.

"It's really nice to see you smile."

Kaleb jumps up out of his chair. "I hate to ruin this moment, but I've got to get going. I'm meeting Paul at Mama's before the meeting, and you, my dear, have a dinner to attend." Calling out over his shoulder as he heads toward the front door, he asks, "Are we still on for church on Sunday?"

"Yeah. Same time; same service. See ya later tonight at the meeting." Catherine smiles as she hears the door shut behind Kaleb.

• • •

The door swings open. Scott looks at his daughter and smiles broadly. "Hi, sweetie. Come on in. Everyone's here."

Catherine steps inside, but hesitates when she hears voices and laughter coming from the family room. Memories of drunken rages and angry faces fill her mind. She looks at her father with shame and remorse.

Putting out his hand, he urges, "Come on. It's okay. Everyone wants to see you. We've missed you." He adds with a lump in his throat, "I've missed you."

Catherine smiles, takes his hand, and draws in a deep breath. Breathing in courage and breathing out fear, she walks down the hall with her dad to face her family.

Megan is the first one to notice Catherine. “Hey sis! Glad you could make it.”

“Hey little sis. Good to see you.” Andrew smiles. “You look good,” he says weakly. Bridgette, Catherine’s sister-in-law, smiles tentatively while pulling her son Bryan into her arms. “Hi Catherine.”

Catherine stiffens slightly at the less than enthusiastic response. “Hi everyone,” she manages to say.

Megan jumps up and gives Catherine a big hug and whispers in her ear, “Don’t mind them. Andrew’s been drinking and Bridgette’s not happy. Actually no one’s real happy about it. I’m *really* glad you’re here. And really glad you’re sober.”

Catherine smiles at Megan and then looks back at Andrew. With clear, sober eyes, Catherine studies her brother. She’s stunned when she notices his sad and distant eyes. Compassion creeps into her heart, and she silently prays that one day he will conquer his own demons.

Sighing, she relaxes a little when her mom sweeps into the room. “Hi Cath! You look great, honey.” With a big hug, she chokes out, “It’s so good to have you here.” Wiping away a few tears, Nancy quickly reigns in her emotions. “Okay, gang. Dinner’s almost ready. Let’s get the table set.”

Catherine lingers in the family room when everyone heads toward the dining room. Nicole bursts through the kitchen doors waving her arms in a huff about something. Her husband, Devon, follows behind just shaking his head. Catherine smiles: some things never change.

“Hi Nicole,” Catherine squeaks out, unsure if she really wants to interrupt Nicole’s latest tirade and face her very pregnant big sister. Nicole stops abruptly and turns to face Catherine. Taking a moment to study Catherine, Nicole wraps her arms around her swollen belly. “Hi Catherine. You look…good. I'm glad you could make it." A slight smile crosses her face when she adds, "It's nice to have the whole family here."

"Thanks. By the looks of it, we're going to have even more family here soon. How's it going?" she asks nodding toward Nicole's tight belly.

Before Nicole can answer, Devon jumps in and gives Catherine the "you don't want to know the answer" look. "Uh…It's going well. The baby is very active these days."

Pulling Nicole toward the dining room, he urges, "Let's go sit down, honey." Nicole waddles over to the table and sits down heavily.

Catherine finds herself observing the interactions between family members all through dinner. Megan looks across the table at her, and they discreetly roll their eyes at Nicole's monologue on the latest gossip from her neighborhood social club. Sighing, she inwardly cringes when Andrew is a little too loud when he asks for another helping. A couple times she notices her mother catching her father's eye. She's not sure what unspoken communication went on between them, but they seem happy. It's like she's seeing them all for the first time.

After saying goodbye to everyone, Catherine sits in her car outside the house for a moment reflecting on how far she's come in the past two months. She needs to make amends to everyone, but Jane says she must work the steps in order. In the meantime, she can make living amends by showing up for family events like this and being an active member of the family. Smiling, she realizes her family isn't perfect, but she's glad she has them.

• • •

Catherine notices a young woman standing alone by the open door to the meeting. She breaks away from her group and walks toward the woman. Surveying her as she approaches,

Catherine smiles to herself. *She looks just like I did at my first meeting.*

"Hi, my name's Catherine," she says while extending her hand. Catherine looks directly into the woman's eyes and sees the scared and sad look she knows so well. The woman weakly shakes her hand and then looks away quickly.

"What's your name?"

"Lynn," she says barely above a whisper.

"Welcome. Is this your first meeting?"

Lynn nods her head and crosses her arms.

"Do you think you have a problem with alcohol?" Catherine asks.

"I'm not sure."

Catherine smiles. "Well, you're in the right place to find out. Come on. I'll introduce you to a few people."

Lynn looks up at Catherine with fear in her eyes and doesn't move. Catherine looks back to her friends and sees Jane smiling at her. She smiles back.

Looking back at Lynn, she says softly. "It's okay. Everyone here understands exactly what you're going through. I was scared at my first meeting, but I made it through. And I'm pretty sure you will too."

Lynn stands there motionless.

"Come on, you'll never know until you try," Catherine urges.

After a quick glance toward Catherine's group of friends, Lynn looks back at Catherine. "Okay, I'll come in."

Catherine introduces Lynn to all her friends, and they promptly surround her, offering welcoming handshakes and words of encouragement. Catherine smiles when Lynn's eyes brighten slightly. As Lynn takes a seat with her group, Catherine prays that this one makes it because she knows not everyone does.

Leaning over, Jane whispers, "Good job. I'm proud of you for helping the new girl. You did a good thing. Plus, by helping her you're helping yourself stay sober one more day." Smiling, she adds, "You're finally getting it. You know, I think there's hope for you yet."

Catherine smiles back. "Yeah, I think there is hope for me."

Thank you God for accepting me when I couldn't accept myself, for caring for me when I wouldn't care for myself, and for loving me when I didn't love myself.

And thank you for Lynn.

Chapter Thirty-Nine

The light radiating from Catherine almost blinds Pexov. Squinting, he crawls unsteadily back into the corner, sits down, lowers his head into his hands, and rocks back and forth for several minutes. The loss of another soul is devastating, but the consequence of his failure is terrifying. He knows exactly what will happen if he goes before Satan. Trembling from the vision of his impending torture and banishment, Pexov frantically tries to think of a way out this mess.

Glancing back at Catherine, his eyes start to adjust to the light of the Divine Three now residing within her. He clenches his fists, harnessing the hatred and evil he needs to fuel his rage. "Catherine is to blame for all my pain," he hisses. "She'll pay for what's she's done to me. Yes, she'll pay dearly. I will not be stopped, not by that pathetic mortal and not by Satan."

Jumping to his feet, he stretches to his full height and howls. "I will not be defeated! I will not be bound by anyone!" he yells defiantly. Thrusting his fist in the air, he vows never to return to Satan and to hunt Catherine for the rest of his days.

• • •

All the angels rejoice with Sarephah as she dances to the rhythm of the Divine Three's song of celebration. Singing and laughing, she thinks there's no sweeter sound in all the heavenlies than that of a soul reborn.

The Divine Three draw Sarephah to their throne. "Sarephah! Welcome, faithful one. You have done well. Come tell us what you have learned during your time with Catherine."

Bowing her head, Sarephah lifts her hands to the throne in humble adoration before she responds. "I enjoyed my time with Catherine. Well, most of it," she admits. "I had heard so much about humans, but didn't really understand them until now. It was quite interesting to watch Catherine's journey from bondage to freedom. Thank you for letting me be part of your plan for her."

Sarephah glances down on the scene below, pausing to contemplate the lessons learned along the way. Looking back toward the throne, she smiles and begins.

"I learned that you, the Divine Three, willingly give humans freewill even though you risk constant rejection. Frankly, I don't understand why you did it with all the trouble humans get themselves into.

I learned that demons will do everything in their power to destroy humans.

I learned that there is an incredible group of people who call themselves alcoholic even though they no longer drink. Their love for each other is inspiring.

I learned that there is an incredible group of people who won't call themselves alcoholic even though they drink alcoholically. Their hatred for themselves is heartbreaking.

I learned that humans have an amazing capacity to endure needless, self-imposed pain and suffering even in the face of pure love.

I learned that evil is a by-product of Satan's will rather than a product of your will.

I learned that prayer really does make a difference.

I learned that not all demons win the battle for a mortal's soul.

I learned that your love is boundless, but that you have boundaries.

I learned that choices begin to define character and that character then defines choices.

I learned that a human's story is never finished until the last stroke of the pen.

I stand ready to serve you, the Divine Three, when another human is in a battle for their very soul. I want to be a there when they are wrestling with choices that will decide their ultimate destiny. After all, by your grace there are divine possibilities."

Laughing heartily, the Divine Three express their pleasure with Sarephah by bathing her in the light of their love. Sarephah bows again before rejoining the celebration.

• • •

The flash of lightning that crosses the horizon momentarily brightens the face of a large guardian angel watching the gate to Nede. His jaw muscles tense as he reaches for his sword. In one fluid motion, he withdraws his weapon and raises it high above his head. With both hands grasping the handle, a stream of light begins to flow from the tip of his sword. The crackling sound of electricity fills the atmosphere and the winds begin to howl as a legion of angels take flight.

The Divine Three rise from their throne.

A group of demons arrive at the gate in a frenzy. Cackling and hissing in excited anticipation, the demons push and shove each other for position. The mightiest demon steps forward, grabs several demons, and throws them aside. Rising to his full height, Satan boldly stands at the gate, waiting to present himself before the Divine Three.

One by one the angels descend on the chaotic scene at the gate and form a circle around the demons. The demons squeal in anger when they're surrounded by the host of armed angels.

The angels draw their swords and move in closer. The demons become even more frenzied.

With one look, The Divine Three silence the horde of demons. Nodding toward the gate, They signal the guardian angel to open the doors. After the gate swings open, Satan bows his head slightly and enters Nede.

"Why have you come?" asks the Divine Three.

"I have come about Catherine: the one who calls you savior."

"What about Catherine?"

"Catherine calls you savior now, but I wonder what will happen when life gets tough for her. Will she still call you savior? Will she still love you? Will she still serve you?"

"Why do you ask these questions? Are you considering Catherine in your unquenchable thirst to destroy what is ours?"

Flashing his blood red eyes, Satan hisses, "I will not let this one fulfill her destiny."

The Divine Three bellow, "Will the one who contends with Us survive forever? Your existence is still in Our hands." The force of the wind stirred up by the Divine Three drives Satan to his knees.

"What makes you think you have any say in matters concerning Catherine's destiny?"

Satan rises to his feet, "Because you have given her freewill, and in spite of her new-found faith, her will is still pathetically weak. Just like so many before her, she will not persevere through the trials ahead, because I will take the freedom you have given her and use it to my advantage."

The Divine Three announce to all the heavenlies, "Satan, your pride continues to be your downfall. We have given ourselves to Catherine. We are in her and she is in Us. We will never leave her nor forsake her. We have plans for her."

Defiantly, Satan declares, "I too have plans for Catherine. I will do everything in my power to make sure she grows disillusioned with you and the life you've called her to live."

As the heavenlies begin to shake with the anger of the Divine Three, Satan spins around, flies out of the gate, and disappears into the depths of the heavenlies with his angry horde of demons following behind.

Satan returns to his throne planning his next move against Catherine.

The Divine Three return to their throne confident in their perfect plan for Catherine, knowing all the possibilities that await her if she seeks them, even in the trials ahead.

Divine Perseverance

Book Two: The Divine Series

Eager to start a new life, Catherine boldly takes a stand for her beliefs. However, it's not long before she's confronted with a series of events that begin to erode her confidence. Pexov embarks on a new quest to silence Catherine when another more powerful demon, Furdon, joins him. The angel, Sarephah, working with the Divine Three, will do everything in her power to assist Catherine in her fight against both seen and unseen enemies. As Catherine's life spirals out of control, how will she respond? Will she turn back toward the only life she's ever known, or will she find divine perseverance to strive toward an uncertain future?

Made in the USA
Charleston, SC
23 November 2010